WRONG PLACE
WRONG TIME

Please Note: This is a work of fiction. Character names, and incidents are products of the author's imagination. Businesses are mostly fictional, but if not, they are referred to in an intentionally favourable, or neutral context. The West African State of Modrisia does not exist.

PEP▶ Pointy End Publishing

First published in 2019. Second printing: November 2019

Email: info@pointyendpublishing.com

Cataloguing-in-publication details are available from the National Library of Australia. www.trove.nla.gov.au

ISBN (Print): 978-0-6484779-0-7

ISBN (eBook): 978-0-6484779-1-4

Cover Design: www.covermint.design

Cover Photograph: Bikeworldtravel: Shutterstock

UK Maps and Drawings: John Young: youngj@netspace.net.au

Paper: 75gsm (FSC grade, and carbon neutral)

Set in 11 pt Athelas

Print typesetting and eBook production by Vellum

WRONG PLACE
WRONG TIME

IT'S THE MOMENT WHEN YOUR LIFE IS
CHANGED FOREVER

LESLIE HENRY

PRAISE FOR WRONG PLACE WRONG TIME

MI6 from the inside — I was there at the time.

— Ex MI6 Officer

I see this as a future BBC drama series.

— CEO International Charity

Hits the jackpot — Masterpiece. I could not put it down. The author's attention to detail is awesome.

— Journalist & Social Commentator

You nailed it! Lots of twists, and lots of surprises.

— International Management Consultant

I loved the author's use of metaphor to underscore the narrative.

— Internationally Recognised Artist

This book was an editor's dream.

— Book Editor & Published Author

CONTENTS

ABOUT THIS BOOK

This book is a work of fiction because of conveniently denied facts.

While attending a conference in London, Tyler Jones overhears a disturbing conversation between an arms dealer, and a West African politician. What Tyler saw and overheard, will affect the national and international interests of Great Britain.

Two weeks later, the politician is dead outside his embassy, and Tyler fears that he will be next.

Learning about the situation, MI6 exploit Tyler's vulnerability, by recruiting him as an agent. They infer that if he's one of them, it will protect him.

Over the next six months, Tyler Jones will be exposed to secrets that MI6 and the British Government, would never want the public to know about.

ACKNOWLEDGMENTS

For Faith Rose Fisher

I am indebted to my disparate group of quality controllers. All of whom are shining examples of creativity in their chosen fields of endeavour.

Activities that include: Painting, Writing, Business Management, Retailing, Science, Medicine, and Teaching.

These amazing people are listed in the order that they offered to invest their precious time to help me.

Karen Fisher, Roslynn McRoberts, Stephen Spurrier, Irene Combey, Julie Reid, Graham Haycock, Cathie Coleman, Sue James, Name Withheld, Franca Smarelli, Lisa Barrand, Robert Scott-Howarth, Juliet Fisher and Craig Hiscock.

Thank you for agreeing to step into my world of spies, and their agencies. A world of lies and hypocrisy.

I am also indebted to the uniquely talented graphic artist, John Young. John created all the street maps, that add so much to my words.

Leslie Henry.
Melbourne, September, 2019.

PAGE LEGEND FOR DIAGRAMS & MAPS

- *London (Map 1):* Charing Cross Hotel, Waldorf Hotel, Italian Cafe, Leicester Square, Trafalgar Square, Savoy Hotel, Adelphi Theatre, and surrounding streets. **Page 36.**
- *London (Map 2):* Piccadilly Circus, Courthouse Hotel, Eve Club, Oxford Circus, Selfridges Department Store, and surrounding streets. **Pages 37 & 100.**
- *London (Map 3):* Charing Cross Hotel, Big Ben, Houses of Parliament, Westminster Bridge, Lambeth North Tube Station, Century House (MI6 Headquarters), and surrounding streets. **Page 101.**
- *Yugoslavia (Map 1991):* Outline map showing the geographic regions, and places referred to in the story. **Page 216.**
- *Brent Cross:* Brent Cross Tube Station (Front & Rear Entrances), The station's Neo-Georgian/Art Deco Rooftop, and surrounding streets. **Page 271.**
- *Mind Map:* How all the people and places relate to each other. If you need to see, or remind yourself of how everything in the book fits together; this is the map you should consult. **Page 289.**

1

EPIPHANY (PROLOGUE)

As his vision adjusted to the glare of the hastily clicked bedside light, the clock on Jemma's bedside table, told Tyler Jones that he'd hardly been to sleep at all.

The sweat that was dripping from his legs, and saturating the bed linen, and the heart that was pounding its way out of his chest, bore witness to the fact that things were not right.

Before falling asleep, he'd kidded himself that everything would be OK. If he didn't think about it, then it didn't exist; it had never existed.

If he found himself thinking about it, he would extinguish the thought, and replace it with a version of reality, that whilst capable of salving his anguish, was a fantasy, and he knew it.

With the mixed emotions of panic, anger, and despair, battling it out for the best seat in Tyler's brain, he'd come to the realisation, that these seemingly disparate emotions, were in fact related, and codependent. He had a vested interest to see that they were fed, and watered; because, while they existed, he existed.

Tyler further contemplated, that by indulging himself with these seemingly irreconcilable emotions, it not only distracted him from aspects of the situation he'd rather not think about; it also catalysed the dual currencies of physical energy, and mental clarity — qualities he so desperately needed.

His barefoot trip down the tiled hallway, to fetch a cup of tea from the freezing cold kitchen, afforded him some immediate psychological comfort. He was moving about doing things, and his mind was totally occupied with the necessary and unnecessary tasks at hand. All proof that he was OK.

Back in Jemma's bed five minutes later, and with his heart still pounding, Tyler knew that his demons were real. To destroy them, he would need to attend the briefing at Century House, and place his trust in Cyril Smart and MI6. A decision from which there could be no turning back from, and a decision that Jemma has serious misgivings about.

He knew what nobody else knew, that he had had no part to play in all this. He had contributed nothing; other than to be in the wrong place at the wrong time. Or was it, the right place at the wrong time?. Or was it, the wrong place at the right time?

Fuck it, who gives a shit anyway, Tyler thought. *The fact is that I was there, and I did see and hear things — things that I can't now un-see and un-hear.*

2

REWARD FOR EFFORT

Late August, 1991.

Without Rupert Murdock, and News International, the provincial firm of Craven Printing, probably wouldn't exist.

As a casualty of the 1986 Wapping Dispute, the dispute that saw thousands of London print workers lose their jobs, Jim Craven had returned to his Birmingham roots. With the assistance of a financier friend, Bill Barrett, Craven had established his own printing business. Working out of a shopfront in Kings Norton, a town just south of Birmingham, Craven Printing offered the first Desk Top publishing service in the area.

By the late 1980s, Craven Printing had relocated to larger premises on a local business estate, changed its name to NuForm-Craven, and become a one-stop-shop media enterprise.

Before the advent of NuForm-Craven, customers, or their

agencies, were required to outsource the various components of a job. This outsourcing increased the cost and time required to get the job done, and it also increased the chance, that something might go wrong. NuForm-Craven's one-stop-shop approach on the other hand, meant that NuForm-Craven assumed full responsibility for every phase of the job.

Maybe it's a point-of-sale flyer, or a full page print-ready ad for a glossy magazine, or a logo and tag line that reflects the aspirations, and values of a shiny new business, or a company that needs a corporate video, or full-on TV commercial, or a trade exhibition stand, complete with halogen lights, huge photo display banners, roll-up banners, and light boxes, or a university, that needs someone to design, and produce a series of 35mm slides, for professor know-it-all, when he flies to Boston for the most important lecture of his career.

NuForm-Craven does all this, and more, out of a tacky warehouse just south of Birmingham, and they do it with a small band of extremely talented people. The admin and graphic design creatives work within the ironically boring, two story, brown brick street-front office. In the warehouse behind, there are two Heidelberg offset printing machines, with their related industrial cutting, folding, and stitching machines. In addition, four fully kitted-out photographic studios have been strategically built into various parts of the warehouse. One for fashion, one for small products, one for high-tech precision machines, and an extremely large one, for TV commercials, and corporate videos.

Tyler Jones, a good-looking, fit, and healthy twenty nine year old male, had started working at NuForm-Craven, about a year after they moved into their new premises on the estate. Beginning as a trainee, he had quickly advanced to his current position, as Production Supervisor.

Because Tyler constantly moved between the different departments at NuForm-Craven, he had become the firm's only multi-tasking employee. He had acquired so much hands-on, practical experience, plus he had the desirable, and endearing qualities, of enthusiasm for life, and the ability to charm.

Jim Craven, who had personally interviewed, and employed Tyler Jones, stuck his head over Tyler's right shoulder, as Tyler was gently lowering a bubble-wrapped display banner into a cardboard box, and whispered, 'See you in my office *Tiles*. Don't rush, finish what you're doing.'

With Craven's warm breath still lingering in his ear, Tyler contemplated the import of what had just happened. That Craven had referred to him as *Tiles*, Craven's term of endearment for Tyler, suggested that more than likely — this was going to be a good news day.

Tuesday, 27th August, 1991.

'Take a seat Tiles. I'll get Julie to make us a cup of tea while I nip out for a moment,' said Craven, as he gestured toward one of the armchairs, in the conversation area of his office, and left the room.

Tyler did as instructed, and although indications were that no bad news would be forthcoming, he couldn't help but feel nervous — quite nervous.

Craven's prolonged absence from his office didn't match Tyler's expectation as to when he should return, such that subtle waves of involuntary tremors, were now passing through the pit of his stomach. He also noticed that his hands were trembling, ever so slightly, but none-the-less visible if he out-stretched his arms.

Is Craven playing mind games with me, or what? thought Tyler. *Is he deliberately trying to un-nerve me? Un-nerve me to improve his bargaining position, with regard to whatever it is, that he has on his mind?*

The answer to those questions, came faster than Tyler imagined, when the silence in the room was broken by the familiar sound of a toilet being flushed, and the cistern refilling.

How quickly the worm turns, Tyler thought, *It's Craven who's given himself the shits* — *he's more nervous than I am.*

Craven reentered the room, closely followed by Julie Clarkson, NuForm-Craven's slim, and stunningly attractive, twenty-seven year old receptionist; her headset around her neck, cord dangling, and the tea tray carefully embraced with both hands.

Julie headed toward the large coffee table, directly in front of Tyler, and with great skill, placed the tray on the table with not a ripple on the surface of the tea.

There are two ways that women perform this task, men seem to only have one. One way, is to bend at the waist, while placing a tray onto a low surface. This is the preferred option of girls with large breasts, and men.

The other way, is to slowly and gracefully bend at the knees, while maintaining a perfectly straight back, and this is exactly what Julie did. Tyler's eyes, followed the descent of the tray, but his central vision was directed toward Julie's pert breasts, hiding inside her crisp white cotton blouse.

'Thanks Julie, you're a gem, we'll be right now.' Craven said with an upward inflection, when he noticed Julie glancing back at Tyler as she negotiated the doorway of his office.

Craven, energetically stirred two teaspoons of sugar into his tea, and with a squirming movement, he settled himself into the soft armchair. 'Oh, I forgot. Could you reach around, and grab that Manila folder, on my desk over there?'

Tyler twisted in his chair, did as instructed, and in the process, gathered that there could only ever be one, or two sheets of paper inside the folder.

Craven leaned forward in his chair, as he began speaking, something Tyler perceived as a good sign.

'You've been with us for over a year now, and you've lived through a lot of the changes we've made, I want to, err..., or better said, we need to make some more changes, if we want to stay ahead of the pack. We need to make changes on the admin side. All the people downstairs, and in design are fine, they just keep doing one hell of a great job, but it's us lot up here where we need to make some changes. We need to change the way we get, and keep our customers.'

Craven paused and gesticulated, offering Tyler that poor me, please agree with me, turned-up palms gesture, to which Tyler, not quite sure what he was agreeing to, and where the conversation might be headed, replied, 'It all makes sense to me Jim.'

Once having received what Craven perceived to be Tyler's

approbation, Craven, without missing a beat, quickly picked-up where he'd left-off.

'I want you to know Tiles, that I've given all this a lot of thought, and I don't want to flatter you into accepting something that you're not completely comfortable with. Putting aside myself, you're the only person in this place, who's got hands-on experience with every single thing we do.'

'So, I want to put a proposition to you Tiles.'

Having got that statement out of the way, Craven relaxed back into his chair, while Tyler, hands loose on his lap, straightened in his chair, and leaned forward in anticipation.

'I want to get someone else in, to do what you're doing, and move you up here next to me, in the smaller office next door.' Craven said, as he swung his arm out to the side.

'I want you to take calls from customers, who don't quite know what they want, or how to get what they want. Take them by the hand, and walk them through a process that satisfies their needs, and delights them such that they'll want to invite you home to dinner. If you haven't noticed it already Tyler, people like you, they really do. People respond to the way you engage with them. You're a credit to NuForm-Craven, and I think we should move our relationship to a new level.'

'What I'd like to do Tiles, is to offer you, the position of Sales Manager. As you know, looking after sales, is a major part of what I do. I think, in keeping with what I said earlier, it's time, to hand that role over to someone else.'

'I'd like to increase your base salary, from £13,500 to £15,500 and...' Craven hesitated at this point, as he reached for, and opened the Manila folder he'd got Tyler to pass from his desk.

'Earlier today, I spent some time going over our customer accounts. Last financial year, we did just over 900K, give, or take a bit. Eighty percent of that, predictably came from twenty percent of our customers.'

'I've created a list of all the customers who I've personally looked after, and I'd like to hand them over to you. Put you in charge of them, and as an added incentive, you'll see that I've also calculated the average monthly spend of all our customers. I'd like to draw a line under these amounts, and offer you a 2% commission on all net monthly sales, above this baseline amount.'

'We'll pay this commission to you monthly, and I've estimated that in the first year, it'll probably add about 3,000 quid to your salary, even if you don't get any new customers, or increase the spend of existing customers, simply because of the price increase that's due in November.'

'In handing these customers over to you Tiles, and to have you out there, it'll take a huge load off my shoulders. I need this time to implement the other changes we need to make, and we can't do any of that without Bill Barrett's support. Bill's our silent financial partner, at NuForm-Craven, and we need to have him on-board with all this.'

'Oh..., I almost forgot,' Craven uttered, with exaggerated intonation. 'A lot of my time is spent out of the office seeing clients, so if you're going to be doing all this, and other stuff too, you'll need a car, so you can have my M3. I've only had it for nine months, and it's got less than 5,000 on the clock, I'll get something new, and anyway, a *Beamer* sends the right message to customers.' Craven didn't elaborate on what he meant, but Tyler got the gist of it.

'This means that your salary will go from £13,500 to around £18,500, plus you'll enjoy the benefits of a company car.'

'It'll probably take a few days to get all this set up,' Craven pondered. 'September's almost with us, so how about we start our new arrangement, from the beginning of September?'

'I'm getting ahead of myself, and it's terribly rude of me,' said Craven.

'I haven't even asked if you'd be interested in taking-on this new responsibility. Maybe it's something you need to think about? Maybe it's something you need to talk over with someone else?'

Craven, now looking straight into Tyler's eyes, proffered a strong non-verbal cue, that it was Tyler's turn to say something, and that that something should be — *yes*.'

'No Jim, I don't need to think about it, or talk it over with anyone else, I'm my own man. And, yes, I'd love to accept your more than generous offer.'

Tyler had reciprocated Craven's direct gaze, as he voiced his acceptance, but it was quickly developing into an embarrassing moment, as each party looked to the other to provide a circuit breaker. Craven obliged by looking away, and saying, 'I think this calls for a beer old boy,' as he rose, and stepped across his office to the bar-fridge, which was concealed inside a cupboard.

With a Heineken in their hands, they stood leaning, half sitting, on the bench-top under the window in Craven's office. As is common in anticlimactic moments such as this, their conversation was embarrassingly banal, and a couple of Heinekens didn't help.

Craven is a person who has difficulty making decisions, and sticking with them once made, particularly decisions relating to the management of others.

In situations where decisions must be made, he will beat around the bush for an eternity, until out of sheer frustration, someone else will proffer a solution. A solution, that he then claims as his own.

Perhaps Craven's most annoying foible, is that whenever he feels the need to make an offensive, or judgmental remark, which is often, he will distance himself, by hiding behind the third person.

He will preface his remarks with the same boring mantra; *My Granny Craven always said...*

During his goodbyes with Tyler, Craven said, 'See you in the morning old son, and remember — My Granny Craven always said, never get your meat, where you get your bread.'

Tyler knew exactly what Craven was getting at, and as he exited Craven's office, he simply said, 'See you in the morning Jim.'

$$* \ * \ *$$

When Tyler Jones, accepted Jim Craven's offer to promote him to the newly created position of Sales Manager, he probably underestimated, the extent to which this decision would change his life.

Tyler would be leaving a position, that he'd held for nearly two years. A position that started out as an unskilled Man-Friday job, but morphed into something far more rewarding, for himself, and for NuForm-Craven as well.

Over time, Tyler had gone from being a Gofer, delivering this here, moving that there, helping out here, helping out there, to being able to perform just about any task in any department. Not only could he perform these tasks, but he could usually perform them with the same degree of skill as a trained operator.

Unbeknown to Tyler Jones, there was a direct connection between what he had brought to his job over time, and the future changes, that were planned to take place at NuForm-Craven.

An amorphous transformation had been taking place at NuForm-Craven, the precise nature of which had evaded conscious recognition. It was Tyler, who had unintentionally demonstrated, that while training and experience were essential to attaining, and to performing basic skills, it was his secret sauce of enthusiasm and creativity, that had added value to them. Tyler's ability to see relationships that no one else had seen, and more importantly, how skills could be morphed to embrace new offerings and opportunities for NuForm-Craven. A new business model that could grow Jim Craven's business, and provide it with a competitive advantage that could last well into the future.

Under pressure from his business partner Bill Barrett, to grow the business, plus fears for his own position, Jim Craven had seen the future. Nothing creative on Craven's part, but rather the sort of divine revelation that only occurs when one is at one's darkest moment.

The movie, that had projected itself on Jim Craven's bedroom ceiling at three am, and the eureka moment that would change the life of everyone at NuForm-Craven; featured Tyler Jones in the lead role.

As is common with eureka moments, a fully-formed plan was revealed to Jim Craven that morning. A plan that embraced all the required changes in departments, personnel and positions at NuForm-Craven. Most important though, was the slight-of-hand necessary to ensure that when the credits rolled across the screen, it would be Jim Craven front and centre; not Tyler Jones.

When Jim Craven performed his little job promotion set-piece for Tyler Jones, he had known exactly where he was going with it. There's a distinct difference, between knowing where one's going, and actually getting there. The last thing that Jim Craven actually wanted, was to relinquish any form of control at NuForm-Craven, but with a looming financial crisis that he'd thus far managed to hide from Bill Barrett — Craven was a beggar, not a chooser.

Barrett was a middle aged *Roller* driving, wily character, who's wealth demonstrated that whatever his skills were, they worked well for him. He had deduced from the financials supplied by Craven, that changes were long overdue at NuForm-Craven. Sales were stagnant, costs were rising, the customer base hadn't grown sufficiently, and the bottom-line had for the most part, been maintained from price increases.

At their last meeting, Barrett had effectively presented

Craven with an ultimatum. If he couldn't come-up with a plan to reposition NuForm-Craven for the future, then Barrett would be forced to reconsider his relationship with the firm.

Craven knew Barrett well enough to know that he'd meant what he said. This was by no means an idle threat. It was a promise, that if the issue wasn't resolved, Craven would be out on his own with nowhere to go, and with debts that he could never repay.

When Craven had had his meeting with Tyler Jones, he had been well aware that he needed Tyler Jones, much more than Tyler Jones needed him. He also knew, that Jones would be blind to this construct, because of his limited life experience, and personality type.

This situation provided Craven with an unfair edge. He could offer Jones a financial incentive that would have little, or no impact on NuForm-Craven's bottom-line, but it would be more than sufficient to satisfy the needs of a young, upwardly mobile male.

Then, right there at Jones's moment of decision; right there when the music stops playing; Craven would present his pièce de résistance; the card up his sleeve — the shiny metallic blue, BMW coupé.

If all went to plan, Craven would only need to relinquish aspects of his current job, that he didn't enjoy anyway. Functions that he found tedious, functions that challenged his comfort zone, and functions that unfortunately, kept his picture square in the frame of blame.

Craven's standing at NuForm-Craven would be enhanced, business would improve, and Bill Barrett would get off his back.

In fact his restructuring changes would be seen as innovative, and Tyler Jones would be seen to have received a more than generous reward for effort.

The final credits, would definitely have Jim Craven's name, front and centre.

As it transpired, things did go according to plan for Jim Craven, and it would appear, for Tyler Jones as well. It had all the outward appearances of having been, a win-win situation.

There was though, one unresolved and lingering pain-point for Jim Craven. The anxiety associated with his unrequited affection for Julie Clarkson. His vision of loveliness, that he would now have to share with Tyler Jones.

Friday, 6th September, 1991.

It was only the fifth day into his new role, and Tyler Jones felt like he had been at his new desk, in his new office, and driving his new car forever. It was as if things had always been like this, that there had never been another time, other than this time — and he was loving every single moment of it.

Tyler had been working through the accounts, making contact with customers, one-by-one to introduce himself, and to explain the changes. He explained that this was the beginning of a whole new relationship, and not just an excuse to call them, because NuForm-Craven has decided to move its human furniture around.

In this regard, he was careful not to shoot himself and

NuForm-Craven in the foot, by hinting at any criticism of Jim Craven, although he was sorely tempted at times.

As Tyler worked his way through the list, there was the odd occasion, where a customer had responded with palpable resentment. Regardless, there had not been one single person, who wasn't eventually won around by Tyler's charm. Won around, because they wanted to be won around, and thus a whole new beginning, for them and for NuForm-Craven.

A growing list of clients, had sought face-to-face meetings with Tyler at their premises, such that Tyler was already sticking coloured pins, into the cork-board map that hung on his office wall. He saw customer journey rounds emerging.

If further proof was needed, that Jim Craven's decision to relinquish his sales role, had been the right decision, then it had come in the form of the unsolicited business that Tyler had received from his phone calls.

Firm orders were placed for work that would have gone elsewhere, and promises were made for jobs that were still in the planning stage. It was only the beginning of the month and already, nearly two thirds of the sales forecast for September had been achieved.

Craven too, had come to terms with the decision he'd struggled with, just three weeks earlier. He now accepted that by moving Tyler into his new position, it had proved beneficial for all concerned. Beneficial for himself, for NuForm-Craven, and for Tyler. All the fears he had had were now gone — even his state of anxiety with regard to Julie, was now easier to bear. Tyler seemed oblivious to her ways, and apart from the odd surreptitious glance down her blouse at reception, she didn't seem to be his flavour.

With only a sharp tap, Jim Craven pushed Tyler's office door open, plonked himself down on one of the chairs in front of Tyler's desk, and said, 'Tiles old lad, I've got an idea that might appeal to you.' He paused briefly, took a deep breath, and repositioned himself in the chair. 'You're probably already aware of it, but I go down to London from time to time, stay a couple of days, and see a few clients. I leave my car at home, catch the train, and stay at the Charring Cross Hotel. I find it easier that way. No car to worry about, and the Charring Cross Hotel, is really close to everything. Most of our top accounts down there are within walking distance, or only a few stops on the tube.'

'Anyway, I've received an invitation to be part of an industry forum being held at the Courthouse Hotel, just off Regent Street — this Friday week actually, the thirteenth of September.'

'I think it'd be good if you went along in my place. There are a few speakers in the morning, then an open forum until lunch. After lunch there's an opportunity to network until mid-afternoon, and then there's a dinner in the evening. It's only seventy-five quid a head for the whole day, including lunch, and dinner.'

Craven did what he always did in situations like this; he stopped, and tested the waters before continuing, 'It's being subsidised by this firm called AcuWrite Media, an international data storage firm, who've got their European marketing office in Slough. No doubt, they've got their own agenda, but because we're all involved in such a fast-changing industry, we have to keep up with what's going on.'

'It'd be nice if we, that's you old boy, were there, to not only keep on top of things, but to spread the NuForm-Craven message at the same time.'

'Wow!' Said Tyler, finding it difficult to hide his excitement. 'That'd be really great Jim. I'd love to do it.'

'OK then,' said Craven. 'I'll get Julie on the job. How about you get down there late on the Thursday, stay Thursday, and Friday night, and then train it back home sometime Saturday? Something to look forward to old boy, eh.'

As quickly as Craven had appeared in Tyler's office, he up, and left, without another word, and Tyler got away to meet his mates down at the pitch, earlier than expected.

* * *

Thursday (AM), 12th September, 1991.

With Jim Craven not due in the office until after lunch, Tyler had arrived at work early, to get as much done as possible, before he had to leave for the industry forum.

With Tyler returning phone calls from the previous day, Julie quietly slipped into his office, and delivered a cup of tea.

Fifteen minutes later, when Tyler's light disappeared from her board, Julie came back to collect his cup. 'You naughty boy. You haven't even touched it. You deserve a smack. Now I've got to go and make you a new one,' Julie said, as she turned to leave his room.

Returning with the fresh cup of tea, she pushed Tyler's

office door closed with her bottom, and with her free hand, reached around, and snibbed the lock.

Walking to Tyler's side of the desk, while still facing him, she squeezed between his knees and the edge of his desk, and after carefully placing the cup of tea behind herself on his desk, she slowly unbuttoned her blouse.

Reaching down, she pulled her skirt up over her buttocks, kicked off her court shoes, and wiggled her knickers and tights down until they dropped to her ankles. Stepping out of them, she leaned over, and undid Tyler's belt and flies zip.

As Tyler lifted his weight, and slid his buttocks slightly forward, Julie pulled his trousers over the front edge of his chair, until, aided by the weight of his belt, they dropped to the floor.

Facing him, she knelt on his chair, by placing a knee either side of his thighs, and hovering over him she reached down between their bodies, to guide him as she lowered herself onto him.

With Tyler eagerly easing her breasts out of her balconette bra, Julie hunched forward, and with the outside edge of her forearms across the fronts of Tyler's shoulders, for leverage and balance, she began to ride him.

At the point, where the pain from the pressure of Julie's forearms on Tyler's shoulders was becoming too much to bear, pleasure overtook her. Straightening herself up, she leaned back, and now with only her finger tips on the tops of Tyler's shoulders to steady herself, she increased the speed and force of her movements, until with eyes squeezed shut, and suppressed screams; she orgasmed.

As they slowly reassembled themselves, Tyler grappled with an increasingly urgent, and perceived need, that he should say something.

As he opened his mouth to utter words, that his brain had yet to construct, Julie bent forward, and with a firmly pressed open hand across Tyler's mouth, she kissed him on his forehead, and left his office.

* * *

Thursday (PM), 12th September, 1991.

After lunch, and just as Tyler was packing up to leave for London, Jim Craven suddenly appeared in his office.

Because of what had happened with Julie earlier in the day, and knowing the devastation it would cause if Craven ever found out, Tyler's response to Craven's sudden appearance, was one of stunned silence. Like some naughty boy, caught in the act of stealing fruit from a neighbour's tree.

'Christine our bookkeeper, has just given me this to give to you.' It's the NuForm-Craven AMEX card, that I had her get for you. It's only just arrived in the second mail, so how's that for good timing on my part?'

Jim Craven's words, instantly put Tyler at ease and told him, that Jim Craven's vision of loveliness, his Madonna, remained intact and safe.

'You know what bookkeepers are like. She's ordered me to tell you, and out of fear for my life, old boy, not to mention yours — pay attention. No personal expenses on the company card. Use the card to pay the big bills like the hotel, and here's two hundred quid out of petty cash to cover incidentals. Make sure you bring her back the change, along with all the receipts, otherwise she'll hunt you down, and don't expect me to come and save you.'

'On a more serious note, thanks for doing all this old boy,' said Craven, 'Intruding on your weekend, and all that. Feel your way at the event, but do try to establish as many new relationships as you can. There might also be the opportunity, to form mutually beneficial arrangements with other suppliers at the forum. Even competitors, can sometimes be customers.'

'Oh, and here's a presentation album, to pop in your briefcase. I've had the graphics people put it together, with examples of some jobs we've done, along with some photos of our equipment and facilities.' Craven extended it in Tyler's direction, letting the album randomly unfurl through some of its pages.

With Craven's face pleading for gratitude, Tyler dutifully responded by saying, 'Gee Jim, what a fantastic idea. It's absolutely beautiful.'

3

WAVING THE FLAG

'Tyler Jones checking-in,' Tyler said to the girl on the other side of the Hotel reception counter. He would have much preferred it, if she hadn't been so immediately available, and eager to attend to him. At least until he'd conquered his briefcase, which was refusing to stay vertical, as he tried to place it down against his right leg.

To add insult to injury, his suit bag had joined the battle. It had taken advantage of Tyler's inattention, and slid off the narrow black, polished marble counter top, landing in an undignified heap on the floor. The type of heap, where the coat hanger hook, totally disappears inside the bag.

On his way into the hotel, Tyler had managed to deflect a porter, who'd needlessly offered his services. But now, having lost the battle, and in danger of losing the war, Tyler leaned down, picked up his suit bag, and reluctantly handed it to the porter, who was now waiting by his side. As he did, his right leg moved away from the briefcase, and with the slap of leather on the marble tiled floor, the briefcase adopted its intended position. The porter bent down, picked up the briefcase, and its relationship with the suit bag was restored. Porter 2 : Tyler 0 : Game over.

The receptionist checked her computer screen, disappeared into a side office, and returned with Tyler's registration card. Placing the card on the marble counter, she gestured to the black pen that was attached to a chrome chain, with the expectation that he should sign it. The moment she spotted that he'd be settling with an AMEX card, she requested the card, took an impression, and placed the sales voucher up on the counter for Tyler to sign; just in case he possessed thoughts of leaving with a suitcase full of towels, and a television set under his arm.

Only when he'd signed the voucher, and it was safely within her grasp, did the receptionist pass Tyler's room key to the porter.

The porter ushered Tyler toward the lift, and took him to his twin share room facing the Strand on the second floor. A bit noisy, but worth it to have a view that embraced the edge of Trafalgar Square, the National Gallery, and the side-rear of St Martin In-The-Fields. The porter hung Tyler's now reassembled suit bag in the wardrobe, and carefully placed his briefcase on the desk next to the TV. He then loitered with an intent, that was only satisfied, when Tyler produced two, one pound coins from his pocket.

Later, following a room service meal, Tyler sat up in bed, and reviewed his notes for the next day. Although he wasn't one of the four people, invited to give a presentation, he knew the importance of being prepared. Tomorrow, after the break, the programme promised a round table open forum, so Tyler knew that at the very least, he'd be required to introduce himself and his firm.

In the event that he'd be asked questions, he'd also need to be able to succinctly articulate, what it was that they did at NuForm-Craven. His game-plan would be to proffer information in a way that begged further questions, in the hope that people might seek him out during the networking session after lunch. Most of all, he knew that he had a really great story to tell, and that went without saying — it was now up to him to do justice to it. It also belatedly occurred to him, what an incredible responsibility all this was — whatever had possessed him to agree to it.

Another job before turning out the light, was to plan his walk to the Courthouse Hotel in the morning. With the London A-to-Z open on the bed, and one eye on the TV, he quickly realised, that it was impossible to find a straight path, to any destination in London.

Being practical, his first attempt was to find the fastest route to the Courthouse Hotel. Achieving his goal, he abandoned the idea, because it involved too much ducking and diving. If he got lost, it'd make him late, so he settled for a slightly longer route, but one where it'd be almost impossible to get lost.

Out the front door of the hotel onto the Strand, across to Trafalgar Square, around Nelson's Column into Cockspur Street to Pall Mall, then right into Waterloo Place, which led directly into Regent Street, across Piccadilly, and on up the right hand side of Regent Street to Great Marlborough Street.

If all went to plan, he'd easily be there in less than half an hour.

* * *

Friday (AM), 13th September, 1991.

When Tyler opened the drapes in the morning, he was greeted by a pleasant and unexpected surprise. Bright sunshine was casting long shadows across the Strand, and judging by the way people were dressed, any fears he may have had about the weather, were quickly dispelled.

A push of the TV *on* button, and *Good Morning Britain* told him that Friday the thirteenth of September, was shaping-up to be warm, with a forecast high of twenty-three degrees celsius.

It was a nine, for nine-thirty start at the industry forum, so Tyler was showered, dressed, breakfasted, and back in his room, putting on his tie by quarter past eight — ample time, for a lovely walk in the sunshine to Great Marlborough Street.

Before leaving his room he made a last minute check of his briefcase. The important items were all there:

- The NuForm-Craven presentation album that Jim Craven had had prepared.
- His notebook and pen.
- A bundle of his new business cards.
- His A-to-Z Pocket Guide to London.

Exiting the Charing Cross Hotel, Tyler followed the mental map that he'd re-imprinted on his mind before leaving his room. He was confident that he wouldn't have to stop, put his briefcase down, get out his A-to-Z, only to experience the embarrassment of someone asking, 'Do you need any help, Sir?' No, Tyler would definitely never court the indignity of presenting himself as some hapless tourist. He was transformed. This was now his town, he knew it like the back of his own hand, he was Tyler Jones Esquire.

This hubristic vision of himself propelled his step, with the surrealistic sensation that he was floating on air.

In this heightened state of consciousness, as he levitated along the course of his mental map, Tyler absorbed into the core of his being, every sight, every sound, and every smell. The sight of the crowds, already starting to make movement on the pavement difficult. The sounds of emergency vehicles, and every accent imaginable other than English. The smell of diesel fumes, from the delivery trucks, buses, and taxis; the vehicles, that collectively, accounted for most of the volume, most of the smell, and most of the noise on Regent Street.

Entering the Courthouse Hotel, through its grand arched entrance, with its heavy oak panelled doors, Tyler headed down the hallway, and into the foyer. Adjacent to the staircase, a notice board told him that the forum was downstairs, in Chamber I; with the number *One* expressed as the Roman numeral.

Descending the stairs he was conscious, that his nerves were beginning to get the better of him. His heart was racing, his armpits were damp, he was trembling inside, and he was experiencing waves of light-headedness; all signs of a panic attack in the making.

As can happen in situations such as this, one's perception can be quickly reversed by a fortunate change of circumstance.

From the group of people, who were milling around at the end of the hallway, and what Tyler assumed, was the entrance to Chamber I; a bespectacled, slightly dishevelled looking chap, in a russet cloth three piece suit, had broken away, and was theatrically walking toward him with outstretched arms. 'Tyler Jones!' He broadcasted, 'I don't believe it. Fancy you being here. How many times has it been, that I've thought of contacting you? How long has it been, since we saw each other last?'

With an exaggerated expression of joy, not so much from seeing Chris Wood again, but rather because he was suddenly feeling so much better, Tyler said, 'Yeah, I think you're right Chris. It must have been just before you pissed-off from the north, to be with your snobby friends in London.'

'Fuck you Tyler Jones, I love it. You haven't changed a bit.'

'And..., fuck you too Chris Wood.'

As they ambled back down the hallway, Tyler said, 'Anyway Chris, what are you doing with yourself these days, and what brings you here?'

'Well, I could answer those questions, in a variety of ways. The short of it is, that the London Leader has sent me along. They think that there's a story to be had here, for the Sunday Magazine Section, and anyway, thanks to you lot, I get in for free. Tonight's booze, and food is on you old boy, and I'm paid by the newspaper to be here to boot.'

'Anyway, I'll only be here until lunchtime, then I've got to get back to the paper, but I will be here for the dinner tonight — most definitely am I coming back for the dinner. So, let's leave the big picture stuff, until we can have a chat over dinner. Anyway, It's not just about me old boy, I need to know what's been happening with you too.'

As quickly as he had appeared, Chris Wood separated himself, and reintegrated with the group of people, from whence he had come.

Once inside Chamber I, Tyler saw that the room, was set-up in a U Shape format, with places set for about two dozen people. Although the room was obviously below ground level, it appeared that natural light was coming-in through Venetian blinds on the side wall. Even if this was a created effect, it worked well, because it made the room feel so much more welcoming.

Tyler placed his briefcase on a seat in the back row; a seat that appeared to be unspoken for. He figured that it offered a great, straight-on, uninterrupted view of the large projector screen, and an easy exit if he needed the loo.

People were securing their seats, pouring themselves cups of coffee, and then either milling around in small groups, or as in Tyler's case, hovering coffee cup in hand, lone-guard, and self-conscious, over their chosen spot.

The programme got underway, and on-time, with an introduction from the UK marketing manager of AcuWrite Media, Jerry Blair. His introduction was followed by four speakers, each person speaking for ten minutes, until morning coffee break.

During the AcuWrite presentations, Tyler got to see things he'd read about, but never seen. AcuWrite had used an interactive whiteboard, and a colour LCD panel, which was placed directly on top of the hotel overhead projector. Instead of using a carousel slide projector, as other presenters were using, all AcuWrite's slides were fired to the colour LCD panel, via a VGA cable from their laptop computer. There were occasional minor issues, with slow transition times, but for the most part, it went without a hitch. After all, how many times, had Tyler witnessed a flustered presenter, having to pause a presentation, while someone rescued one of his 35mm slides, that was jammed inside the projector.

Tyler felt that the morning talks alone, had made his trip to London worthwhile. The talks had supported his belief, that the changes already made at NuForm-Craven, had definitely been the right changes at the right time.

Before breaking in readiness for the open forum session, attendees were asked to ponder the following points for discussion:

- Are there things on the technology horizon, that we should be preparing ourselves for?
- What should existing businesses be doing, to future-proof themselves?
- Will design, and print technology become so DIY, that customers, will move these functions in-house?
- If so, will this be tantamount, to the industrial revolution all over again?
- Do we need to reinvent ourselves, and if so, how should we go about it?

In a short, and casual conversation, with Jerry Blair's

assistant Jennifer during the morning coffee break, Tyler sensed, that frustration existed in AcuWrite's relationship with their London agency. He decoded Jennifer's loose remarks, to mean that their agency was overpriced, and arrogant. Tyler immediately sensed a business opportunity.

Tyler also sensed that this seemingly out of her depth girl, with the title of marketing assistant, somehow wielded inordinate decision-making power within AcuWrite Media.

After their conversation, and as Tyler turned to walk away, he realised that the unexplained glances, Jennifer had been casting over his right shoulder, were directed toward AcuWrite's marketing manager, Jerry Blair. In a flash, Tyler saw it all.

During the break, and driven by a sense of need, Tyler quickly reinvented the script he'd spent so much time creating, and memorising last night. He rewrote it, such that if engaged in conversation, or if questioned, he would now reveal as little as possible, about the already implemented changes at NuForm-Craven.

Tyler's original intention, had been to use the open forum as talk-bait for the networking session after lunch. By now deciding to limit the amount of information about NuForm-Craven, it would certainly disadvantage him in that regard. In Tyler's mind it was now a balancing act, between trying to get new business on one hand, and giving away trade secrets on the other. He would now play his cards much closer to his chest.

During the open forum session, Tyler made the following points, and peppered his contribution with comments, that were shamelessly directed toward the ear of marketing assistant, Jennifer.

- Satisfying customer needs must always be the overarching focus of any brief.
- Customers must be engaged in every step of the process.
- Only a one-source agency such as NuForm-Craven can truly fulfil those needs.

By Tyler raising these points, it also conveniently helped to answer the questions of *survival,* that had been posed before the coffee break. If Tyler had got anything at all out of the open forum session, it was that not one single person in the room had a clue.

As the group broke for lunch, and people were leaving their seats, a timid Jennifer sat herself down on the edge of the chair next to Tyler, and leaning forward said, 'I'm sorry to interrupt you Mr Jones, but Jerry Blair our marketing manager, has asked me to ask you, if you wouldn't mind giving us some of your time up in Jerry's room after lunch?

'I'd be delighted to. In fact, I'd be more than delighted. What time?'

'Would one-thirty be OK with you? Jerry's in room 204.'

'Look forward to seeing you both. One-thirty in room 204 it is.'

After lunch, and as promised, Tyler gently tapped on the door of Room 204. Within a millisecond, Jennifer's face began to reveal itself through the crack, as her delicate form struggled against the overwhelming opposition of the automatic door-closer. Tyler, sensing her distress, assisted by gently pressing on the outside edge of the door.

'Oh..., what a struggle, thanks Tyler. Anybody'd think we didn't want you to come in. Do come in and sit down. Can I get you a cup of tea, or coffee? Jerry's just had to nip downstairs, he'll be back any moment.'

Any moment as it turned-out, was only a couple of minutes away. Tyler heard the characteristic click of the door-lock release mechanism, as Jerry's keycard told the system, that he was friend, not foe.

'Ah. You're here,' said Jerry, 'that's lovely. Let's get on with it then, shall we? I've been looking forward to talking to you. Of course, I heard what you said during the session, and Jenny's filled me in on some of the other stuff. Has Jenny offered you some refreshments?'

'Yes.' Said Tyler. 'I'm fine thank you, but if you feel like a cup of whatever, then I'll join you.'

'Maybe a big pot of Cafetière coffee, pretty-please Jenny.'

'Yes Sir, coming-up Sir. Right away Sir.' Was Jennifer's instant rejoinder, underscored with a salute gesture, and a quick poke of her rolled-up tongue.

This playful exchange confirmed Tyler's earlier suspicions, and he felt happy for them. From a selfish perspective, he actually found it enjoyable, and relaxing to be in their company, but at the same time, somewhat disarming with regard to his earlier resolve, not to give away trade secrets.

'Now, Jenny tells me that you've got a folio of your firm's work, and it's got some pretty cool stuff in it. Do you mind if I take a look?'

Tyler pulled his briefcase up onto his lap, and handed the album to Jerry.

'Wow, this is really, really nice work.' Said Jerry. 'Jenny was right. Your company seems to be a perfect fit for where we see ourselves going next. Our current agency just doesn't seem to be able to image us, to capture an identity that fits our values. We just seem to be hitting one brick wall after another. They just don't get it.'

At this point the Cafetière, three cups, and saucers, a little jug of milk, and some sachets of sugar were delivered to the coffee table by Jennifer. Taking a seat next to Jerry on the two-seater sofa, she played mother, and poured the coffee.

'Thanks Jenny. We'd better be getting back downstairs to the networking session, but what I'd like to quickly propose, is that you, Jenny, put a brief together, and for Tyler to get back to you with a proposal, after he's had a chance to work on it. Then, if all goes to plan, you can personally manage the account with NuForm-Craven, and I can stay out of it. Hopefully, this will mark a new beginning for both our firms.'

As Tyler departed Jerry's room, he was elated. He'd achieved much more than he could ever have wished for. He had almost certainly, scored the account of the forum organiser. *How good is that*, he thought, *What a boast this is going to be when I get back and tell Jim Craven.*

When Tyler reentered Chamber I, and poured himself a cup of coffee from the side table, it dawned on him, that he'd barely managed one sip of Jennifer's coffee. The stress of having to stay on-message, lest he blow his one and perhaps only, opportunity to nab the AcuWrite Media account, had left no room for much else.

It also occurred to him, that he'd totally lost his appetite for the networking session. He was apathetic and tired. He just wanted to go back to his hotel room, and lie down. Anyway, he'd spent enough time observing and listening to the other participants, to conclude that apart from not having much in common with any of them, he didn't see any business opportunities there either. For them it seemed that *self interest*, and *status quo* were the only two horses in the race.

It was only just after two, but for Tyler the day had already been too much for him emotionally. His mind had progressed beyond the networking session. The plan now was to only stick around long enough to keep-up appearances, and then vamoose.

Less than half an hour later, Tyler was out on Great Marlborough Street, and headed back to his hotel.

LONDON (MAP 1)

CHARING CROSS HOTEL, WALDORF HOTEL, ITALIAN CAFE,
LEICESTER SQUARE, TRAFALGAR SQUARE, SAVOY HOTEL,
ADELPHI THEATRE

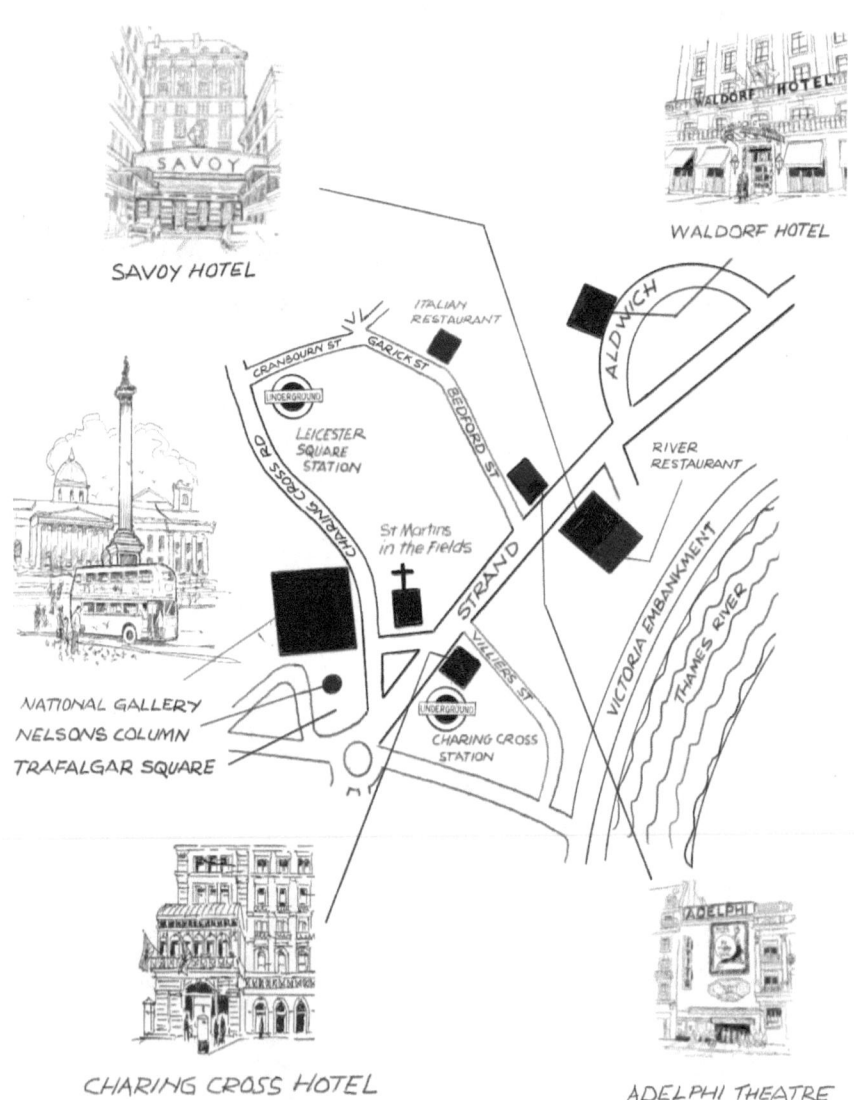

SAVOY HOTEL

WALDORF HOTEL

ITALIAN RESTAURANT

CRANBOURN ST

GARICK ST

BEDFORD ST

ALDWICH

UNDERGROUND

LEICESTER SQUARE STATION

CHARING CROSS RD

St Martins in the Fields

RIVER RESTAURANT

STRAND

VICTORIA EMBANKMENT

THAMES RIVER

VILLIERS ST

UNDERGROUND

CHARING CROSS STATION

NATIONAL GALLERY
NELSONS COLUMN
TRAFALGAR SQUARE

CHARING CROSS HOTEL

ADELPHI THEATRE

LONDON (MAP 2)

PICCADILLY CIRCUS, COURTHOUSE HOTEL, EVE CLUB,
OXFORD CIRCUS, SELFRIDGES DEPARTMENT STORE

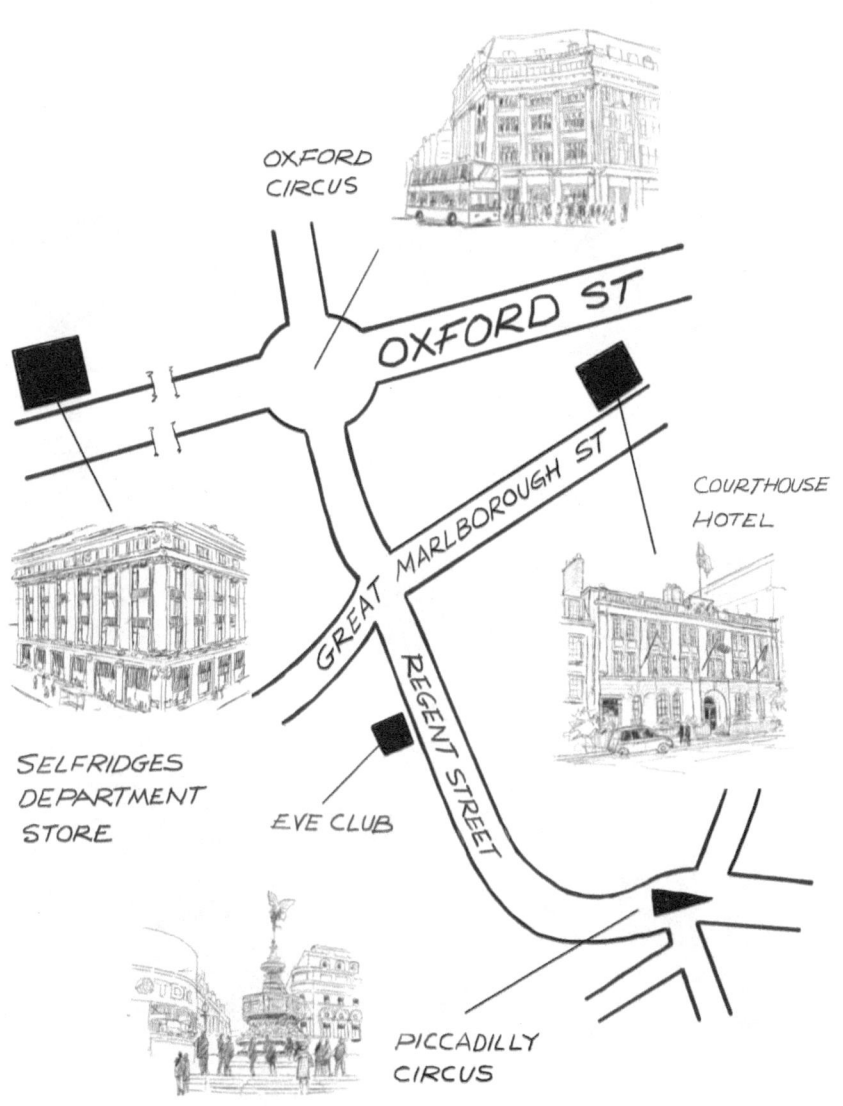

OXFORD
CIRCUS

OXFORD ST

GREAT MARLBOROUGH ST

COURTHOUSE
HOTEL

REGENT STREET

SELFRIDGES
DEPARTMENT
STORE

EVE CLUB

PICCADILLY
CIRCUS

4

CONVERSATIONS

Friday (PM), 13th September, 1991.

It was just on three in the afternoon when Tyler Jones walked back into the Charing Cross Hotel — much earlier than he'd anticipated.

The thought of hanging about in his room until he changed for dinner held no appeal, and anyway, because of his walk in the fresh open air, he wasn't tired anymore. All of a sudden, it seemed like a long time between now, and when the minicab was due to pick him up at six-thirty.

Unsure of what to do, but knowing that the universe rarely speaks to a person with a full bladder, Tyler paid a quick visit to the public loo, on the ground floor.

Two minutes later, and the universe had rewarded Tyler as a true-believer. Atop a polished brass stand at the foot of the grand staircase, a sign advised guests that afternoon tea was now being served in the upstairs bar lounge. An invitation that Tyler would normally have walked past, and not even noticed, but on this occasion, he found the offer strangely appealing.

Entering the lounge, he surveyed the scene, and intuitively headed toward a coffee table with two sofa chairs, halfway along the left hand wall. He purposely chose to sit in the chair that angled back toward the entrance and the interior of the lounge, because he could observe people inside the lounge, or those entering or leaving. The drinks bar, out of view behind him, was of no interest to him.

There were only a few people in the lounge, but after all it was just after three on a Friday afternoon. A couple of older ladies were seated at a table with upright chairs in the centre of the lounge. On another table, three expensively dressed women in their early to mid-forties, were washing down their afternoon tea with a glass of Moët. On the opposite side of the lounge in the front corner, a middle-aged man was seated at a table facing back into the lounge. Tyler decided that he was probably a tourist, because on his table was an expensive SLR camera on a shoulder strap, and he was reading a London travel guide.

Within moments of Tyler seating himself, a waiter appeared, and stood alongside, order pad and pen in hand.

Flashing his room card, Tyler said, 'Just a pot of Earl Grey tea, and a Florentine please.'

'Are you sure you wouldn't prefer our full afternoon tea offer, at just eight pounds fifty, Sir? It really is better value.'

'No, I'll just stick with the Earl Grey, and the Florentine, if I could please'.

Apart from the male waiter, a waitress was moving about in

a housemaid's uniform, suggesting to Tyler that the girl had been seconded from housekeeping; probably because the usual waitress was unavailable for her shift. With a confused expression on her face, she nervously popped in, and out from behind the servery, tending to the needs of the ladies, and it was she, who a few minutes later, delivered Tyler's afternoon tea.

As Tyler signed the order docket, he was vaguely aware that two men had entered the lounge, and seated themselves at the coffee table immediately behind him.

After the waitress left his table, Tyler began checking the objects she'd placed on the table. He reoriented the plate with the Florentine, the teapot, the strainer, the milk jug, the sugar bowl, and the hot water jug, to allow for the most practical, and efficient use of the objects.

Wait, stop, no hot water jug — alarm bells. Tyler raised his arm just in time to catch the waitress's eye, as she was about to disappear behind the servery wall. Profuse apologies, and she quickly returned with the missing jug of boiling water.

Next, lift the teapot lid and check. Will it be loose tea, or will it be tea bags? To Tyler's relief, huge leaves of loose tea and the strong aroma of Bergamot greeted him, and said, *Good afternoon sir, my name is Earl Grey, and I'm here to delight your senses.*

Moving to the next item on his late mother Edna's list of essential steps to serving the perfect cup of tea: pour the milk into the cup first, then slowly turn the teapot, three times clockwise, and then three times anti-clockwise, before pouring. This step is essential to release the flavour from the leaves without bruising them, and most importantly, under no circumstances should the pot be stirred with a metal spoon.

At the moment that Tyler had concluded his tea ceremony, his attention was drawn to the voices of the two men who'd seated themselves behind him. It was their contrived whispering that had drawn his attention — no doubt contra to any intentions that the two men may have had.

Intrigued, Tyler straightened up, twisted his torso, and feigned a backward glance over his left shoulder, as if he were about to order something from the bar.

The two men were seated in sofa chairs and facing, what until now, had been the back of Tyler's head. Because he found himself looking straight into their faces, he quickly released the twist in his torso, and his right buttock obliged by settling itself back down onto the seat of his chair.

Once again he was facing toward the lounge entrance, and to Tyler's relief the men continued their conversation, as if nothing had happened.

In the brief moment, that Tyler's eyes had met theirs, Tyler had registered that one man was of black African appearance, while the other was Caucasian. The black man's face projected a warm curiosity, whilst the other man's face was cold and expressionless. A look that Tyler had found unnerving.

The man of African appearance seemed to be in his late forties, with a balding head, and heavy tortoise spectacle frames. He was moderately overweight, and more extravagantly dressed than the other man. He was wearing an expensive suit, white shirt with double-back cuffs, gold cufflinks, floral tie, gold wrist watch, and a large yellow gold diamond ring on the little finger of his right hand.

The Caucasian man was about the same age as the African,

but taller, slimmer, and had a more muscular build. He had a neatly trimmed moustache, shaved head, and a British accent with what seemed to be a South African click to it. He was dressed in an unbuttoned, and crumpled pale-blue linen jacket, blue jeans, and a white open necked shirt with long sleeves.

As Tyler returned to pouring his tea, he was now more conscious of the whispered conversation taking place behind him, than he had been before. The Caucasian man was saying something along the lines of: 'I've locked in place the package that you signed-off on last time we met. The armoured vehicles, the heavy weapons, the small arms, and the offsite training for your men. With regard to the training, I've arranged for the men to be flown to the island of Bougainville, where they'll be looked after by our ex Special Air Service, and Special Boat Service people. As promised, there will be no direct link, with regard to any of this, to either yourself, or myself.'

Following a brief pause as if to underscore his comments, he continued. 'In your position as the Modrisian, Minister of Finance, I'll deal directly and only with you. Apropos what I said a few moments ago, no-one else will communicate at this level. That is how it needs to be. Under the circumstances, it's better for you, and it's better for me.'

'Once everything's in place, day-to-day contact can begin between your people, and my third party facilitators. Any issues concerning the facilitators must be directed through me. You do not need to have direct contact with these people.'

'Once your funds have been received and cleared, it will automatically trigger the delivery of your Rolls-Royce, and the amount of eight hundred and fifty thousand British Pounds, will be transferred to your offshore bank account.'

When commenting on what had just been said to him, the black man's voice, was so muddy that Tyler had difficulty understanding him. What was clear to Tyler though, was that there had been a surprise gearshift in the tone of the conversation taking place behind him. The black man's voice had become more strident, and the other man was responding with signs that he was in a simmering state of cold rage. His speech had slowed, and his volume had lowered. His words were now being articulated with exaggerated precision, and they were being delivered staccato, like a steady stream of rounds from a machine gun.

For Tyler, the non-participant observer to the conversation, the impact of the caucasian man's words were instant, profound, and totally unexpected. It was as if he had channelled the fear that the black man was feeling at that moment.

'We are way past the point of negotiating the arrangement. You did enough of that last time we met. Don't fuck with me. Do you hear? Do you understand me? If you go back on our agreement, I will personally come after you — along with all the other democratically elected leaders of Modrisia. There will be no place on earth where you will be safe. You are a greedy cunt, but you can't be that fucking stupid. You will honour our agreement as it stands. There will be nothing beyond what was agreed to last time.'

'Anyway, I don't want, or need to meet with you personally again,' he continued, 'After we part company today, if you need to contact me, I'll give you a new mobile phone number.

Commit it to memory, and don't stick it in that electronic gadget of yours. Zero double seven, double zero nine, double zero seven, double zero. That's, Zero double seven, double zero nine, double zero seven, double zero.' Tyler heard the muffled, but now contrite voice of the black man as he repeated the number.'

Suddenly, the voices of the well-dressed, Champagne-sipping, tittering women, stomped their way back into Tyler's consciousness, and with that he realised, that the two men were probably just about to say their goodbyes, and leave. He was disorientated, and his heart raced as he fought to suppress an almost irrepressible urge to get out of his chair and run — an action that would only make a bad situation worse. He decided that considering his state of fear and confusion, the last thing he needed, was for the men to get a good look at him, on their way out, and that could only happen if they were first to leave.

Tyler straightened up, took a series of slow, deep inaudible breaths, and while continuing to face the entrance, he stood up, pushed his chair back, picked-up his briefcase, and slowly walked toward the entrance.

As he descended the curved staircase, he maintained a gaze, that was always 180 degrees away from the lounge entrance, until he was well below the level at which his face could be seen. When he stepped onto the carpet runner at the bottom of the staircase, he avoided the lift, and rather took the other staircase back to his room on the second floor.

As Tyler swiped his key card, and received the *hello, you're back again,* click and green light, his brain was numb. He struggled to recall one single thought he'd had since leaving the lounge. It was as if his brain had deactivated itself, because it was dangerously close to being full.

He had seen, and heard things that disturbed him. It had invoked a weird sense of fear, that he had never experienced before.

On the other hand, logic was telling him that his fears were almost certainly groundless. Even if the men had been aware of him, they probably wouldn't give a rat's arse anyway. It was none of his business, it didn't concern him, and it didn't pose an immediate, or real threat to him — move on, and forget about it. It was simply a case of him having been, in the wrong place at the wrong time.

His mental state, had fast descended, into a cul-de-sac of vacillating extreme thoughts. Intense fear, with an urge to make a run for it, to be instantly replaced by calmness, and equipoise. Paradoxically, these emotions were interspersed with states of excitement, if not elation, and an intense desire to share his experience with others.

At this point, at precisely ten past four in the afternoon, Tyler's brain did what all normal brains do when faced with an insoluble, and unresolved problem; it created a diversion — it was time to take a bath.

Tyler's soak in a deep hot bath, with a couple of sachets of complimentary pine needle bubble bath, relaxed him, and moved his emotions to a much more balanced and happy place.

A place where he suddenly saw the irony of his situation — today just happened to be; Friday the thirteenth.

* * *

When Tyler eventually hit the hotel forecourt, it was already twenty to seven, and to his relief, there was no evidence of an unclaimed minicab. It was now a matter, of the minicab being late, not Tyler.

At that point, it also crossed his mind, that maybe the minicab had already been, and gone, perhaps even with someone else in it. Maybe a non English-speaking tourist, who had responded to the driver's call-out for *Jones,* by clambering in.

At quarter to seven, a dark blue Volvo 440 hatchback, pulled into the forecourt, the driver got out, peered over the car roof in Tyler's direction, and said, *Mr Jones?*

Deposited safely back at the Courthouse Hotel, courtesy of an unnecessarily apologetic minicab driver, and with his return journey reconfirmed for a ten-thirty pick up, Tyler reentered a room that in no way resembled the one that he'd left, only a few hours earlier.

Gone was the U shape conference setting, replaced by six round tables, each set for six, soft side wall lighting instead of the overhead halogen spotlights, and from the corner of the room, came the soft, sweet sounds of a jazz quartet. Keyboard, double-bass, drums, and the jewel in their crown, a female songbird, who's slender fingers, gently caressed the neck of a vintage Gibson arch back.

People were milling around the room, and chatting in small groups, while two, or three waitresses, skilfully danced in and around them, with trays of drinks and canapés. Most faces Tyler recognised from the forum earlier in the day, even if he'd forgotten the names that belonged to them.

Some faces were missing, maybe yet to arrive, or maybe never to arrive, because they'd already packed up and gone home. Overall, it seemed to Tyler that numbers had been maintained, or even increased, because some attendees were now sporting previously unseen partners. Most partners were women, probably the wives of delegates who'd seized an opportunity to accompany their husbands, for a stint of retail therapy in London.

Conversely, there were a couple of unfamiliar males, who Tyler assumed, were husbands of women delegates. Either way, male, and female partners could be identified by their nervous, awkward disposition, and their bizarre overdressing.

When Tyler entered the room, he immediately spotted Chris Wood, dressed in the same clothes, drink in hand, and standing at the back of the room talking to Jennifer and Jerry. Not wanting to appear too eager, or needy, Tyler milled around until it seemed the right psychological moment to approach.

That moment presented itself, when Jennifer looked away from Jerry and Chris, spotted Tyler, and said, 'Tyler, we've just been talking about you. Do come and join us.'

Like most people there, Jennifer had changed during the break. The dark blue business jacket and skirt, the white cotton blouse, the barely-black tights, and the sensible black wedge heel court shoes, had been pushed aside for a stunning, well above the knee, floral print silk dress, nude tights, and beige high heels. Tyler immediately understood what it was that attracted Jerry to this surprise package, and he was more than a little bit envious.

'Actually,' said Jennifer, 'We know Chris, because he writes our advertorials, and as you know, he's been here today, to gather material for a feature article he's preparing for the Sunday Leader. Chris has been telling us that he's known you from secondary school days. We would never have guessed there was any connection. Don't worry though, everything he's said about you, has been complimentary.'

'Touché,' said Jerry, 'And hey, seeing as we're all about to be sitting down, and you guys obviously want to catch-up, why don't we all sit together? The way the numbers have worked out, we'll be the only ones on this table, and Jennifer, and I want to move-on, about nine o'clock anyway. Under the table, is a bottle of 1978 Saint-Emilion Grand Cru, that you're welcome to. The dinner menu, offers one bottle of house red, or white per couple; after that, the same wine is fifteen quid a bottle from the bar.'

Tyler, and Chris glanced at each other, and in a heartbeat, Chris Wood said, 'We accept. Yes Sir, Mr Jerry, we accept. Not quite the quality I'd normally drink, but much better than the house wine.' Tyler, highly embarrassed by Chris Wood's insensitivity, was rendered speechless. Proof that uncorked, and unseen, the 1978 Saint-Emilion Grand Cru, had already begun to weave its magic.

At the close of such an intensive day, no one at the table had any desire to talk shop. Their conversation, flitted from holidays, to live music, to fashion, to dysfunctional families, and finally as the *J-Birds* were visibly itching to leave, the sorry state of the British economy.

As Jerry rose, to ease Jennifer's chair back, lest she risk a departure, significantly less elegant than her arrival, and true to his word, he simultaneously reached under the table, grabbed the bottle of Saint-Emilion Grand Cru by the neck, and placed it on the table in front of Chris Wood.

Tyler immediately noticed that the cork had already been removed and placed back. He figured that this was probably to avoid getting into a dust-up with the wine waiter, or perhaps it had been a prior arrangement, and its presence on the table was Kosher — sort of. Either way, neither Tyler, nor Chris Wood gave a damn, as they urgently unplugged the bottle.

At the point when Jerry, and Jennifer had said their good-byes and left, Tyler and Chris, had not managed one single moment of conversation between themselves.

It was just on nine-thirty, the dinner was over, the plates had been cleared, and the jazz band had skilfully transformed their offering to match the mood of the room.

Freshly brewed coffee had begun hitting the tables, and for Tyler and Chris, sitting on what was now a table for two, it provided the perfect setting to enjoy their superb Bordeaux, while having their long-awaited chat.

Tyler Jones shared with Chris Wood, the major events of his life since they'd last seen each other, sometime in the early-eighties.

Tyler reminded Chris, that unlike him, he'd never quite completed his A-levels. He'd left school, and tried a variety of jobs, until he'd stumbled into the one at NuForm-Craven, at the age of twenty-seven.

He explained how Jim Craven, as a refugee from the Wapping dispute in 1986, had returned to Birmingham, and with finance provided by a friend, had started his own desktop publishing business.

The business had grown quickly, because it just happened to be doing the right thing, at the right time, and in the right place.

Tyler explained how he'd started as a Trainee Supervisor, but had recently been promoted to Sales Manager, and hence, his reason for being at the forum.

Tyler, suddenly aware of the hour, and interested to hear Chris Wood's story, navigated a quick biographical tack, away from himself.

Chris for his part, began by linking his own career success, with what Tyler had just said about Jim Craven, and the Wapping dispute.

'There I was, just out of the London School of Economics, with a degree in Politics and International Relations, and the Wapping thing started. While all those Journo dicks were out there on the picket line, in sympathy with their printer mates, I simply walked in, and took one of their jobs, well actually, I took two.'

'The Leader seized the opportunity to create one new job out of two old ones, hence my position as, National Political and International Relations Correspondent for the London Leader. It would seem then, that your boss Craven and I, have progressed very nicely thank you, out of the misfortune of others. Very Darwinian, don't you think?'

'I live on my own in a posh flat, on the edge of the Thames, looking down on Tower Bridge, and I've got a Porsche and a Harley in the car park under the building.'

'I am quite often out of the country, on assignment, which also provides me with the opportunity to combine pleasure with business. I really do have a very good life.'

'I get paid more than thirty-five thousand quid, plus expenses, to chat with senior politicians, overseas leaders, dignitaries, celebrity entertainers, sporting greats, and believe it, or not, even senior spooks from MI5 and MI6. I get regular *off the record* briefings from these people, during nosh-ups at London's best restaurants; presumably at Her Majesty's expense.'

When Chris Wood had boasted about his connections at MI5 and MI6, the disturbing events of Tyler's afternoon broke through, and in a Tourette-like moment, Tyler said, 'You won't believe what...,' and just as he was about to add, *I overheard this afternoon*, he edited his words midstream, to become, '...the time is. I'll have to be pushing off, my minicab's due in a few minutes.'

While the replacement clause, may have been less than perfect, it nonetheless allowed Tyler's mental lapse to pass unnoticed, such that Chris Wood said, 'What a shame, never mind, it's an excuse for us to do this all again; we need a plan. I propose this side of Christmas, which gives us a couple of months to arrange something.'

Producing a business card from his wallet, Chris Wood said, 'Call me when you know you're coming back down to London, so I can make sure I'll be around.'

'It's been really great, to see you again Tyler Jones. I'm already looking forward to next time. Don't miss your cab, and don't feel sorry for me old boy. When you leave, what's left in this bottle, will all be mine.'

At just before ten-thirty, and to the accompaniment of the songbird, as she delivered a slow, and husky rendition of *Summertime*, Tyler Jones headed up the stairs, and out on to Great Marlborough Street, to meet his Indian minicab driver.

5

LIFE CHANGES

Saturday, 14th September, 1991.

When Jim Craven had suggested to Tyler, that he attend the industry forum in London, it had all seemed, a bit of an indulgence — an excuse to get away from work for a few days.

It was only now when it was all over, that Tyler realised, just how exhausting it had all been. It had taken more out of him, than he ever could have imagined.

How then, would he spend his six hours of freedom, before he needed to be back on the Northern Line to get to Euston Station by four?

As he was checking-out of the hotel he realised that it was fresh air and exercise he needed, not the inside of a gallery, or museum.

At just after nine in the morning, and with his check-out completed, Tyler consigned his briefcase and suit bag, to the hotel porter for a few hours of safekeeping.

Stepping out of the hotel onto the Strand, he intuitively turned right into Villiers Street; the narrow street, bordering the side of the Charing Cross Hotel, leading down to Embankment Gardens, and the river Thames.

With Cleopatra's Needle visible through the trees, Tyler sat on one of the park seats, consulted his map, and came up with a plan.

He would take the river walk, on the edge of the Thames, to Tower Bridge and St Katharine's Dock, and somewhere along the way, he'd stop for lunch.

He calculated, that it was probably a couple of miles each way. He would go at a steady, but relaxed pace, take-in the attractions, have lunch, and still be back to pick up his things by three o'clock; just enough time to get to Euston by four.

Tyler also questioned whether his desire for fresh air and exercise, had less to do with his physical wellbeing, than it did with something else. That his need for physical exercise, although justified by his day of inactivity and stress yesterday, plus his overindulgences at dinner last night, may in fact be a diversion, designed to avoid him facing issues that need to be addressed.

What to make of his lapse into madness with Julie, a couple of days ago, and what to do, if anything, about the conversation he overheard, in the hotel lounge yesterday.

Tyler had had many relationships with women over the years, probably more than his share, and it had always been the same. Sometimes there would be lots of sparks; sparks that would set off a series of explosions, before fizzling out. Other times, the fuse would sputter and die, only moments after it was lit.

Tyler had given great thought to his dalliance with Julie, in an attempt to better understand what had happened. He had replayed the mental video, over and over again.

He had been aware for some time, that Julie had fancied him, and for his part, he had found her physically irresistible at times too, but he had never actioned those desires.

Rightly, or wrongly, he had been moved to a better place emotionally by what had happened, and that must count for something. Julie had entered his room with a need, and in accepting her advances, Tyler had demonstrated that he too had a need. One's need, satisfied the other's need, and in some weird sense, they cancelled each other out.

Confirmation that this had in fact been the case, came when Craven had suddenly and unexpectedly appeared in the office later that afternoon. The Julie who greeted him, was the same old Julie. There was no sign, overt, or subtle, that something might have happened between herself and Tyler. Things had returned to the way they always had been, and Tyler was determined that from his side anyway, they would remain that way.

He also rehashed his overheard conversation in the upstairs lounge bar, and as he had concluded yesterday, the fear that he felt at the time was illogical. He was not in any imminent danger, best forget about it and move on.

Having dispensed with his major concerns, and with inner peace restored, the sensory delights of the river potentiated every experience he encountered for the remainder of his walk.

* * *

Friday, 20th September, 1991.

Tyler Jones would get together with his mates after work on Friday afternoons. They'd meet-up during the warmer, daylight saving months, around five-thirty, to kick a ball around on one of the pitches, down off Pershore Road. It was a loose arrangement, totally devoid of obligation. Whomever showed-up, showed-up.

They'd play for an hour, or so, and then predictably for a bunch of young guys, score an own-goal, straight through the front door of the local pub.

Most of them had gone to the same Secondary School, leaving at various stages, and ending-up in a variety of jobs. In some cases, they'd gone in to a trade, while others had continued their education at nearby colleges, or universities. In Tyler's case, he'd left school without taking his A-Levels, and knocked around, until finding his feet at NuForm-Craven.

They'd all considered joining a team, in the Birmingham and District, Amateur Football Association, but the thought of any commitment turned them off. They just wanted to kick a ball around and have fun.

On this particular occasion, it was only Tyler Jones and Tim Hadley who arrived at the pitch. It was such a lovely day, and with daylight saving still in force, the others had probably decided to confine any physical activity to their elbows.

After kicking the ball around, until they were bored silly, and with no-one else there, the logical thing was to pack up, and head up the hill to the pub.

Their decision was also logical, because they hadn't seen each other for quite some time. There was much to catch-up on, and to sit out the back of the pub, in the soft late afternoon sunshine, was such a wonderful way to do it.

Tyler told Tim about his new job promotion, and how he'd bumped into their old school chum, Chris Wood, when he was down in London. How Wood had bettered himself by moving down south, certainly faring better than those who'd stayed in Birmingham. A notion, that only served to reinforce their long held, and well entrenched local prejudices, with regard to people who moved down south.

For his part, Tim Hadley talked about his own new job, as purchasing officer at a local plumbing supply company, and how his sister Jemma, had recently given birth to a baby boy at Selly Oak Hospital.

Over the years, and because of his friendship with Tim Hadley, Tyler had certainly been aware of Tim's sister Jemma. Tyler remembered her well. She was drop-dead gorgeous, but she was spoken for.

Through Tim, Tyler had even been invited to Jemma and her husband Mark Knightley's house-warming party. It was a warm and muggy summer evening, and every room in the small house was packed with people, holding a glass of something. The music was loud; The Waterboys — The Whole Of The Moon, the words of which had for inexplicable reasons, transported Tyler to another place. A place of mixed emotions; exhilaration and passion, paradoxically wrapped in nostalgia and sadness.

In a desperate need for fresh air, Tyler had found his way

out into the back garden. It was there, while the long outro riff was playing in the background, that Tyler had found himself alone with Jemma.

Words, long forgotten, had passed between them, but it was the locking of eyes and the accompanying unexpected emotions, that Tyler had not forgotten. The fact that neither party could shift their gaze from one another. A situation, that had only been resolved, when Tim had come looking for Tyler. If Tim Hadley had been wise to Tyler and Jemma's sudden display of self-conscious embarrassment, then he hadn't shown it.

'Well,' continued Tim Hadley, 'the fact is, that Jemma's husband Mark, just up, and left her earlier this year, right when she needed him the most. She was less than half way through her pregnancy at the time, and they already have one child, Annie, who's nearly four years old. We're led to believe, that Mark, has settled for the bachelor life, in the oil fields of Bahrain, but we don't really know. With his SAS background, maybe he's taken some sort of paramilitary, security job. Since leaving the army, Mark Knightley was one of those chaps, who found the transition back into civilian life very difficult. It's as if, in his mind, he had never considered himself married.'

'Where Jemma's concerned, since the arrival of baby Cameron, emotionally, she's not been in a good place. Mum helps out where she can, but I think Jemma has become quite depressed. She doesn't have a job, which would offer the company of workmates, so she's stuck at home on her own for most of the time. She's got a couple of girlfriends, but they're busy with their own small kids and families.'

'Perhaps one positive, is that for the past six months, or so, Mark's continued to pay the mortgage, and he's also been putting, one hundred and fifty quid, into their joint bank account each week. So, it looks like he's going to do the right thing by her, financially at least.'

'Anyway Tyler,' said Tim, 'Sunday week, the twenty-ninth, we're having a lunch at mum's place. Mum's just had some home renovations completed, so we're going there to celebrate. Why don't you come along, It'll only be the family, plus a couple of close friends like yourself — and of course, you'll get to see Jemma again.'

You'll get to see Jemma again — were the only words that Tyler Jones heard.

* * *

Tuesday, 24th September, 1991.

At his desk, Tyler was feeling that life was pretty good, and getting better by the moment.

Tyler's high spirits were almost entirely due to Tim Hadley's words last Friday afternoon; *You'll get to see Jemma again*. Those words, just like the parable of the mustard seed, had assumed disproportionate significance in his mind. In of themselves, the words had little meaning, but for Tyler, the words invoked fond memories of a warm summer evening, with the most beautiful woman he had ever seen. Sunday lunch could not come fast enough.

Jim Craven had decided to take the week off; a decision that had pleased Tyler no end. It meant that Craven wouldn't be hovering around when he went down to Slough, for his meeting with the people at AcuWrite Media.

His aim being, to return home with the biggest customer NuForm-Craven has ever had.

* * *

Thursday, 26th September, 1991.

Tyler pulled into AcuWrite Media's car park for his lunchtime meeting, with only minutes to spare.

The J-birds were sitting chatting in reception, when Tyler entered the building.

It was obvious to Tyler, that a bond had formed between himself and these people, whom he'd met for the first time only two weeks ago; a bond that went beyond business. He liked them, and it seemed that they liked him too.

'We've booked a table, at a Bar along the High Street,' said Jerry. 'Only a five minute walk from here. The air is brisk, but the walk'll do us good.'

The bar restaurant was a rambling place, with bare wooden floorboards, bare wooden tables, and bentwood chairs. It was bustling, it was noisy, it was chaotic, and obviously successful. Tyler decided that the place was populated by a mixture of creative types, property agents, and prestige car sales people, all in their mid-twenties to mid-forties, and all addicted to immortality.

The place had the inviting smell of some sort of cheese bake, and combined with everything else, Tyler felt more alive than he'd felt in a long time.

Following their vegetarian lasagna with salad, and a shared bottle of Bordeaux, Jerry said, 'Being Friday, we're not much in the mood to talk business, more in the mood to relax, and enjoy ourselves. We have made a decision though, and that's all that matters for the moment. We want to come up to your firm, and maybe spend a few hours with you and your team.'

'Last financial year, we spent over a quarter of a million quid with our London agency. Based on your rate card, we would have spent considerably less, and received much more. Those savings could be better used, to grow our European business.'

Jennifer then took the lead, 'Your involvement with us, primarily relates to what we plan to do in Europe. Our other offices look after their own local geographic regions, but overall authority for Europe, resides with us.'

Jerry resumed, 'As I said in London, once we've set all this up, I want Jenny to handle the day-to-day operations directly with you. Jenny will also co-ordinate the other local European offices, that she just mentioned.'

Lost for words, Tyler said, 'Wow, I'm flattered. I really can't believe that you'd make such a major decision so quickly, and on the basis of our brief meeting in London.'

Back on the motorway, and pointed north, Tyler's thoughts were so profuse, that they log-jammed as they fought with each other for Tyler's conscious acknowledgement.

The thought that kept forcing its way to the top over and over again, was: *I've just grown NuForm-Craven's overall business by more than twenty percent in one day. This twenty percent increase may well translate to a fifty percent increase in our net profit. How good is that?*

* * *

Sunday, 29th September, 1991.

When Tyler Jones, parked his car outside Mavis Hadley's semi-detached in Lazy Hill, and knocked on her front door, he had lost all connection with space and time. There was, last Friday week, when he'd had dinner with Tim Hadley, and then there was now; Standing on Jemma's mother's front doorstep with a bottle of white wine, and a bunch of flowers. All events in-between, had been obliterated, because nothing in-between seemed to matter.

'Tyler! Please do come in,' said Mrs Hadley, 'We're all down the back. Follow me.'

As she began to turn away, Tyler held out the bottle of wine, and the flowers.

'Oh, you dear lovely boy, bless you,' she said as she leaned over and pecked Tyler on the cheek, before heading off down the long hallway; the end of which, Tyler could see was bathed in sunshine.

The large extension with its large south-facing end wall, had cleverly embraced what would have been the original kitchen, and dining rooms; converting them, into one large open-plan living space.

As Tyler entered the area, to his left was the rebuilt kitchen, and to his right was the new dining area. The original hallway walls had been removed, and replaced on the kitchen side, with a large granite bench-top, while the dining room had gained the space that had previously been wasted on the hallway.

There they all were; Tim, Tim's brother Simon, their mum Mavis, little three year old Annie, and sitting in an armchair against the floor to ceiling glass window, was Jemma.

The glowing autumnal sunshine transformed Jemma's image into something akin to a Byzantine icon. The only person who seemed missing from the room, was the baby, who Tyler quickly decided, was probably sound asleep somewhere else in the house.

There was though, one sudden, heart-sinking moment when Tyler realised, that there was someone extra in the room. A man was standing by the window, staring out at what little remained of Mavis Hadley's back yard.

Tyler immediately perceived the man as a threat. Was he there with Jemma? He was tall, about Tyler's age, and as he turned to acknowledge Tyler's presence, Tyler saw that he was very handsome indeed.

Announcing Tyler's presence, Mrs Hadley said, 'Here's Tyler, someone get him a drink, and top-up our glasses at the same time. Jemma darling, pretty-please, could you come and give me a hand to get the lunch on the table?'

Annie ran toward Tyler, wrapping herself around his right leg, as she dragged him toward her nest of toys in the middle of the carpeted floor. Tim stepped forward as did Simon, to shake Tyler's hand, and as they did, Tim said, 'Oh, Tyler, this chap over here is Trevor, he's a friend of Simon's, I don't think, you've ever met Trevor before?'

Still in the process of shaking hands with Tim and Simon,

Tyler, out of the corner of his eye saw Trevor approaching; unbuttoned casual floral shirt, tanned face, heavy gold necklace, and large ebony earrings. As Trevor extended his hand toward Tyler, he said, *Hello Tyler*, and Tyler knew that he had absolutely nothing to worry about.

Tim twisted around, grabbed a Tuborg from a large plastic bowl of crushed ice on the kitchen bench top, and thrust it into Tyler's right hand. Annie, simultaneously, and out of sheer persistence, had inched Tyler closer to her toys on the floor and away from the others. To guarantee that he remained on course, she had changed her grip from his right leg, to his right arm, before finally changing to her ultimate hold; a neck lock, from which submission was the only escape.

Tyler now faced the embarrassing choice, of either falling flat on his face in the middle of Annie's toys, or dropping on his bum from a great height, with a kid draped around his neck, and a beer in his hand. He wisely, and successfully executed the later option.

This risk-taking activity, of not wanting to disappoint a small child, had temporarily obliterated everything else from Tyler's mind.

With Annie, now seated happily amongst her toys, Tyler was suddenly aware that Jemma was crouched down on her haunches, beside him.

With her face close to his, she whispered, 'I don't know how you feel about seeing me again, but I'm certainly excited to see you. It'd be good to catch-up. How are you placed for coming around to my place on Tuesday evening? After dinner, and when the little ones are both hopefully, asleep in bed.'

* * *

Tuesday (PM), 1st October, 1991.

When Tyler arrived at Jemma's Terrace house, in Lifford Circle, he knew, that this would be a make-it, or break-it occasion.

To believe that something is as it is, or how it appears to be, is one thing, but in reality, it may turn out to be something quite different.

Tyler's mental processes were a mess. His state of anxiety, was tantamount to standing, on the edge of a cliff. *Is what I feel for Jemma, a construct of what I want to believe? A belief that in reality, probably has no foundation in fact.*

Jemma's house, was the last in a row of terraces, and possessed the enviable asset of having its own driveway and garage. Considering the unlikely prospect of finding a parking spot in the street, Tyler took advantage of the driveway which was vacant.

As Tyler got out of his car, and walked along the narrow pathway to the front door in the crisp night air, the scales fell from his eyes. He finally saw things how they really were. Yes, it was all a construct of his desires, and thank God, it was revealed to him now. Now, as a blurred image appeared through the frosted glass panel of the front door. Thank God, for being saved from saying, or worse still, from doing something that he would regret for the rest of his life.

Yesterday, when Jemma had phoned to reconfirm their arrangement, she'd said that eight-thirty was a good time, because the little ones should be asleep. Once again, this comment, had been conveniently knitted-in to Tyler's machinations.

'Come in Tyler. Thanks for coming. Come into the sitting room where we can talk without waking the little people.'

The room was brightly lit, and on the mantelpiece, was a framed photo of three soldiers, taken in what appeared to be a desert. Having not seen Mark for such a very long time, Tyler assumed that the person in the centre of the photo, must be Mark.

There were no soft lights, or soft music playing, and Jemma, although attractive in a knee-length floral cotton print dress, was certainly not wearing anything curve-hugging, or revealing.

Gesturing Tyler toward the sofa, Jemma headed to a facing armchair on the other side of the coffee table. Pushing her court shoes off with her toes, she sat down, tucked her legs up, and sat on her feet.

Although now considerably more relaxed, Tyler was none-the-less somewhat lost for words, such that his opening comments barely qualified as ice-breakers, but they sort of made sense.

Jemma, who'd remained silent throughout what was now, fast becoming an embarrassing moment for Tyler, broke the ice by saying, 'You see, I've got this problem, that I need to talk to you about.'

Nervously sensing that Jemma was about to reveal something terrible; something akin to having been diagnosed with a terminal illness, Tyler remained silent. Suitable words could not be found fast enough.

Letting her legs slide out from underneath her, so that she

could straighten up, and while fixing Tyler with a steady gaze, Jemma said, 'My problem is you, Mr Tyler Jones — you are my problem.'

With that, she stood up, made no attempt to put her shoes back on, took a couple of side steps to avoid the coffee table, and without taking her eyes off Tyler, she stood there, perfectly still.

Now, pleasantly surprised, but somewhat confused by what had occurred, Tyler also stood up, and after slowly moving toward her, wrapped his arms around her upper body.

They stood there, in total silence, not moving for a long time; enough time for Tyler to feel Jemma's tears, gradually soaking their way through his shirt. Moving his arms from around her upper back to below her waist, he gripped her by her upper thighs, and pulled her in to himself, with a firmness that said he wanted her.

Jemma, now with her face pressed so firmly into Tyler's chest that it was difficult to speak, sobbed, 'I love you Tyler Jones, I love you like I've never loved anyone before. I love you so much it frightens me. When we were all having lunch at mum's place, and I know this will sound terrible, but all I could think about, was for you to get up from where you were sitting, collect me, drag me under the table, and fuck me. The fact that my mother, my brothers, and my children were all there, meant absolutely nothing to me at that moment — nothing mattered to me, but you.'

As he kissed her face and neck profusely, Tyler turned Jemma's body slightly to the side, allowing her to breathe more freely, and so that he could lift the skirt of her dress. With the sound of elastic, and cotton crackling, Tyler forced his left hand, down the inside front of Jemma's knickers.

Jemma's knees were no longer able to support her. For minutes now, she'd gradually relinquished all control of her body to Tyler, who now, slowly and ever so gently, lowered her down onto the carpeted floor.

Saturday (PM), 12th October, 1991.

Since last Tuesday week, Tyler and Jemma's relationship had strengthened by the day, if not by the hour, and his evening visits to Jemma's place, resulted in a superglue bond to form, between himself and three year old Annie.

Two nights ago, Tyler, and Jemma had decided to celebrate their togetherness, by going out to a restaurant on Saturday night.

Arriving at Jemma's place late on Saturday afternoon, Tyler suggested, 'Why don't we head on down, to The Arcadian Centre?'

'What a wonderful idea,' said Jemma, 'We'll go in my car. Annie'll be beside herself. We haven't been out to a restaurant, since Mark left.'

'I was only reading the other day, about a new Latin American place, that's opened-up at The Arcadian. Can we go there please, pretty please. Also my darling, because I'm such a scheming and possessive bitch, maybe after such a busy week, my man will be so exhausted, that he'll need to have a sleepover. Don't answer that question.'

'Who's for dinner at the Arcadian? Who's for yummy Latin American food?' Tyler said, as they got out of Jemma's car.

'Yes, yes, yes, yummy Latin American food,' blurted Annie, bouncing up and down, without the foggiest idea what Latin American food was. 'I'm really, really hungry. Come on Tyler, let's go now.'

'Are we allowed to come too?' Jemma chimed, as she winked at Tyler, and extended Cameron, up and out from her body with both arms. 'After all, we might have played some part in all this too, you know — little miss bossy boots.'

In anticipation, that this situation might eventuate, Jemma had parked her car at a car park close to the Arcadian. This meant, that within a flash of adult-time, but an unacceptable eternity in four-year-old-time, the little family was being escorted to a table for four, at Cafe Sofrito, by their waiter.

After removing a chair from the table to provide space for Cameron's pram, the waiter offered menus, and quickly returned with a complementary flask of Hibiscus and Yerba Mate tea.

Lowering his height by bending his knees, the waiter looked straight into the eyes of Annie, and with a strong Spanish accent said, 'And what may I offer this beautiful young lady? We have Coke, Fanta, and Sprite, but might I recommend Jugo, which we prepare ourselves, and is greatly enjoyed by children of lovely parents who come to dine at Cafe Sofrito. Jugo is sweetened berries, and fruit, blended with a dash of lime, and served with crushed ice, in a tall glass.'

Wise to Annie's confusion, and that she was just about to blurt-out something that would prove embarrassing, Jemma quickly intervened. 'That sounds absolutely lovely, what a lucky girl you are to have your own special drink.' As Annie's brain struggled to make sense of the conversation, Tyler seized the moment, to enquire about the house white wine.

'The house white wine, yes it is a wonderful choice Sir. It's a lovely Sauvignon Blanc-Semillon from the Casablanca Valley, in Chile. It's our most popular white wine, Sir.'

'That sounds great, thank you' said Tyler, 'We'll have a bottle, and two glasses.'

While this exchange played itself out, Annie had quietly decamped to another table on the other side of the room. A boy her own age, was embarrassing his parents, by crawling under the empty tables, and little miss busybody had decided that they needed her assistance. 'Get up Julian. Stop being a baby. Why don't you behave yourself, like this lovely little girl? What's your name, sweetheart...?'

Meanwhile, back at the Jones, and Knightly table, the waiter, had returned with their drinks, and after safely depositing them, he stood order pad in hand, ready to take their food orders.

Typical of patrons, they'd been so engrossed in conversation, and settling in to their environment, that they hadn't even opened their menus, so they did what most people do — seek guidance from their waiter.

During a summary, of the most complex, and expensive meals, from the specials board that the waiter carried around with him, Jemma interjected, and said, 'We'd really like to have something simple, more kid-friendly — you know how it is with small children — something perhaps we could all share.'

Without missing a beat, and as if he knew it was coming, 'Ah, dear lady, I thoroughly understand, I have two small children of my own. Might I recommend, a large plate of our house speciality — Taco Sofrito. These are Tacos, generously filled with a sauce of sautéed tomatoes, garlic, onions, roasted peppers, and our own special blend of fresh herbs.'

Exercising good judgement, combined with a gut feeling to stay away from any mention of price, Jemma said, 'That's, exactly what we need. Thank you.'

With Cameron dead to the world in his pram, and with Annie still residing, with the family three tables away, Jemma seized the moment. Stretching her upper body across the table, she grabbed Tyler around the neck with both arms, and pulled his head across the table toward her, 'God I love you, you sexy bastard. You've got no idea, how much I love you. I shouldn't say it, but I can't live without you. It's only been just over ten days, and I'm a mess. I don't want you to go back to your place tonight; I don't want you to ever go back to your place.'

Having delivered such an unambiguous statement of intent, she released her mutually uncomfortable grip, and with a straight back, gracefully slid back onto the seat of her chair.

Blindsided by events, Tyler was rendered speechless. This was supposed to be his moment to declare his commitment to her — not her to him. This was supposed to be the man's job.

Although the initiative had been taken from him, Tyler felt it much better to accept Jemma's proposition as a given, and then work together to put form to it.

With Jemma's erotic Opium perfume, still lingering in his nostrils from her embrace, Tyler shared his innermost feelings with Jemma. They were now, Tyler and Jemma — two peas in a pod.

Was all this a case of too much too soon in a relationship? In a very forthright manner, Tyler and Jemma bravely challenged the notion, and with a quorum of two, unanimously agreed that it wasn't.

With their Tacos delivered, it took them barely twenty minutes, to map-out their immediate future. Putting aside the odd sleepover, and the temptation to do otherwise, Tyler would remain in his one bedroom flat. They would draw a line in the sand, and make a list with regard to what of any importance belonged to whom. On Monday, they'd go to the bank to open a current account in joint names. For practical purposes this account would be used to take some of the day-to-day financial pressures off Jemma, and indirectly, her soon to be ex-husband Mark.

It had already been verbally agreed, between Mark and Jemma, that Jemma would stay in the house, and remortgage it in her own name. As Tyler was in effect, now being gifted a wife, and as he had no reason whatsoever to seek financial, or material benefit from Jemma and Mark's marriage, his presence would none-the-less provide additional financial security for Jemma and the children. Future support for the children of the marriage, was obviously a matter for a Court to decide, with Tyler prepared to assume ongoing responsibility, as required.

With the advent, of NuForm-Craven's newest customer, AcuWrite Media, Tyler was confident that his income was destined to increase far beyond the predictions of Jim Craven.

After Jemma's divorce settlement, he'd be in a position to pay Jemma's mortgage, from his salary alone if need be.

* * *

Monday, 14th October, 1991.

Following Tyler, and Jemma's night out at Cafe Sofrito, a number of changes had already been made.

They had visited their local RBS branch, and opened a joint Current Cheque Account, with linked Highline Cards, and in a due diligence exercise, Tyler had seen his rental agency to discuss his options, with regard to discharging the lease on his flat.

Regardless of their plan, for Tyler to remain in his one bedroom flat, he had, with considerable encouragement from Jemma, replicated all his personal bits and bobs at Jemma's house. This replication had extended well beyond the contents of a toiletry bag, to include, a dedicated drawer for his smalls, and in Jemma's wardrobe, a supply of shirts, jackets, trousers and shoes.

Most days, Tyler simply came straight home to Jemma's place after work and spent the evening with her and the children, before returning to his flat, sometime during the wee hours.

6

NINE O'CLOCK NEWS

Monday (PM), 14th October, 1991.

It was just before Nine o'clock in the evening, when Tyler arrived back at Jemma's place, and inserted his new duplicate key, into the lock on her front door.

Tyler had reluctantly agreed to meet a client over dinner, because the client had difficulty getting away during business hours.

There was only the soft light of a Jasmine candle on the hall table when Tyler entered, and save for the soft music, there was no other sound. Absent were the now familiar sounds of little people; he was too late home to see them before they went to sleep.

'Is that the love of my life, I hear? I'm tied to the kitchen sink and waiting. Actually, forget the kitchen sink, pop the news on, and I'll meet you in the sitting room.'

Placing his briefcase down alongside the hall table, Tyler

followed Jemma's instructions, and turned into the sitting room — the room from which Jemma's voice was now beckoning.

With the TV remote controller in his outstretched right arm, and aimed over the top of Jemma's head, they giggled and smooched, until they fell backwards onto the soft three seater sofa that faced the TV.

With Tyler suitably pinned face up, between Jemma's body and the back edge of the sofa, Jemma said, 'Who's in control now Mister Jones? How does it feel, to be helpless under a women?'

'If I could just breathe, I'd be able to tell you, Mrs Boss Lady.' Tyler said, as Jemma shifted her weight so that her body dropped sideways, between Tyler and the back of the sofa. Now released, Tyler rolled onto his side, dropped his legs over the edge of the sofa, and sat up facing the TV.

...and over on BBC2 it's, The Second Russian Revolution, but right now here on BBC1, it's the main news.

The Modrisian Finance Minister, Mr Baako Attah, shot dead on the steps of his embassy in London.

Jacques Delors calls on the EU to double its size.

Saddam Hussein says the war is not over as the UN says Iraqis beat its team to nuclear secrets.

The UN peace Convoy fails to break the siege of Dubrovnik in Yugoslavia.

Good Evening.

As Tyler sat up, the static screen graphic that accompanied

the lead item, flooded him with confusion and fear, as he struggled to make sense of what he was seeing.

He now had a name, for the face of one of the men he'd seen at the Charring Cross Hotel, and if Mr Baako Attah had been murdered, not only did Tyler know who did it, and why, but maybe his life was at risk too. His worst fears were being realised.

The body of Mr Baako Attah was found on the steps of the Modrisian embassy in Chelsea just before one o'clock this morning. He had been shot in the head. Mr Attah was the Modrisian Minister Of Finance.

A nearby resident who did not wish to be identified said that he had heard what he now understood to be a gunshot just after midnight. Because there were no further noises he did not investigate, or call the police.

In a prepared statement an attaché from the embassy said that forty-seven year old Mr Attah had been in London to receive treatment for a heart condition. The embassy was not aware of any threat to Mr Attah's life, and were assisting police with their investigation.

A police spokesman said that anyone with information should call Crimestoppers.

The way Tyler was now feeling, reminded him of how he felt four weeks ago, when he left the hotel lounge to return to his room.

Jemma, now up on her knees, and running her fingers through his hair, had drawn no connection whatsoever between the TV news, and Tyler's sudden change in appearance, and behaviour.

'Are you OK my darling? Are you sickening for something? You've gone all pale and sweaty.'

'No, no, I'm fine.' Said Tyler. 'Well, in the way that you ask the question I guess, but perhaps, not in another way; no I'm not alright. I actually need to talk to you about something that happened when I was down in London last month. Something that's been troubling me ever since, and something I haven't been able to understand — that is until I watched the news tonight.'

With the TV now turned off, Tyler told Jemma about his overheard conversation. He emphasised that he'd come to the conclusion, that the whole thing was probably a misinterpretation on his part, and that if it hadn't been for the news tonight, he had made up his mind to forget about it.

'This man, Mr Attah, the man who was shot, is definitely the man I saw at the hotel. He's definitely the man who was being threatened by the other man, and God knows who he is. I saw, and heard it all.'

'Maybe you should call Crimestoppers, like they just said on the news. Or, is there someone else you can talk to, outside of me of course my darling. Someone who you can trust, or maybe someone, who can put you in contact with someone else who can help you?'

'Actually,' said Tyler, 'it's been going through my mind as we've been talking. There is someone who fits that description, and that's my old friend Chris Wood, the journalist chap I told you about. In fact when we had dinner together, he told me that he's in regular contact with senior government, police, and spy agency people as part of his job.'

'It's only nine-thirty, maybe it's not too late to give him a call. Have you got his number?'

'I do. I'm sure Chris's business card is in my briefcase, and no, it's probably not too late to give him a call. The thing is though, he travels a lot, and he may well not be home, or even in the country for that matter.'

'What can I do you for, Mr Tyler Jones.' Chris Wood humorously said as he answered the phone.

'I'm really, really sorry to interrupt your evening Chris, but if you've got a few minutes, I need your advice. It relates to something that happened, while I was down in London, at the Charing Cross Hotel actually. The same day we saw each other, and had dinner together. If you've seen the news tonight — about that man from the Modrisian Embassy who was shot dead — well, that's what it's about.'

Tyler explained the situation in great detail, including how close he'd come to talking about it, but pulled himself up when they were having dinner together.

'OK Tyler, yes, I did see the news tonight. A gruesome business indeed, and based on what you've just told me, I'm sure there are people who need to hear your story. Let me give it some thought, and maybe make some discrete phone calls. I'll get back to you in the morning when I've worked something out.'

* * *

Still leaning with his back against the internal corner of his kitchen bench, where he'd taken Tyler's call, Chris Wood, with one deft movement of his middle finger, terminated the call from Tyler, and took a new line; a line with an atypical dial tone.

'Good evening Cyril, apologies for the late hour, but I've got something for you. Apropos the gunning-down of this Modrisian man in London earlier today, I have an acquaintance, Mr Tyler Jones, who overheard a conversation between this Baako Attah fellow, and another man at the Charing Cross Hotel, four weeks ago.'

'Tell me more, tell me more, my good man,' said Cyril Smart.

'Well, that's pretty well it, but he has more detail of course, that wasn't discussed with me. The gist of it is, that he apparently overheard a lengthy conversation in the upstairs lounge at the Charing Cross Hotel. During the conversation, an overt threat was made to the West African man, by the other man who was with him.'

'Wonderful information Mr Wood. Simply wonderful. We knew about the meeting, and positioned one of our officers there, but not knowing where the pair would seat themselves, we got no audio, and only a few photos from the other side of the room. I've seen the photos, and your man must be the chap sitting at the table against the wall with a briefcase. Our officer said that this man left a couple of minutes before the targets, but he had no idea who he was, where he came from, or where he went after he left.'

'The man who was with the Modrisian man, is well known

to us, he's a Jewish, South African arms dealer, by the name of Aaron Hersman. We also believe that Hersman is an agent working with the Mossad. It seems that he had negotiated an arrangement, with, or without the Mossad's knowledge, to supply arms and men for a planned coup in Modrisia around Christmas time. This Baako Attah chap was not only positioning himself for leadership after the coup, but he would also be clipping the ticket on the arms deal with Hersman — and that's probably why he's now dead. Something's obviously gone wrong with the deal. Hersman is a cold and ruthless killer, you betray him at your own peril. Interestingly, it's only recently that Hersman's reappeared on our radar.'

'So the question is,' continued Cyril Smart, 'what's the possibility for us to enlist the services of your Mr Tyler Jones? Normally a reports officer would work with you on a matter like this, but for reasons I can't discuss at the moment, I need to deal with it personally, and quickly. I'd like to meet with you tomorrow to discuss the matter further. It's important that we deal with it as quickly as possible.'

'If we decide that this Mr Jones can assist us, I'll personally clear it with "C", and then you can arrange for this Mr Jones, to meet with me on Thursday. As usual, morning tea, ten o'clock in the downstairs bar lounge at the Waldorf.'

'Thanks Cyril, see you there in the morning.'

Tuesday, 15th October, 1991.

Cyril Smart, Special Operations Manager at MI6, and a

person who reported directly to "C", the chief of Britain's Secret Intelligence Service, the SIS, was sitting waiting in the Waldorf bar lounge when Chris Wood arrived. Cyril Smart is also the person who journalist, cum MI6 agent runner, Chris Wood reports to.

Chris Wood with his degree in politics, and international relations, from the London School of Economics, combined with his position at the London Leader, made him an ideal candidate, for recruitment by MI6. In so doing, Wood became one of Six's chosen few, from the Fourth Estate. His education, his job, the circles that he moved in, and his frequent trips overseas, ideally positioned him, to be an MI6 agent.

'Good morning Mr Wood.'

'And a lovely, crisp Autumn morning it is, Mr Smart.'

'So now Mr Wood, tell me more about this Mr Tyler Jones.' Cyril Smart said, as he slid a ten by eight black and white print, out from inside a Manila folder. Pinning the print with his finger for a few seconds, he then slid it back, and closed the folder.

'Yes, that's Tyler Jones.' said Chris Wood.

'So what would it take to motivate this Tyler Jones to work with us? Would it be money, excitement, ego, or something else?'

'Well Cyril, at the moment fear would be the most likely motivation. After all, that's what motivated him to call me late last night. He's a decent chap, he's not flashy, or boastful, so there's not much ego there to stoke, but money, for purely practical reasons probably wouldn't go astray. He's just received a promotion to sales manager at his firm, which by definition brings more responsibility, but also provides more freedom, so if whatever you've got planned for him, involves a cover story, then he'd be in a good position to pull it off. Some sort of financial compensation would also appeal to him, because he's just taken up with a woman, who's got a young child and a baby.'

'Good man. Just the news that I hoped to hear.' Smart said as he rose, hands on the edge of the table as he pushed his chair back. 'Mr Jones seems perfectly suited for what I have in mind. Before I give you the green light to arrange a meeting between Mr Jones and myself, let me first go, and make a phone call to clear it with "C".'

Smart, leaving his Crombie overcoat neatly draped over the back of his chair, and his Christys Fedora on the table, gathered up his folder, and headed off to the public phone booths in the hallway near the ground floor loos.

Returning a few minutes later, Smart said, 'Yes, I do need you to arrange for Mr Jones to meet me. Let's say, here at the Waldorf, at eleven o'clock tomorrow morning.'

'Call Mr Jones, give him the instructions, and then confirm the arrangement with me in the usual way.'

7

DECISION TIME

Wednesday (AM), 16th October, 1991.

It was just before lunch, when Julie switched the call from Chris Wood, through to Tyler.

'I know it's short notice, but I've arranged a meeting for you in London tomorrow morning. It's with a senior person from military intelligence. His name is Mr Cyril Smart, that's his real name, it'll only involve the two of you, no one else will be there. He told me to tell you that considering what you witnessed, and the subsequent death of Mr Attah, it's critical that you meet with him as soon as possible.

'Jesus, that's less than twenty-four hours away, and in London, for fuck sake.'

'As I said, it's short notice, but don't forget, it was you who called me, late on Monday night, in a somewhat anxious state of mind. I've worked hard to get this meeting for you so quickly, and I think its pretty clear what's most important.'

'I know. I'm sorry Chris, it's just that it all comes as a bit of a shock, and I guess my reaction just proves how important it is, that I meet this Mr Cyril Smart.'

Chris Wood jumped back in, 'Something I learned that should be of interest to you. Mr Smart knew about the meeting, and he even knew the name of the other man who you saw. Military Intelligence apparently had someone observing, and taking photos. They even have a photo of you in the lounge.'

'So, if you've got a pen; it's the ground-floor bar lounge at the Waldorf Hotel at eleven o'clock tomorrow morning. Mr Smart's middle aged, very dapper, and will almost certainly be wearing an overcoat, hat, and gloves. I speak about his appearance from personal experience.'

'You probably already know where the Waldorf is, but it's in Aldwych, just a short walk down the Strand, on the opposite side from the Charing Cross where you stayed when you were in London. You can also get off the tube at Covent Garden if you're on the Piccadilly Line, and you're almost there. Oh, and just a small request, Mr Smart has asked, that apart from your partner, it might be best if you don't discuss this matter, with anyone else before you meet with him.'

After Tyler hung up, he realised that he'd suddenly lost his appetite for work. With Jim Craven away, and no one there to tell him what he could, or couldn't do — he went home.

Tyler proffered Julie a lame excuse as to why he was disappearing for the rest of the day, plus all day tomorrow, and with that duplicitous act, Tyler Jones had inadvertently taken his first step, on the path to developing a cover story.

* * *

Wednesday (PM), 16th October, 1991.

'How come my darling man's home so early? Did he get the sack?'

'Oh, if only.' said Tyler, 'My day was going really well, until Chris Wood phoned to say that he's got me a meeting, with a spook in London tomorrow morning.'

'You've got to be joking. In London tomorrow morning. I was hoping he'd be able to pass-on your information to the right person, and keep you out of it. It might have been better, if you'd simply called Crimestoppers anonymously, like the police suggested on the news.'

'Yes, I understand what you're saying, and in one sense, I want to agree with you,' said Tyler, 'but I guess it really comes down to the fact, that I'm scared stiff that this bloke's coming after me. In my mind, I keep going back to what I was thinking at the time, when all this was happening. The general conversation of these men was disturbing enough, but when you hear one man threaten the life of the other, it suddenly registers that if you've seen him, then he's seen you. Maybe not at the time, but maybe later, he forms the opinion that you represent a threat to him, and he comes after you.'

'Anyway,' said Tyler, 'I learned something else, really important. Apparently they already know who this other man is, and they know about the meeting. They even had someone there taking photos, and thinking back, I now remember seeing a man who was obviously pretending to be a tourist. He had an expensive camera and a tourist guide book on his table in the lounge.'

'Oh, my darling, I've obviously contributed to your worries by encouraging you to talk to this Chris Wood,' said Jemma, 'and now you can't put the genie back into the bottle.'

'No, please don't feel like that,' said Tyler as he gently cuddled Jemma's face into his chest, while running his fingers through her hair. 'Chris Wood seemed to suggest that this chap I'm seeing tomorrow, also believes I've got good reason to be concerned.'

'Maybe that's what they want you to think,' said Jemma. 'Maybe they've got some agenda, that's served by encouraging you to believe that. Is this Chris Wood mixed-up with these people in some sort of way? I just know that I love you, and I don't like to see you upset — take me to bed.'

Thursday, 17th October, 1991.

As happened, Tyler Jones, and Cyril Smart entered the Waldorf Hotel only moments apart.

Tyler had trained it from Birmingham, arriving at Covent Garden in good time. Enough time in fact to have a quick poke around. Something he'd planned to do when he was down in London last month, but simply ran out of time.

There was instant recognition as their eyes met, which demonstrated that Chris Wood's description to each of them had worked.

'Mr Jones, I presume. Follow me,' said Cyril Smart as he led the way down the passageway to the bar lounge.

Taking an inordinate amount of time to select a table, Smart took a white handkerchief out of his trouser pocket and began wiping, what to Tyler, seemed to be a perfectly clean table.

Following a visual check of his handiwork, Smart took off his slate-grey Fedora, and carefully placed it on what was now destined to be his side of the table; the side that faced back out toward the entrance. He then removed his black leather gloves, and his grey woollen overcoat. Tyler noticed that both Smart's coat and his hat, shared an attention-seeking red satin lining; *paradoxical for a spook seeking to operate in the shadows,* Tyler mused. Smart then held his coat vertically by its collar, before folding it inwards, and carefully laying over the back of his chair.

It was only then, when his disrobing ceremony was over, and he was pulling his chair back to sit down, did Smart gesture to Tyler to also take a seat.

Here was a neatly dressed, slim man, who Tyler guesstimated to be in his early fifties, and about five feet six, or seven tall. His hair was thinning, but still had plenty of colour; he wore bifocals with gold wire frames; his suit was two-piece, and mid-grey; his white shirt was ironed, but the collar was crumpled from wear; his tie was burgundy, and clipped to his shirt with a gold, hand engraved tie bar; his nails were manicured, and he wore an engraved gold signet ring on the little finger of his right hand. Accompanying all this, there was, Tyler detected, an odd, but not unpleasant smell of floral soap.

Special Operations Manager, Cyril Smart, was an MI6

career spook, who'd progressed his way through the ranks, by never offending those who ranked above him.

His beginnings had been intriguing.

As a young MI6 officer during the early nineteen sixties, Cyril Smart had spent most evenings, sipping fruit-cup, or champagne, at the Eve Club. A sophisticated nightspot in Regent Street, where he was posted as a case officer during his field training.

In that murky environment, he not only handled his agents, but he socialised with cabinet ministers, foreign spooks, business tycoons, and world famous stars of recording, stage and screen; not to mention the Eve Club showgirls and dancers.

Club members, and their guests, had access to a full bar, but showgirls and dancers, when invited to join private tables, were strictly limited to drinking Champagne, or fruit-cup. Fruit-cup being, chopped fruit, marinated in apple cider, and served in jugs with crushed ice.

Cyril Smart had ingratiated himself with the co-owners of the club, Helen and Jimmy O'Brien, and could often be seen, sitting with them at table number one. What Cyril Smart never knew, because his masters never told him, was that Helen O'Brien, a Romanian who's real name was Elena Constantinescu, was, just as he was, a British SIS operative.

Resident showgirls and dancers, were ideally positioned to glean valuable information when they were invited, or instructed by Helen O'Brien, to join guests at their private tables. Eve Club protocol ensured that table invitations were the remit of the Eve Club head waiter, with guests being discouraged from approaching girls directly. For a girl to join a private table, five pounds would be added to the guest's bill by the head waiter. The aggregate of these five pound amounts would then be paid to the girl as part of her wages. The base wage for a dancer at the Eve Club; two shows a night, six nights a week, ten o'clock at night through two-thirty in the morning; was only five pounds a week.

After retrieving and curating information gathered by the girls, Helen O'Brien would pass this information on to her handlers, during her twice weekly debriefings, at an SIS safe house in Hampstead.

Cyril Smart's time at the Eve Club, as a servant of Her Majesty's Secret Intelligence Service, came to an abrupt end in 1967. He had become overly friendly with an Australian girl, who, while dancing at the club each night, was also training to be an opera singer with John and Aida Dickens, during the day. While sex on the premises was strictly forbidden, girls *going-case* as they called it, off the premises, was reluctantly tolerated by Helen and Jimmy O'Brien.

Cyril Smart's relationship with this girl, had not only broken an Eve Club rule, it had also compromised his SIS cover role.

'Thank you for meeting with me Mr Jones, particularly at such short notice, I appreciate your help, and without overdramatising things, it's important that we deal with these matters quickly. There are circumstances associated with all this, that I can't discuss with you today.'

Smart then performed exactly the same sliding picture show that he'd performed for Chris Wood the day before, but this time, there were four images on the ten by eight, black and white print. Images that spanned the whole time that the meeting had been taking place. The last image in the series, and the one that Smart's finger was strategically positioned over, clearly demonstrated the caucasian man's interest in Tyler, as he rose to leave the lounge.

'Mr Wood has explained your situation to me, and these photos prove that you were in the lounge at the time that Mr Aaron Hersman and Mr Baako Attah had their meeting. We believe that Mr Hersman is almost certainly the person who killed Mr Attah. Not only that, but this man, Mr Aaron Hersman, demonstrated particular interest in you when it occurred to him that you may be there to observe him.'

'We also have reason to believe that Mr Hersman is currently trying to find out who you are. It may seem ironic, but you are in far less danger if he concludes, or we help him to conclude, that you are an MI6 officer — you are one of us. Therefore, an ongoing and more formal relationship between yourself and us, would seem to be mutually beneficial. A quid pro quo, you might say.'

'So with all this in mind Mr Jones, and until the matter is resolved, I'd like to offer you the opportunity to work with us here at MI6. The work would not require you to give-up your regular day job, in fact it's to our mutual advantage that your life goes on, as if nothing has changed. Whatever your current salary is, as sales manager of your firm, we will pay you half that amount again. This means that for the time you are with us, you'll be earning one and a half times what you earn at the moment.'

'If you agree to join us, we'll start you off with three days of intensive training. This training will provide you with the basics of our normal six month, SIS officer programme. We will also assign a dedicated team, who will work with you to develop a cover story. A cover story is designed to logically explain any changes in the way you would normally be expected to do things, especially any suspicions that might arise from those who deal with you on a day-to-day basis.'

'I don't want you to make a decision right now, I'd like you to consider my proposal overnight, and I'll call you in the morning. Feel free to discuss it, devoid of any detail, with your partner, and as I said earlier, there is urgency in getting you briefed and trained up. In this regard I can warn you in advance, that for most of the week after next, you'll need to be with us down here in London, maybe the Monday to Thursday inclusive.'

Having delivered his proposal, Smart offered no opening for further conversation, or questioning. He immediately ceased eye contact with Tyler, pushed his chair back, and began restoring his attire with the same degree of fastidiousness, that had visited its removal.

Tyler stood dutifully by the table as Smart picked up his hat and gloves, and as he resumed eye contact, Smart said, 'Once again, many thanks for meeting with me Mr Jones. What number shall I use to call you in the morning?'

Tyler offered the direct line to his desk phone, the one that would bypass Julie, and without further ado, Smart shook his hand and departed.

Tyler's impression of Cyril Smart was that he didn't particularly take to the man. He saw him as an obsequious, patronising ex-public school boy who suffered from OCD, but then Tyler was currently conflicted, and all things considered, he was in no position to bargain.

* * *

Friday, 18th October, 1991.

Tyler arrived at work just after eight thirty, because he figured that Smart would probably call mid-morning, and he desperately needed to get his thoughts sorted out beforehand.

As he attended to the back-log on his desk, Julie appeared, and placing a welcome-back cup of tea on his desk, gave a résumé of what had happened during his brief absence. Thankfully it amounted to not much at all, demonstrating that he could probably disappear more often and for longer periods.

Last night, he and Jemma had discussed the frustrating inequity that existed in Smart's proposed relationship, over and over again. They had looked at it from every which way, trying to find some sort of balance, between being all in, or all out, and they just kept going in circles.

On one hand, do nothing, go it alone, don't involve other people, because his life is not in danger, and never has been, it has all been a misunderstanding — but then, how can one test that assumption.

On the other hand, accept Smart's photographic evidence and the recent murder of Mr Attah as proof that his life really is in danger, therefore his best chance is to place his trust in Cyril

Smart; but then there's no way to test that assumption either. The all-in option does though, abrogate personal responsibility, handing all decision making to Smart and MI6.

Of all the concerns, this was the one that upset Jemma the most. What if Smart's strategy was to engage Tyler's services, by inferring that he's in danger when he's not — taking advantage of him, by reinforcing his foolishly voiced fears to Chris Wood.

'And, what about Wood himself?' Jemma had said, 'What do we know about him? What part has he played in all this? How do you know what the real relationship is, between him and Smart? How do you know exactly what information he's passed on, because I have the feeling that he's passed on much more than you will ever know about? Maybe he has the same agenda as Smart, maybe he has his own agenda — neither of which are in your best interests.'

At precisely nine thirty, Tyler picked-up his desk phone, to the dulcet tones of Cyril Smart.

'Good morning Mr Jones, Smart here. After we parted company yesterday a number of things have been arranged for you. At ten on Monday, the twenty-eighth, I'll meet you outside the entrance to the Lambeth North Tube Station, on Westminster Bridge Road and take you to the *Office* at Century House. Prior to being briefed, you'll need to sign a statement saying that you agree to be bound by the restrictions pertaining to the Official Secrets Act. After our meeting, and if you've agreed to join us, I'll pass you over to our induction team, who'll work with you for the rest of the day. On the Tuesday afternoon, I'll have a car take you down to Fort Monckton for your three days of training. I'll then have you picked up on the Thursday afternoon, and dropped to Euston Station for your trip back to Birmingham ready for work on Friday morning.'

'I'll call you again if there are any last minute changes, otherwise I'll meet you on Monday the twenty-eighth at ten o'clock in the morning, outside the entrance to Lambeth North Tube Station.'

Having got all that out of the way, and as happened yesterday, no further conversation was entered into, not one single word — Smart didn't need to discuss the matter any further.

Tyler's distress, related to the fact that once again, he'd let Cyril Smart go unchallenged, and by default, virtually signed-up to Smart's proposal.

Tyler attempted to rationalise his feelings, by trying to identify what it was that motivated him. Hopefully, he could then feel better about himself. Unfortunately, the process left him feeling gutless, making his already bad situation worse.

He hadn't challenged Smart once, even when he knew he should have. He had actively avoided conversation with Smart, because his state of indecision offered no platform from which to mount an argument, one way, or the other.

And worse than all that, there were other deeper reasons that made Tyler feel even more uncomfortable. He had been brought up to believe that the Cyril Smarts of this world, were important and knowledgeable people, that's how they got to be where they are. They were to be respected, and trusted, because they could be relied upon to always make the very best decisions, on behalf of ordinary folk like us.

There was also another weird, and seemingly paradoxical feeling that he was loath to admit to. If he had turned down

Smart's offer, or if he had offended Smart, such that Smart withdrew his offer, then he would deny himself, the thrill and excitement of living dangerously.

Had all this introspection merely uncovered the possibility that he was a wolf in sheep's clothing. In reality, he was actually, the thrill-seeking personality type.

* * *

Friday, 25th October, 1991.

After his call from Cyril Smart, Tyler had vacillated between fits of extreme anxiety and depression.

After dinner, when Annie and Cameron were asleep, Tyler discussed Cyril Smart's call with Jemma.

When discussing Smart's proposal, Tyler held nothing back. He revealed all his inner-most thoughts and fears to Jemma, including the paradoxical fear, that if he had turned down Smart's proposal, or offended him, and Smart had withdrew his offer; who would he turn to for help if he needed it. He'd be out on his own, and considering his present state of mind, that was a risk that was too terrible to contemplate.

While Tyler had Jemma's total support regardless of whether he accepted, or rejected Smart's offer, she continued to question Smart's motivation. Was it a genuine desire to help Tyler, or was it something else?

No matter how much they discussed it, Jemma could see that Tyler's mind was made-up, he would meet Cyril Smart and accept his offer, so she quickly shifted their conversation to the infinitely more positive topic of love.

LONDON (MAP 2)

PICCADILLY CIRCUS, COURTHOUSE HOTEL, EVE CLUB, OXFORD CIRCUS, SELFRIDGES DEPARTMENT STORE

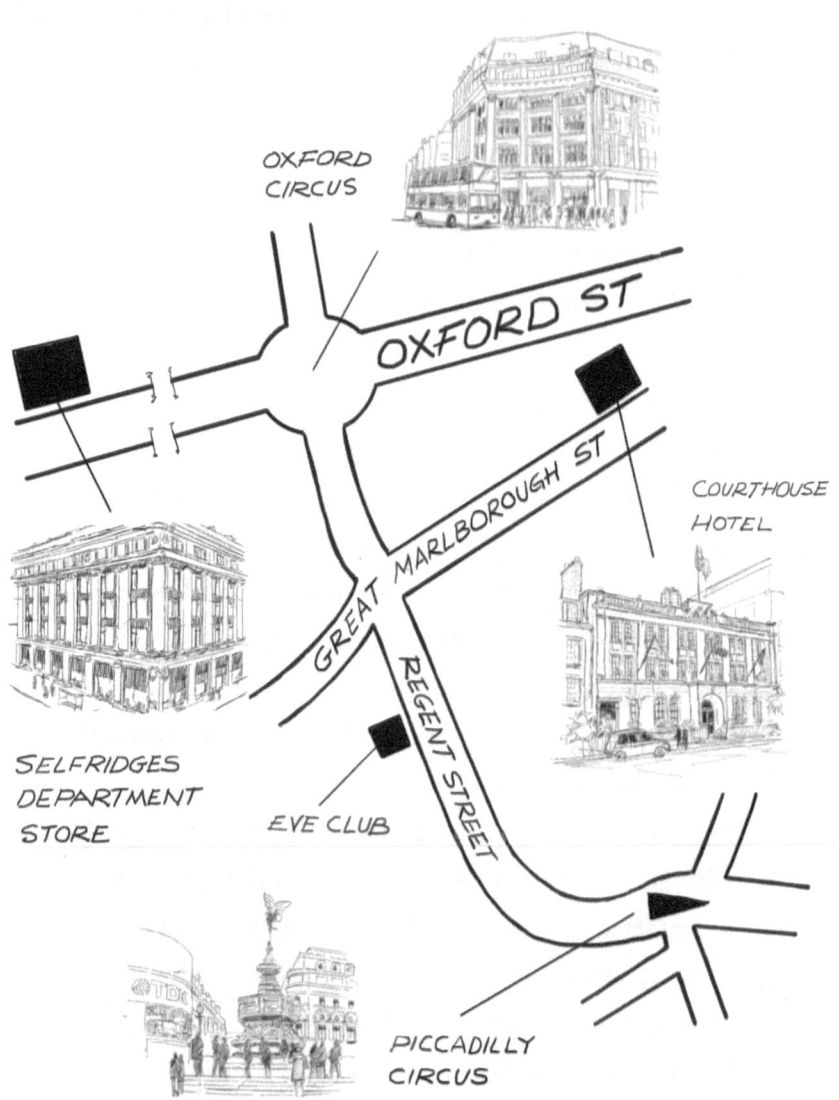

OXFORD CIRCUS

OXFORD ST

GREAT MARLBOROUGH ST

REGENT STREET

COURTHOUSE HOTEL

SELFRIDGES DEPARTMENT STORE

EVE CLUB

PICCADILLY CIRCUS

LONDON (MAP 3)

CHARING CROSS HOTEL, BIG BEN, HOUSES OF PARLIAMENT,
WESTMINSTER BRIDGE, LAMBETH NORTH TUBE STATION,
CENTURY HOUSE (MI6)

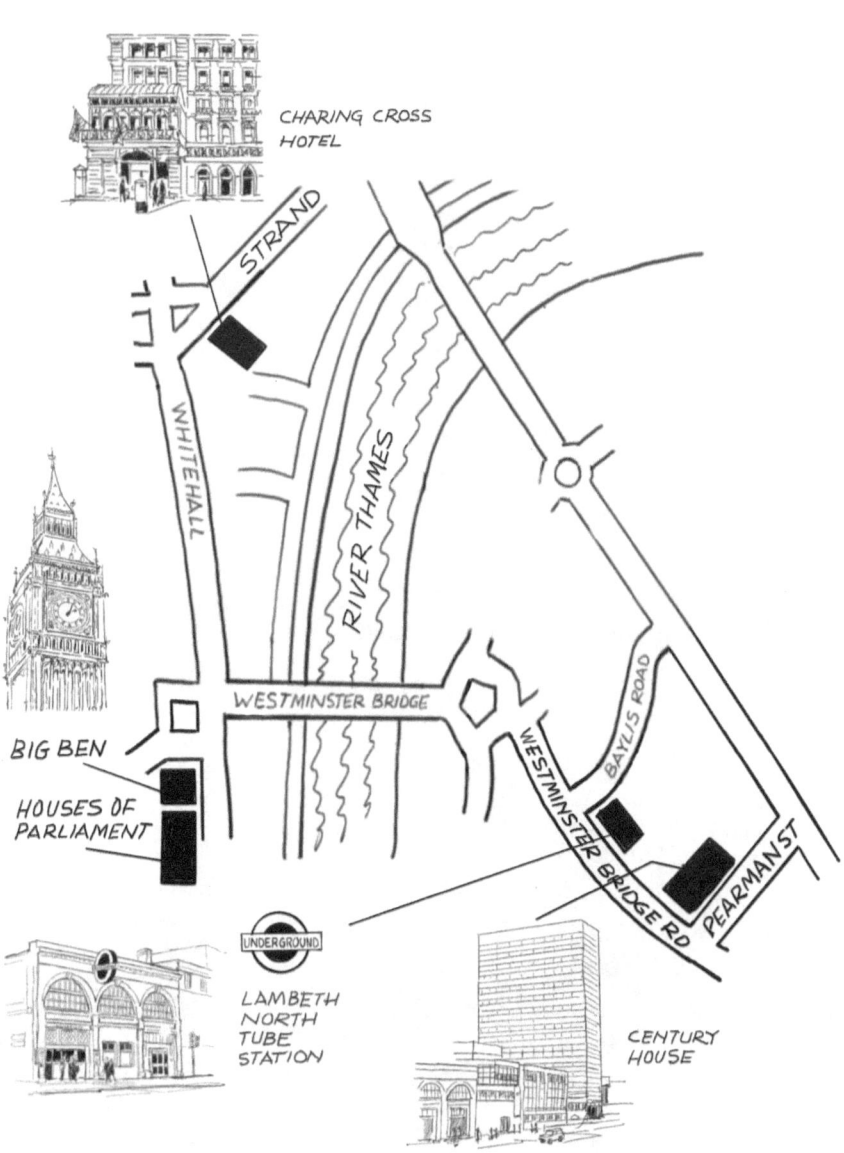

CHARING CROSS HOTEL

STRAND

WHITEHALL

RIVER THAMES

BAYLIS ROAD

WESTMINSTER BRIDGE

WESTMINSTER BRIDGE RD

PEARMAN ST

BIG BEN

HOUSES OF PARLIAMENT

UNDERGROUND

LAMBETH NORTH TUBE STATION

CENTURY HOUSE

8
SIGNING UP

Monday (AM), 28th October, 1991.

To meet Cyril Smart, outside the Lambeth North Tube Station at ten o'clock in the morning, Tyler had needed to be dressed and ready to catch the bus to Birmingham New Street Station, by twenty past six. The six fifty-five train, from New Street to London Euston, would give him time to get the underground to Lambeth North, and baring unforeseen holdups, still have time for breakfast when he got there.

Tyler, relieved that he'd made it to his destination in good time, stepped out of Lambeth North Tube Station at twenty past nine. After quickly convincing himself that Cyril Smart was nowhere to be seen, he crossed to a cafe on the corner of the street to his right; it was time for breakfast.

Following his meal of poached eggs, grilled tomatoes, mushrooms, bacon, and baked beans on toast, and a cup of coffee, it was coming-up to ten o'clock; time to meet Cyril Smart.

Dressed exactly the same as when Tyler had seen him last Thursday week, Cyril Smart was standing just to the side of the station's arched entrance.

'Good morning Mister Jones. Come with me. Let's walk on down to the Office. Good trip? How long did it take?' Smart said, not bothering to wait for a reply as they walked along Westminster Bridge Road, in the direction of Westminster Bridge.

In less than fifty yards, Smart, with an outstretched right arm, guided Tyler over to the left, and toward an office block that was setback from the street. Above the large anodised aluminium and glass front doors, was a polished stainless steel sign that spelled out *Century House* in relief lettering.

If this building really is the headquarters of MI6, thought Tyler, *It's a fine example of nineteen-sixties London ugliness. There's even a crappy looking drive-through petrol garage across the end corner of the building for fuck sake.*

With Smart leading the way they entered the building, were cleared past the security desk, and then via the lift they went up to the twenty-second floor. Access to all floors above the ground floor required key access.

Exiting the lift, Smart turned left into the passageway, and unlocking the door at the end, ushered Tyler into his enormous and sparsely furnished office. With the same precision that Tyler had witnessed at the Waldorf, Smart removed his outer garments and placed them, one by one, on the hat and coat stand, just inside his office door.

With an instinctive need to orient himself, Tyler walked across to the corner windows. 'Wow,' he said, before literally holding his breath as he gazed out onto the uninterrupted and magnificent views of Westminster Bridge, the Houses of Parliament and Big Ben.

'I'll just go, and rustle-up some coffee for us. How do you take it?' Smart said, as he beckoned Tyler to take a seat on one of the chairs in front of his desk. 'While I'm away, in front of you, there's a statement I need you to sign. Read it, sign it and date it. It simply says, that you agree to be bound by the provisions of the Official Secrets Act. You'll also be asked to sign it again, if, and when we terminate our arrangement, and..., if you're up for it, the Act itself, is over there on the bookshelf.'

'After you do that, we'll have a chat about what you'll be doing over the next few days to serve your country, and that's the aspect I want to impress upon you Mr Jones. Whatever you do, or we do together, we do it with our country's best interests at heart.'

When Smart returned, he was carrying a tray with a Cafetière coffee pot, cups and saucers, a little jug of milk, a small bowl of Demerara sugar, and a plate of mixed biscuits. He carefully placed the tray on his desk, sat down, scooped-up the document that Tyler had duly signed and dated, and slid it into a Manila folder on the other side of his desk.

Passing Tyler a cup and saucer from the tray, Smart said, 'I'll leave it for you to do yours, and now that we've got all the paperwork out of the way, let's have a chat about what you'll be doing with us.'

'You've probably already pieced together that Mr Wood is

associated with us in some way, but as I'm sure you'll understand, I can't discuss the exact nature of that relationship.
Maybe in the future there will be a need, but at the moment
that isn't the case.'

'The important thing, is that the account you gave to Mr
Wood, of what you saw and heard at the Charing Cross Hotel,
helped us enormously. It gave us information that our officer at
the scene could not obtain on the day.'

'Last time we met, I told you that if Mr Aaron Hersman
knew that you were one of us, it would protect you. So now that
that is in fact the case, not only will you be assisting us to secure
our strategic interests, but our relationship will also mitigate
any personal risks you may have incurred up to this point.'

'I'll be giving you a call later in the week, to arrange another
meeting so we can talk about what you'll be doing. I won't go
into detail now, other than to say, that your chance involvement
with us has been most fortuitous. We otherwise, would not
have had the time, nor the resources, to do what we need to do.'

'More housekeeping. With regard to communications
between scheduled meetings, or in an emergency. Before you
leave Monckton, they'll give you a secure mobile phone for that
purpose. I know it's a bit of a drag, to have to lug around
another mobile phone, but it'll be one of those new small
MicroTACs.'

'After lunch I'll be passing you over to our cover story team.
Actually two people Mandy, and Ben, both about your own age.
They'll work with you to establish a cover story that's airtight;
well, as much as is humanly possible, that is.'

'Developing a cover story, is just a matter of following a

logical process. They will examine everything you do; when you do what you do, and why you do what you do. Then when you need to be doing something different, with us for instance, it will all seem logical and plausible to those around you — so plausible, that your modus operandi will never be questioned by people close to you, or anybody not close to you for that matter either.'

'Once your cover story been been developed, Mandy, and Ben will test it. They will rehearse it with you from every conceivable which-way. In that regard, I'll warn you in advance Mr Jones, that you will probably find the experience stressful and embarrassing, because, at a certain point they will stop playing nicely. They will take their gloves off and be the Devil's advocate. They will try to break you, and your cover story by picking holes in it. The good news is — they will mend it, and put it all back together again if it's found to be lacking.'

'When the rehearsal process is over, everything will seem natural to you. Everything will have become second-nature to you. You will feel as if that's the way things have always been. If you believe it — everyone else will believe it too.'

'You'll spend this afternoon, and tomorrow morning with Mandy and Ben, and then after lunch tomorrow, I've arranged for you to be driven down to our Ministry of Defence facility at Fort Monckton.'

'Monckton is a totally different kettle of fish. Things are more structured down there and may I say, more confronting. Nothing too bad, so don't worry about it, nothing you won't be able to cope with, but they may test your limits.'

'They'll test you by putting you in hypothetical situations

where if you had a choice, you'd rather not be in. That's the point of the exercise though. Better to face an issue under conditions where if you make a wrong choice; you get to come back, and have another go.'

Apart from the odd query to clarify his understanding, Tyler, added, nor subtracted anything substantial to the conversation.

When they finally broke for lunch, Tyler switched on his mobile phone, and went outside to call Jim Craven; NuForm-Craven duty called.

Putting aside his initial nervousness, the call went precisely as he would have hoped. He could have asked for the moon and Craven would have agreed, and at no point did Craven convey even the slightest interest, as to why Tyler was in London, or when he'd be coming back.

Tyler felt, for the first time in his life, that he was now a free agent.

* * *

Monday (PM), 28th October, 1991.

Smart, gently tapped, and entered the small meeting room on the fifth floor. The room where Mandy and Ben were working with Tyler on his cover story.

'If we could wrap things up for the day please,' Smart said. I've got a taxi coming in a few minutes to take Mr Jones to his accommodation over in Pimlico. He'll be back here at nine in the morning, so you'll have him until he heads off to Monckton after lunch.'

It was just before five o'clock when Tyler was taken by taxi to a terrace house close to Victoria Station.

'My name's Meg. You must be Mr Jones. Mr Smart called a few minutes ago to say you were on your way.'

Tyler was intrigued. *She's done this before*, he thought. *This must be some sort of MI6, B&B, Safe House. I wonder what her connection with the Office is; or was?*

'Now Mr Jones, you're up on the Second floor, follow me up the stairs, and I'll show you to your room. You'll have the bathroom to yourself, no one else's with us at the moment.'

The premises were scruffy, with paintwork and floor coverings that had seen better days, and soft-furnishings that were in desperate need of an open window.

The woman was on the wrong side of sixty, with bright red hair, and lipstick to match, an electric blue jumper, a bright floral scarf, a long flowing sunflower-yellow skirt, and brown leather sandals.

As she led the way up the narrow staircases, Tyler noticed that her sandals where spattered with what appeared to be coloured paint. As they passed the first floor passageway he could see small stacks of unframed paintings leaning against the walls, and on the walls themselves were abstract nudes and impressionistic scenes.

'Are you an artist?' Tyler enquired.

'Very well spotted, Mr Jones. 'My husband Fred's an artist too. His studio's up on the third floor, and mine's on the first. We bought this house in the late fifties when properties were cheap. The overheads are monstrous though, so accommodating guests takes the pressure off us financially. It also means that we don't have to produce commercial art to survive, and so we get to be choosy about who we sell our work to.'

Entering into the passageway on the second floor, Tyler didn't have to wait long, to meet the other artist in residence. The door to what would be Tyler's room was open, and halfway up a step ladder, replacing a lightbulb was Fred. He too was spattered with paint. In Fred's case it was all over his carpenters bib and brace overalls and the backs of his hands.

Fred, of untidy appearance, and similar vintage to Meg, was rangy, slightly stooped, and had large boney hands. *Not the sorts of hands one would expect an artist to possess*, Tyler thought.

When Fred spoke, it was with a mellifluous, and cultivated tone. A voice honed by decades of smoking. A voice ideally suited to presenting authoritative news bulletins on BBC radio.

'There you go Mr Jones,' said Fred, flicking the light switch, 'let there be light. Now after you've got yourself settled, you've got a sink and tea making facilities over there, and feel free to use the telephone, because the Office pays the bill. Your bathroom is at the end of the hallway and no-one else will be using it. Do have a lovely evening. Oh..., and I nearly forgot. We'll bring breakfast up on a tray at seven thirty, give you a tap, and leave it outside your door. Mr Smart has ordered a taxi for you at quarter to nine.'

After Meg and Fred took their leave, Tyler, with a sudden and desperate need for fresh air tried to open a front window. Defeated and dejected, he reached for the corded phone on his bedside table to call Jemma. Upon second thoughts he changed his mind, and got his mobile phone out of his briefcase — keep the call brief and bear the cost. After his day at the Office, it seemed highly likely, that someone out there would be listening in.

'Hi sweetie-pie it's me.' Tyler began, 'I'm on my mobile at a B&B in Pimlico. First chance I've had to say hello all day — I've had a really busy day of it, I'm exhausted. Anyway, more importantly, how's your day been since I slipped out in the early hours of this morning?'

'Oh, as you can imagine my handsome man, my day's been absolutely riveting. Nappies and more nappies, playing with mummy toys like dishwashers, washing machines, floor mops, and Hoovers. Not to mention my exciting trip down to Sainsbury's with a baby, and a small kid who never shuts-up, and that pretty well sums it up.'

Devoid of detail, Tyler conveyed to Jemma the gist of what had happened over the course of his day, his call to Craven, and his understanding of what was still yet to come, down at Fort Monckton. Following that, the conversation quickly turned to matters of love.

Tuesday (AM), 29th October, 1991.

Smart was proven correct. Tyler *had* found his time with Mandy and Ben, both stressful, and embarrassing.

Stressful: Tyler now understood why Smart had used that word — he got it.

Embarrassed: Yesterday, that word seemed inappropriate, and wrong — but today, he got that too.

When Mandy and Ben wrapped-up their session yesterday,

they had achieved their goal. They had mapped out and neatly packaged a cover story for him. It was plausible and it was bullet proof.

This morning Tyler would rehearse his plan with them, he would demonstrate how well he could handle a series of hypothetical, but highly likely situations.

Ninety minutes into the session, and Tyler proved unconvincing. He had allowed Mandy and Ben to blast holes in his cover. When they stopped for morning tea, Tyler was not only stressed out of his brain — he was *embarrassed*.

True, Cyril Smart had warned Tyler yesterday, that Mandy and Ben would stop playing nicely. In fact, the scenarios they presented to him this morning, were actually quite benign, and should have been easily dealt with — if Tyler had simply stuck to the script.

If he couldn't handle this situation, then how would he handle a situation where he was likely to fall into the hands of the wrong people; or God forbid, was already in the hands of the wrong people.

Fortunately, the lessons learned from the first session, ensured that Tyler handled the second session much better. Out of sheer embarrassment, Tyler now understood that being in possession of a bullet proof cover story was important, but equally important, was to rehearse the script, over, and over, and over, again. As Cyril Smart had said yesterday, *if you believe it, then everyone else will believe it.*

* * *

Tuesday (PM), 29th October, 1991.

Caressed by the autumn sunshine that fell across the back seat of the dark grey Vauxhall Cavalier, plus the comforting aroma of leather, Tyler soon succumbed to sleep.

Aside the A3, small picturesque villages, held captive within the folds of the rolling green hills, swished by unnoticed, and unappreciated. It wasn't until the more narrow, and twisting roads at the end of the M27 that Tyler, roused by the changes in movement within the vehicle, opened his eyes.

'I have Mr Tyler Jones for Mr Harold Smith,' the driver said perfunctorily, as he handed Smart's letter to the guard at the entrance to Fort Monckton. Inspecting the letter, the officer stooped for a peek inside the car, made a brief intercom call, and then waved them through to the car park, on the other side of the checkpoint.

As the driver opened the car boot, to fetch Tyler's briefcase and small suitcase, a man approached from the direction of the gatehouse building.

Addressing Tyler, he said. 'Mr Jones? My name is Harold Smith, and I'll be your trainer for the time you're with us. Follow me, and I'll take you up to your room.'

Smith, Tyler thought. *His first name might be Harold, but I bet his surname, isn't Smith.*

Smith, a wily, semi-retired training officer, had been brought in by Smart to provide fast-tracked, one-on-one training for Tyler. He took Tyler upstairs to a room that looked back down across the courtyard and carpark. 'So, here you are Mr Jones, two nights board, and lodgings, courtesy of the MOD. When you're unpacked, come back downstairs, and we'll have some afternoon tea and get started. You'll find me in the Officers' Mess.'

Waving Smart's referral letter in his hand, and as the waiter approached with the afternoon tea tray, Smith gestured Tyler to take a seat. 'Mr Smart has asked me to take you through some basic training in the four main areas of what we refer to in the intelligence community as, *tradecraft*. These areas are, surveillance, counter-surveillance, dead drops, and other communication techniques, and in the unlikely event that someone doesn't like you, avoiding capture and resistance to interrogation.'

'We'll spend four hours on each topic, which will take us through to lunchtime on Thursday. To put this in perspective Mr Jones, I should point out, that our *New Entry Course for Intelligence Officers,* runs for six months. In your case and in just forty-eight hours, we'll be doing a crash course in all the tradecraft skills, that is, minus small arms training and unarmed combat. A big ask, but with your cooperation, it can be done.'

Harold Smith pushed an A4 legal notepad and pen across the table, pulled the mobile whiteboard across from the side wall, and said, 'Let's do things in the reverse order, and focus on *avoiding capture and resistance to interrogation.*'

'Mr Smart told me on the phone earlier this afternoon, that he'd already warned you that you may find this session confronting. So, let's bring it forward, and get it out of the way.'

'Cyril told me that you had a rather hard time of it with your cover story session this morning, but that it all turned out OK in the end. I mention that, not to sprinkle salt on the wound, but to tell you in advance that by default, you've already done most of the work for this session. What happened to you this morning, was a positive, not a negative.'

'When Cyril requested this introductory training course, he emphasised the sorts of things that he might, and might not, want you to be doing for him. Therefore, each of these sessions, has been designed with those needs in mind. So, Mr Jones, when it comes to avoiding capture, and resistance to interrogation, you had already done most of the work, when you created your cover story.'

'In a nutshell, if you successfully master the art of the cover story; to live your double, triple, or even quadruple life, and never be questioned about any aspect of it; or if questioned you can instantly deflect the issue, with a natural, and plausible response. If you can do all that, then you've removed the main reason why you'd ever find yourself captured in the first place — and if you're not captured, then you can't be interrogated. There's a sort of inverse relationship at work here between capture and interrogation.'

'So, to advance the topic further. As I mentioned earlier, small arms, and unarmed combat training, is not something we'll be doing, but even if we were, when it comes to being captured, or getting yourself out of capture, those skills wouldn't help you much anyway. It's only in the movies that spies fight, and shoot their way out of sticky situations. Actually, your best and most lethal weapon is your tongue. In the first instance, your tongue should always be used to avoid capture, and if you are captured, your tongue will hopefully get you out.'

'Your cover story, and how you defend it, is actually your frontline defence against suspicion and capture. Your cover story should be watertight, such that it doesn't invite attention, because attention just leads to questioning, and questioning leads to trouble. As I said earlier; If you're not captured, you can't be interrogated. In the context of *tradecraft* Mr Jones, and at the risk of appearing to be melodramatic, I need to warn you that interrogation is unfortunately synonymous with torture.'

'When you were with Mandy, and Ben, they focused on developing a cover story for you. Then they tested how well you could defend it. What I've been asking you to consider, is more what happens to you when your efforts to defend your cover story have failed — the moment the shite hits the fan — the moment when your head is literally on the block.'

Tomorrow, we'll talk about surveillance and counter surveillance, and on Thursday morning, we'll deal with the various aspects of communication; but before I let you go back up to your room to freshen up for dinner, there's something I want to say to you. Your first name might be Tyler, but I bet your surname, ain't Jones...'

'Touché!' Said Tyler.

Thursday (PM), 31st October, 1991.

Tyler was collected after lunch, and driven straight to Euston station, ready for his train back to Birmingham.

Yesterday, his surveillance, and counter-surveillance sessions, had by comparison with the day before, seemed boring and predictable. Once he'd got the principles into his head, and grasped what it was all about; it had all seemed quite predictable, and what he would have intuitively thought and done anyway. Maybe boredom had crept in, because apart from a few video tutorials, the sessions had been theory based. Nonetheless, he had correctly answered every single question on Harold Smith's multiple choice exam paper, following each session.

At the end of the communications session this morning, Harold Smith produced the mobile phone that Smart had promised when Tyler was at Century House — the MicroTAC lightweight GSM phone. If the intention was to stoke Tyler's ego, then it succeeded. Smith explained that the phone's SIM card limited its operation to SIS encrypted lines, and that the three auto-dial buttons had been pre-programmed for quick use. The phone is the only phone that can be used for SIS communications, and when Cyril Smart calls in the morning, he will call this phone; not Tyler's personal mobile phone, or the NuForm-Craven landline.

During his postprandial drive back to Euston, Tyler meditated on the events of the past four days. His state of reverie only ending when he realised, that he was not the Tyler Jones who had left Birmingham four days ago. He had entered a strange state of consciousness, where all his bits and pieces, no longer seemed like they fitted together.

This feeling was particularly evident, when he realised that since he'd spoken to Jemma on Monday evening, he hadn't spoken to her since. Sure he'd been busy; sure he'd been exhausted; sure it would have been difficult to get privacy, but none of these things would have stopped him in the past. A fundamental change had taken place within him, and it troubled him.

Although this thought consumed him for most of his journey home, he eventually rationalised it so that he could feel better about himself.

Confirmation of his success in that regard, had come when he called Jemma from the train to arrange their meeting at New Street Station. There was not the slightest hint, of her having been upset, or offended by his seventy-two hours of silence. If anything, her lively conversation suggested that their separation had actually brought them closer together.

For right, or wrong reasons, Tyler Jones, was once again, internally reconciled.

9

THE BRIEFING

Friday, 1st November, 1991.

Back at work at eight-thirty on Friday morning, was akin to walking onto the set of an American sitcom. Everyone was in their expected place, and everything was picture perfect.

Any fears that awkward questions may be asked about his four day absence, were quickly dispelled.

Jim Craven was back, and in fine fettle; more eager to boast about his new projects, and how, thanks to Tyler, NuForm-Craven's October sales, were considerably better than forecast.

Julie was her beautiful, ebullient, and professional self. She was eager to report that, in Tyler's absence, there had not been one single issue, that she wasn't able to resolve on her own.

Tyler now had confirmation, that he could come and go as he pleased. At all levels within NuForm-Craven, he was now accepted as being his own man. The default and essential precondition that had been structured into his cover story, by Mandy and Ben at Century House.

Tyler sifted through the telephone messages, faxes, and mail, that Julie had neatly placed in date, and time order on his desk. Amongst the phone messages, were two that begged to be attended to first. One was from the lads wanting to meet-up down the pub after work; it was Friday after all. The other was from Jennifer at AcuWrite. She, and Jerry wanted to set a date for their meeting at NuForm-Craven. The meeting they'd talked about at lunch.

Logic demanded that he dealt with the AcuWrite message first. Speaking with Jennifer, Tuesday the twelfth was locked-in as the date for their meeting. Where the lads were concerned, Tyler took a rain check, having promised to take his little family out to dinner.

Tyler had barely placed the corded handset of his desk phone back on its cradle, when the MicroTAC mobile phone in his jacket pocket began to ring. Cyril Smart was calling, just as Harold Smith had promised he would. He was about to receive, his very first call on his SIS phone.

'Good morning Mr Jones.'

'Good morning Mr Smart.'

'What a lovely clear line we have,' said Smart, 'How would you be placed for next Tuesday? We'll need most of the day, but you will be able to get away late afternoon. Can we say ten o'clock at the Office?'

'Is there anything I need to bring?'

'Just yourself, good man. Oh, maybe while you're moving

about on your journey, give thought to reviewing those surveillance skills that Harold Smith introduced to you.'

'Thanks, I certainly will, and I'll see you in your office next Tuesday.'

* * *

Tuesday (AM), 5th November, 1991.

'Tyler Jones for Mr Cyril Smart.'

'Please take a seat Mr Jones. He'll come down and collect you.' said the middle-aged women at the security desk, situated in front, and to the side of the lift doors.

Smart stepped out of the lift, handed Tyler a visitors lanyard he'd taken from a box on the security desk counter, and took him up to his office on the top floor.

As they entered, Smart said, 'Coffee, or would you prefer tea?'

'You choose, I'm happy with either.'

'Maybe tea then — maybe Darjeeling?' Smart said, as he picked-up his desk phone to call catering.

'First things first,' Smart said as he gestured Tyler toward the two seater Chesterfield in the conversation area of his office, while he seated himself in one of the two leather armchairs.

'Harold Smith tells me that you were an outstanding student. You breezed through the lessons, to the extent that it allowed Harold to include some extra material. He was very impressed.'

'Thank you, Mr Smith is too generous.'

'Now, Mr Jones, while we're waiting for our tea, I'd like to begin our briefing by telling you, that just after Mr Attah's untimely death, Mr Aaron Hersman, the man you saw at the hotel, and almost certainly Mr Attah's killer, made contact with us.'

'But that hardly makes any sense,' said Tyler, 'Why would he do that? Considering everything, why would he draw attention to himself?'

'You have to think like an arms dealer, who has a very close relationship with the Israeli Intelligence Service, to have any chance of answering that question. It might be that he wants something from us, or he's in possession of something he thinks he could trade.'

'I still don't get it. He must know that the SIS would suspect him of killing Mr Attah?' Why would he make himself available, considering that the killing took place on British soil?'

'He doesn't give a damn about that,' said Smart, 'That wouldn't worry him in the slightest. He knows we'll never do anything about it. He knows we won't touch him. So what; he murdered a man. A treacherous man. A man who was about to overthrow, and probably kill, the democratically elected leader of the West African State of Modrisia; not to mention the innocent civilians who would be caught up in it all.'

There was a sharp tap on Smart's door. 'Enter,' said Smart, as he rose to hold his office door open for the tea-lady, as she struggled to get through the doorway. Entering the room, she placed the tray down on the coffee table in the conference area, and before taking her leave, dutifully asked, 'Anything else Mr Smart?'

After pouring the tea for Tyler, and himself, Smart resumed where he'd left off.

'It might be best if I offer you a fuller understanding of who this Aaron Hersman actually is, what he does, and how he does what he does.'

'Hersman is a South African Ashkenazi Jew from Johannesburg, who was educated in England. He has strong ties to Israeli arms manufacturers, senior military personnel, senior Israeli and white South African politicians, and most importantly, the Israeli National Intelligence Agency — *The Mossad*; with whom we believe he's now an operational officer.'

'I know it's counter-intuitive to imagine, because Hersman is Jewish, but for more than forty years, Israel collaborated with the Apartheid regime in South Africa. In fact, without the military and economic support provided by Israel, the Apartheid regime could never have survived for as long as it did.'

'Aaron Hersman is a person who has made his living out of brokering arms deals between Israel and South Africa, plus many other nefarious activities. Aaron Hersman is not a very nice person.'

'Now that the Apartheid era is over, and Israel has recently stated that military and economic ties with South Africa have ended, Mr Hersman has had a much closer relationship with the Mossad. It's this aspect, that I need to brief you on; but first things first, let's go downstairs, and have some lunch.'

Tuesday (PM), 5th November, 1991.

'OK then Mr Jones, let's pick-up where we left off,' Smart said as they reentered his office after lunch.

'As I said earlier, Hersman is actively trying to talk to us. This probably means that he wants something, or if he's offering help, it will not be out of the goodness of his heart. Maybe something's gone wrong, and he wants to use us to help him fix it. If that's the case, what that something might be is anyone's guess, but based on our intelligence, we can make some calculated guesses.

But before we get ahead of ourselves, with the personal machinations of Mr Hersman, we need to establish what a possible quid pro quo might be, because believe me, if we're right about all this, there will be a quid pro quo.'

'With the greatest respect Mr Smart,' Tyler interrupted, 'I'm struggling to understand why you're telling me all this. It seems obvious to me, that you plan to involve me in some sort of way. Wasn't my cooperation with you supposed to protect me from Hersman?'

'Good man Mr Jones,' Smart's rejoinder came with lightning speed. 'I expected you to challenge me about this.'

'You may remember Mr Jones, that when we first met, I told you that, yes, Mr Hersman did perceive you as a threat. I also said that, if he believed, or we could encourage him to believe, that you are one of us, then he will forget about you. You will no longer be a threat to him. As I also said this morning, in relation to the killing of Mr Attah, Hersman is not the slightest bit worried about what we know. He knows we won't touch him.'

'That's why there was urgency to get you on-board, and trained up. We have a window of opportunity here with regard to something, I can't talk about at the moment; that is, until we know where we stand with Hersman. We need to prove to him that you definitely do belong to us, and then hopefully, we'll find out what it is that he wants; then we can form a strategic response plan.'

'By him approaching us, maybe all's not well within the Mossad. He may even be considering switching sides, or maybe he's prepared to work both sides from the middle, and if so, our side may, or may not be, the other side. Alternatively, Hersman's relationship with the Mossad may be absolutely hunky-dory, and they simply want him to negotiate some sort of deal with us.'

'In fact my plan is for you to meet with Hersman, face to face, and very soon. I know what you must be thinking, but you have nothing to worry about. You will be perfectly safe.'

'When you actually get to meet with him, he may even offer you an inducement to switch sides, or maybe work for both. To be prudent, we must assume that any one of the scenarios I've canvassed with you today is possible; or it may be something, that we haven't even thought about.'

'Whatever the reason turns out to be, your involvement in the operation will definitely get Hersman off your case.'

'So, Mr Jones, I hope that answers, why it has to be you, and not someone else.'

'Let's talk now, about what Hersman's been doing now that the arms trade with South Africa has stopped,' said Smart.

'As luck would have it, Hersman's Mossad masters, have provided him with a new opportunity. As one door closed, they opened another one for him here in London.'

'In the same way that Israel propped up the Apartheid regime in South Africa, Israel has also been propping up military dictatorships in Central and South America, and more recently the Serbs in Yugoslavia.'

'Over the past year, and as I'm sure you would be aware, trouble has been brewing in the Balkans; trouble that right now, is spiralling out of control. Serb militiamen supported by Montenegro, are shelling the Croatian towns of Vukovar in the north east, and Dubrovnik down on the Adriatic.'

The Serbs, who have dominated the Yugoslav Army since the days of Tito, are right this minute shelling Dubrovnik with shells that are made in Israel, even though there is a UN Security Council Arms Embargo in place. Shell casings have been photographed by our agents in Dubrovnik, that clearly show the Israeli manufacturer's serial numbers. We believe that Hersman is the Mossad's chief negotiator, for the Israeli arms that are currently being supplied to Yugoslavia.'

'Our intelligence from on the ground, and through our Government Communications Headquarters, GCHQ, in Cheltenham, tells us that huge supplies of these Israeli weapons are finding their way into Serbia using private arms dealers. These deals are negotiated directly by the Israeli National Intelligence Agency, deliberately using supply channels that are designed to circumvent the UN Arms Embargo. Sales are brokered between private arms dealers in Serbia, and private arms dealers in Israel. In this way the Serbian, and Israeli Governments can, and do, plead ignorance; it's called *plausible deniability.*'

'As I said earlier, we have cause to believe that this Hersman-Mossad relationship, is about to change in some way, or maybe it's just a ruse, to encourage us to believe that that's the case.'

'Any questions Mr Jones?'

'No doubt I'll think of something when I walk out the door. Quite frankly, it's all been a bit too much for me to take in.'

'Yes, I understand your situation. In fact it's something I anticipated, after I called this meeting, so over there on my desk is a briefing paper I've prepared for you. It covers everything we'll discuss today, and more. The only trouble is, the information is classified, so you'll need to read it while you're here in my office.'

'Now that I've got the salient aspects of Hersman's backstory out of the way, Let's move on, and discuss your upcoming meeting with him.'

'First. We need to give him a call on the mobile phone number you overheard — the one that he gave to Mr Attah. The purpose of your call, is to arrange a meeting in central London.'

'Once you've established a mutually agreeable date, you will tell him, that he will need to be waiting outside Leicester Square Station, at midday for further instructions. You will also tell him that the precise location for your meeting will be less than a ten minute walk from Leicester Square. He's the one begging the meeting, so he must accept our terms with regard to the arrangement — you must be firm.'

'We won't disclose the exact location for your meeting until the day itself, but it will be central, busy, and open. As this will be your first operation, we'll also support you with some under-cover officers. A good opportunity for you to practice, both your surveillance, and counter-surveillance skills.'

'You can also tell him, if he asks, that you'll be alone, he'll know you're lying, but it won't stop him from coming, because he's eager to meet, and risk-taking is part of his everyday life anyway.'

'We'll discuss things more on the day, but when you actually meet him, you'll listen, but agree to nothing. You'll tell him that any matters raised, will need to be referred to your masters, and that you'll get back to him in due course.'

'Well, that's the bones of it, but don't stress, we'll go over it all again on the day. Perhaps we'll rehearse some likely scenar-ios, and work out how you might best manage them'

'Let's go and have a cup of tea, and when we come back, we'll give Mr Hersman a call.'

With his heart pounding, Tyler dialled Hersman's mobile phone number. Following an initial ring burst, the line went silent for a couple of seconds, before resuming again, this time with a different ringtone.

'He's diverted the phone to another number,' whispered Smart, cupping his hands over his headphones, that along with Tyler's SIS phone, were connected to a recording device.'

'Yes, hello,' were the only words uttered, but for Tyler, the voice was instantly recognisable.

'My name is Jones, our paths may have crossed at the Charing Cross Hotel a few weeks ago. I understand that you want to arrange a meeting with us.' Tyler said, sounding as casual, and relaxed as his state of nerves allowed, before moving on to recite from Smart's dot-point list of instructions.

As Tyler conversed with Hersman, he had been crossing-off, item by item, the points that Smart had scribbled on a notepad on his desk. When it came to the issue of cementing an agreeable date, to Tyler's surprise, and relief, Hersman's response was immediate and positive, 'Yes, that's all fine with me. Midday this coming Friday outside Leicester Square Station would work best for me.'

Tyler leaned forward and wrote, *This Friday?*, to which Smart responded with a double thumbs-up gesture.

After pausing long enough to hear Tyler say, 'Okay, Friday's fine for me too, I'll call you at midday.' Hersman hung up.

'Well done. Good job,' Smart said, 'If you could be here around nine-thirty, ten o'clock on Friday morning, it'll give us enough time to go over things before you go to meet him.'

It was just after six-thirty in the evening when Tyler got back to Jemma's place. Their plan was, that he should get the bus from the station, while she prepared the meal, set the table, and got the little ones, bathed, and ready for bed.

All went according to plan, and unlike his previous guilt-inducing experience, when he arrived home too late to see the children before bed; this time, he was home in time to play with Annie, and read her to sleep.

During their candlelight dinner, Tyler detected a welcome change in Jemma's attitude with regard to his relationship with MI6. He had discussed, to the extent that he was allowed, the events of his rather exhausting, and stressful day; including his forthcoming meeting with Hersman. Throughout his conversation, there had not been one single interruption from Jemma, and she posed no awkward questions afterwards. Her mood throughout had been ebullient, and now skittish to the extreme.

Acting out the characters, and events that she had somehow channelled from Tyler's conversation, Jemma delivered to her audience of one, a stage ready parody of Tyler's day.

The distinct advantage of attending *Jemma's Theatre Restaurant* that evening, was that the bedroom; was only one staircase away.

10

THE MEETING

Friday (AM), 8th November, 1991.

Tyler's Friday briefing before his meeting with Hersman, simply reinforced things that Smart had already spoken about on Tuesday.

Smart went over Hersman's nefarious activities including his connections with the Mossad, his ruthless killing of Baako Attah, the supply of Israeli arms to Serbia, and the possible reasons why he'd requested a meeting.

Actually, thought Tyler, *this has all been a bit of a performance for my benefit, or more accurately, Smart's benefit. A performance to get me all psyched-up, like a football coach does with his team before they go out on the pitch, and another thing, Smart never did explain how Hersman came to make contact with MI6. Maybe the story isn't even true, it never happened, or maybe MI6 approached him rather than the other way around.*

In the remaining time available, activities switched to the

specifics of how Tyler could best manage his meeting with Hersman.

Smart brought-in some other people, and together they fleshed-out some what-if scenarios. Tyler saw all this as an exercise in futility, because as Smart had said, no one had the foggiest idea why Hersman had sought the meeting in the first place; it was all a matter of guesswork.

When it came to locking-in the logistics for the meeting, difficulties arose for the same reason. It was eventually decided that Tyler would meet Hersman, clean of any covert listening, transmitting, recording, or photographic device. Considering Hersman's background, they decided that risk outweighed benefit. Tyler would present himself in a state that would instantly tick all the boxes on Hersman's security clearance check-list.

Tyler would be dropped-off just before midday, and picked-up afterwards on the corner of Garrick and Bedford Streets. He was reassured and encouraged to relax, put his mind into neutral, listen carefully, and make a mental note of everything, verbal, and non-verbal that transpired. All this in readiness for his debriefing back at Century House after lunch.

When Tyler calls Hersman's mobile phone number at midday, he'll tell Hersman to walk east on Cranbourn Street away from Leicester Square Station, and to cross St Martin's Lane into Garrick Street. At the top end of Garrick Street he'll find an Italian Cafe on his left hand side, and that's where Tyler will be waiting outside.

As Tyler rose to leave Smart's office, Smart said, 'We've

made a booking for two. Here's a hundred quid in twenties. Get a receipt, and bring back the change.'

Just before midday, and as planned, Tyler was dropped off at the top end of Bedford Street, close to the Italian restaurant in Garrick Street. He chose to stand outside the pub on the opposite side of Garrick Street, because it offered better area surveillance, and a position where he felt was less conspicuous.

With Hersman's number on his screen, Tyler pressed the *Call* button on his MicroTAC. A simple action, but one that somehow infused him with an unexpected sense of calm.

'Yes, hello,' answered Hersman, to which Tyler responded by delivering the set of instructions that he'd rehearsed in Smart's office. Before terminating the call, Tyler impulsively said, 'I'm no more than a few minutes walk away from where you are at the moment.'

Even before the words had left his lips, he realised the absurdity of what he'd just said. There was no guarantee whatsoever, that Hersman was anywhere near where Tyler imagined him to be.

With only minutes before Hersman should arrive, Tyler turned his attention to counter-surveillance. He had been assured by Smart, that undercover officers would be there to support him, but where were they? From his vantage point standing on the forecourt of the pub he had clear line of sight back along Garrick Street, across into Bedford Street, plus a number of other smaller streets, and laneway openings.

No matter how carefully he surveyed the scene, everything appeared normal, and in place. There was so little time to properly apply his newly acquired tradecraft skills — techniques that are designed to reveal the concealed.

As Tyler gazed in the anticipated direction, at the anticipated time, Hersman appeared. Walking up the cafe side of Garrick Street, and carrying what appeared to be a rolled-up newspaper in his right hand, he walked with the casualness of someone taking a Sunday morning stroll. If he was stressed, then he hid it well, and if he was the Trojan horse for something more heroic, then there was no indication of that either.

As Hersman came closer, Tyler, now feeling quite relaxed and confident, stepped out from the pavement, and crossed the road to meet him.

'Mr Hersman?'

'Mr Jones?'

Following a quick handshake, they turned their bodies, and walked toward the front door of the restaurant.

'Table for Jones.' Tyler said to the waitress as they paused at the *Wait Here To Be Seated* sign.

Devoid of any form of welcome, she ushered them into a room to their right, and a table against one of the windows that bordered Garrick Street.

'Do you mind if we sit at that table over there in the corner?' Said Tyler, pointing to the back of the room. Seemingly unfazed, the girl scooped-up the menus she'd just placed on the table, handed them to Tyler, and escorted them to the other table at the back of the room.

As they stood removing their topcoats, and noisily dragging

their chairs back across the floorboards, Hersman leaned forward, placed his newspaper on the table, and whispered, 'Thanks for doing that.'

Tyler understood exactly what Hersman meant.

When the waitress had led them to the window table, Tyler's mind had instantly processed the situation in pictures — his words only came later.

After all it was he, who had stood on the pub side of Garrick Street, looking back across to the cafe windows bordering the pavement. It was he, who had watched the two business men, deep in animated conversation, sitting side-on at the very next table to where Tyler and Hersman were initially taken. To anyone intent on observing, they may as well have been sitting at one of the outside tables on a warm, sunny day.

Perhaps it's drawing a long bow thought Tyler, *but I believe that Smart knows this restaurant, and I bet he's used it for this very same purpose before. The situation is perfect. Have the target, and a wired-up operative, sit at one of the window tables, while another loiters on the wide curved forecourt of the pub across the street. People mill around the pub all the time, as I'd instinctively done earlier. It's also a position that affords views in all directions, and the good thing about it, is that no one else on the pavement gives a fig. Yes, I'm sure Smart requested that window table, and if he could read my mind right now, he'd be less than pleased.*

As Tyler and Hersman pulled their chairs in, and the waitress took their orders, it suddenly occurred to Tyler that he was sitting almost cheek-by-jowl with, in Smart's words, *a ruthless killer*. It was bizarre.

This thought became the catalyst, for a surreal paradox to

start unpacking itself inside Tyler's head. The surreality related to the sudden juxtaposition, between how he was feeling ten minutes ago, and how he was feeling now. Tyler was not feeling the way he should be feeling.

The fear and dread that had resided in him for so long, had now been supplanted by a feeling of indifference.

Hersman may not be a man one would actively court as a friend, but equally, he was not a man one would go out of one's way to avoid either.

In the time provided by Hersman placing his order with the waitress, Tyler decided that this was not the moment to resolve a paradox. If he allowed his brain to run away with itself, he would lose focus. He must lock himself into his pre-meeting state, and display no outward hint of inner turmoil. He must stick to the hard-coded script that he'd been sent with, and for the moment at least, push the pause button on any further thought.

'So Mr Hersman, why are we here?'

To Tyler's relief, there was no embarrassing pause. Hersman's response was fast, and seemingly unpremeditated.

'OK. Well..., officially I'm here to enlist your services. My masters want to establish a relationship between your agency, and mine. An officially unofficial, back-channel relationship between MI6 and the Mossad.'

'Governments have official Government to Government relationships, and they also have their unofficial Government to Government relationships. This principle also applies to agency to agency relationships. There is nothing strange, or unusual about this proposal.'

'These relationships serve a very useful purpose. Information, particularly verbal, can be traded under conditions of anonymity and deniability. Using people such as you, and I, normal channels that are open to scrutiny can be circumvented.'

'My masters take a pragmatic approach,' he continued, You're in a position to provide information that could add value to what we have, and in return we can reward you in the same way.'

'Why would you propose something like this to me,' Tyler said, 'When you know that all I can do is to take your proposal back to the Office. I have no authority to agree to anything. You'd essentially be asking me to trade information, in the belief that there exists, this so-called, official, but unofficial relationship; a relationship that can be officially denied, and therefore leave me out in the cold as a double agent — hung-out to dry as a traitor.'

'Ah, that's where you are wrong. I tell you Mr Jones, I know you better than you think, and I put myself at great risk to even broach such a matter with you. You may not see it at the moment, but I'm offering you something that's in your own best interests as well. This relationship can, by default, also afford you with personal benefits and protections. Any concerns you may presently have shouldn't relate to me — your worries are much closer to home.'

'I have my own personal reasons for being here Mr Jones, as undoubtably you have yours, but we don't always share those reasons, nor is it wise to do so.'

'I know you're not wired-up because the little gadget in my

pocket tells me you're not, otherwise I wouldn't be so fucking stupid. I place inordinate trust in you to even raise these matters.'

'You'll need to decide what you relay about our conversation, and what you don't. It doesn't matter how you slice and dice it, at the end of the day it's the only power you have. You surely understand Mr Jones, people like you and me, have little say in whatever it is that we do.'

After a long, and reflective pause, Hersman picked up where he'd left off.'

'There are things you know because your masters tell you; there are things you don't know, because they don't tell you, and then there are things you think you know, but you don't know all there is to know.'

'Apropos what I was saying earlier about information sharing, and as you'd be aware from the news services, Yugoslavia is breaking up. The situation has taken the lid off ethnic hatreds that have existed for centuries.'

'At the end of the Second World War, President Tito formed these dissident states into one independent socialist union, known as the *Second Yugoslavia*. This *Modern Yugoslavia* remained unaligned to the major powers, including the Soviet Union. After the Soviets invaded Hungary, Tito saw the Soviet Union as the greatest threat to the future of Yugoslavia, so he increased the resources of the Yugoslav People's Army to the extent that it became second only to the Soviet Union itself.

Employing a strategy he'd used in his fight against the Nazis, he established tens of underground depots of food, weapons, and fuel across the rural areas of Serbia. It's this enormous cache of resources that is now giving the Yugoslav People's Army the edge, in their struggle to prevent the Federal Republic from breaking up.'

'The States of Slovenia, and Croatia have both declared independence, and Macedonia along with Bosnia-Herzegovina have also voted for independence. Although Serbia doesn't have the prosperity of the other States, they do dominate numerically within the Yugoslav People's Army in their fight to stop Slovenia establishing its own independent border posts.'

'This conflict in Yugoslavia is not happening by accident, or because Serbia has designs on its more prosperous neighbours, as the mainstream media would have you believe Mr Jones.'

'It's happening as a direct result of American interference designed to foment ethnic tensions, and armed conflict. This interference has been encouraged by your government, and the governments of Germany, France, and Italy; all of whom stand to benefit from a breakup of the Socialist Federal Republic of Yugoslavia. What you see now Mr Jones, is only the beginning.'

'Since January, the CIA, the Pentagon, the DIA, and other American secret service agencies, have been on the ground in Bosnia, spreading fear that the Serbs are about to attack. They've targeted the Muslim Bosniaks, and the Bosnian Croats in their campaign to incite violence against the Bosnian Serbs. The Bosnian Serbs are led by Radovan Karadžić, who in turn is supported by the Serbian government of Slobodan Milošević, and the Yugoslav People's Army, which as I said earlier, they largely control.'

'With vast amounts of money, the American CIA and the DIA have funded non-government agencies, opposition parties, and nationalist politicians, to spread misinformation designed to instil fear in the non-Serb population. They have also supplied arms to nationalist counter-revolutionary forces led by Franjo Tudjman in Croatia, and Alija Izetbegovic in Bosnia.'

'There's a catch-22 here in all this that you need to consider. Because of the Americans, the Serbs now feel that they're the ones under threat of invasion from the Bosniaks and Croats, so that's why they're conducting preemptive strikes on them in Vukovar, and Dubrovnik. Either way, the Americans, and their allies including Great Britain have achieved their objective — they will have broken-up Yugoslavia as we know it today.'

'We also know that MI6, that's your firm, is prepared to influence the outcome by literally removing people Britain doesn't like. To do this they use a small group of highly trained Special Air Service, and Special Boat Service operatives, secretly known as *The Increment* — even though British law precludes involvement in black ops including of course, assassination.'

At this point Tyler's mind was all over the shop. *Why's he telling me all this crap?* '*Why is he giving me this incredibly detailed backstory? He must be grooming me to change sides? Smart did exactly the same thing; same tune — just different words. Either way, what's my role in all this? Do I need to form an opinion based on facts as presented to me by Smart, or now Hersman? Is it really necessary for me to have an opinion anyway? An opinion that forces me to take sides. Surely, my job is to report the facts verbatim, and leave interpretation and decision making to others. But then, as Hersman has just said, There are things you think you know, but you don't know all there is to know, so who's facts are the real facts?*

'Well Mr Jones,' said Hersman, 'give thought to what I've just told you, and call me. Information can be transferred during meetings, or through the use of dead drops; we can work these things out together as we go along. Don't call me on this number any more, and whatever you do, never call me using your firm's phone. I'll give you a new temporary number; it's zero, double seven, double zero nine, double five seven, double five.' Hersman, unlike when he was with the black man, wrote the number down on the back of a business card, and pushed it across the table to Tyler. 'Commit it to memory as soon as you can, dial the number, and when it rings, hang up, and then use that phone whenever you call me, and please, never use the firm's phone.'

A Spaghetti Marinara each, a side salad each, and a shared bottle of the house Bordeaux, and their lunch was over.

It was just after one o'clock when they rose from their table, and shook hands.

As he had done earlier, Hersman moved his head closer to Tyler, and whispered, 'Don't forget your newspaper, and for what it's worth; it wasn't me who killed the black man. I did not do it. Go figure.'

Friday (PM), 8th November, 1991.

When Tyler crossed to the east side of Bedford Street, the dark grey Vauxhall Cavalier was parked against the kerb.

He'd walked out the door of the restaurant struggling to make sense of his meeting with Hersman. In ten minutes, or so, he'd be stepping back into Smart's office for the debriefing. There was so little time.

What would he reveal? What would he conceal? He had to be so careful. So many issues, and not enough time to consider them rationally. Not enough time to pick winners from losers. Not enough time to stitch a plausible narrative together. A narrative just like his cover story, capable of withstanding scrutiny without unravelling.

Three things kept pushing their way to the front of Tyler's mind. Hersman had said, 'There are things you think you know, but you don't know all there is to know; you'll decide what you relay to your masters, and what you don't, because it's the only power you have; and your worries shouldn't relate to me, your worries are much closer to home'.

As Tyler crossed into Bedford Street, he decided to only mention Hersman's invitation and the reason for the meeting. The officially unofficial invitation for off-the-record meetings. This is the vital piece of information that must be communicated, because it answers the question: what is it that Hersman wants?'

To go back to the Office, and broach clandestine interference by the major powers in the internal affairs of Yugoslavia, now seemed to Tyler, to be akin to the pot calling the kettle black. Considering everything, why even mention it. Even when he was with Hersman, he'd decided that his job was to report, and for others to analyse, and as Hersman had said, the power resided with him to report what he chose to report.

Out of the blue, and for no plausible reason, it crossed Tyler's mind, that to Hersman, and Smart, he was merely a pawn. An expendable complication, required to get a job done — a means to an end.

Inexplicably, Tyler had a strange feeling that Hersman had known all along that of all the issues, Tyler would only relate the officially unofficial invitation.

Settled in the back seat of the Cavalier, feeling snug and secure, Tyler's consciousness slowly reassembled itself. Clenched in his left hand was the newspaper that had started its journey with Hersman, but now resided with him.

Loosening his grip, the paper uncurled to reveal an unsealed, plain faced, B5 Manila envelope. Inside the envelope was a wad of neatly folded, single-sided, photocopied A4 sheets of paper.

The papers seemed to document recent arms shipments to Yugoslavia, in direct contravention of the UN arms embargo. The papers if genuine, suggested that the shipments came from not only Israel, but also the USA, Germany, the UK, France, Italy, and Russia. They documented the countries involved, the secret service agencies involved, the exit and entry ports, and the nature of the shipments.

As the car turned into Westminster Bridge Road, Tyler carefully placed the documents back into the envelope, pulled the peel-to-seal tab, and pressed the flap down.

With a decision based on emotion rather than logic, he reached into his jacket pocket, pulled out his personal phone, and the card with Hersman's hand written phone number. Following Hersman's instructions, he memorised the number, which wasn't all that difficult, dialled it, let it ring a couple of times, and then hung-up. He tore up the card and while the driver was distracted in traffic, he eased the window down and let the pieces be blown from his fingers.

A few minutes later, and back in Smarts office, the debriefing session was already underway. Apart from Smart, there were three other people in the room, two young males, and one young female.

Tyler had never met these people before, but he had seen them. During the ten minutes he'd waited for Hersman, they'd been moving variously around the area. At the point when Tyler had crossed from the pub side to greet Hersman, one of the young males had crossed from the opposite side of Garrick Street, such that they passed each other, with no more than a couple of yards between them.

With his flash-bulb memory now invoked, Tyler recalled that at the moment of shaking hands with Hersman, behind him he could hear, bonhomie as the pair outside the pub greeted their friend who'd just crossed the road.

Tyler's counter-surveillance musings flooded back. He now had confirmation that switching tables at the restaurant had been a good idea.

Tyler chose to feign ignorance with regard to the young trio when Smart said, 'Let me introduce you to your hidden minders.'

Tyler recounted the bones of Hersman's officially unofficial offer to use him as a back-channel for the exchange of information.

Leaning forward Tyler handed the rolled up newspaper to Smart, and as Smart opened the enclosed envelope, Tyler related how it'd come into his possession.

Smart flicked through the enclosed sheets, carefully examining them as he went. After assembling them into some sort of order, he laid them out in a series of neat rows on his desktop.

'Well,' said Smart, 'so now we know why he wanted to meet.'

'I don't get it,' said Tyler. 'What's the point in him putting this official unofficial back-channel proposition to me, when he surely knows I'd come straight back, and deliver it all to you?'

'You're reading too much into this Mr Jones. You're over-thinking it. It all makes perfect sense, and I'm delighted. So with your support, let's take him up on his offer.'

'He's either acting alone in the sense that he's following his own agenda, or his masters have genuinely sent him to explore the possibility of setting-up this back-channel line of communication.'

'With regard to what's going on in the world at the moment, having a mechanism like that in place with the Israelis, is not such a bad idea.'

'If he's acting alone, then that's a different matter. He's creating a situation where he's indirectly trying to run you as an agent, and this officially unofficial relationship is just a euphemism. If that's the case then they've done something to upset him, and he wants to get even. He's a shrewd piece of work, and he'll be using you to do the job for him if he can.

He'll achieve this by manipulating the feed of information we pass to him, because after all, he'll be the gatekeeper.'

'Either way, they'll view whatever gets through to them as highly suspect anyway. You might say then, what's the point of it all? The point is that to them it's all about information. Accurate, or less than accurate; it's information they wouldn't otherwise have.'

'They'll run it through their filters to determine what corroborates, and reinforces things they already know; what flies in the face of things they already know, and then; what's new, and currently unknown to them. It's the unknown stuff that represents the tricky bit for them.'

'Imagine for a moment, that through him we tell them things, that they don't already know; serious things. Do they react to the information, or do they just sit on their hands, and do nothing? Whichever way they choose to go, and regardless of how they obtained the information, it has the potential to precipitate a serious miscalculation on their part.'

'If I had to hazard a guess,' said Smart, 'I'd say my first scenario is probably the case. I get the feeling that he's following his own agenda. I think he's acting alone. He's inviting us, through you, to bait them into doing something stupid. That's how he'll get his revenge.'

'And, do you know what Mr Jones? We may just have the perfect bait for them. This could not have come at a better time. I told you on an earlier occasion that time was of the essence, because we have a time-critical issue coming up. So this provides a better opportunity than I could ever have imagined.'

'Hersman has helped us enormously. Our original plan was

to try to run him as an agent, but this is a much better arrangement. Far easier for us, far less complicated, and far less risky.'

'Oh, and by the way. If this all proceeds, what did he say about communication? How was he going to contact you, and how were you going to contact him?' Tyler had guessed that this question would be forthcoming, 'He'll call me on my personal mobile, not the SIS phone. Out of mistrust I presume, he refuses to call the SIS number' Smart screwed-up his face in a way that indicated, reluctant agreement.

'What about the documents in the envelope,' said Tyler, 'what were they all about?'

'Let's just say that he was proving to us, or someone else is proving to us, that first, he has access to restricted material, and secondly, that they know much more than we thought they knew about what's going on in Yugoslavia. Information about the nature of illegal arms shipments. The nations involved, the secret service agencies involved, the entry ports, and then how those shipments are being moved to their destination. I'll get our chief weapons analyst at GCHQ, Ivan Burzic, to see what he makes of the information. Get him to run it through his filters, and check its authenticity. It's unlikely, but these documents may reveal things that we currently don't know about.'

Interesting, thought Tyler, *That confirms what Hersman said over lunch. There are things you think you know, but you don't know all there is to know.*

* * *

It was just before six-thirty in the evening, when Tyler got off the bus from New Street Station.

As he put his key in Jemma's front door, it occurred to him that he'd been living this double-life for hardly any time at all, but nevertheless, it was all becoming second nature to him. He found this almost instantaneous habituation alarming. If change could be invoked so quickly, and easily, what did it say about him as a person?

The smells, and the sounds of cooking, drew Tyler to the kitchen as if he were on rails.

'How's your day at the Office been, my super spook man? Don't think you can sneak in here without me knowing. My super spook detecting device picked you up before you even got to the front door.

'Where did Tyler go mummy? I heard him come in but he's completely disappeared.'

'Boo.' Said Tyler as he stepped from behind the kitchen door, and scooped her off her little feet with both arms, while he nuzzled his face into her bare tummy, to the accompaniment of punctuated squeals of delight.

'Stop Tyler, I need to tell you something important.' Annie said as Tyler, figuring that she'd had enough, restored her to her upright position.

'Mummy said she was worried about you, so I was looking out my bedroom window for you, and there you were.'

'You, young lady, you should be in bed. Little girls are made of sugar and spice and all things nice, but that's only if they go to bed on time.'

'But Tyler I love you.'

'Don't change the subject. That's a completely different matter, and I love you too. You're just trying to trick me young lady. I tell you what, how about a story in bed while mummy does her work?'

'No, you're trying to trick me Tyler. You just want to get rid of me, so you and mummy can kiss each other all the time. How disgusting.'

Just at the point when all attempts at reason and logic on Tyler's part had failed, Annie, in a decidedly sleepy voice said, 'Well Tyler, what are you messing about for? My legs are killing me. You need to carry me up the stairs for our story.'

Over dinner, Tyler did his best to relate the events of his day to Jemma, minus the detail. Most difficult, was how to explain the paradigm shift with regard to how he felt about Aaron Hersman.

How earlier in the day, and in the space of only minutes, his fear of Hersman had morphed into a state of indifference. Considering everything, Tyler found this transformation the most difficult to understand and to put into words.

Equally difficult to explain, was Hersman's claim that it wasn't he, who had killed the black man.

If that was true, then who was it, and why?

11

BRAVO WELL DONE

Friday (PM), 8th November, 1991.

When Chris Wood picked up the phone in his kitchen to Cyril Smart, Smart said, 'About this Tyler Jones, Aaron Hersman affair. How about another trip to Saudi Arabia?'

'As per usual, it's the story that gets you where you need to be. It's the story that justifies the travel, and the expenses. On this occasion, it'll get you back into our forward operations base in Saudi Arabia. That's where the story has its beginnings, and that's where I need you to be. I need you to do another little job for me.'

'You can tell your masters at the London Leader, that this story will be the scoop de la scoop for 1991. A story that their rivals, would break their necks to get.'

'We'll deny that it ever happened of course, but you'll have enough verifiable facts, that credibility won't be an issue.'

'About the story. It concerns an eight man SAS patrol, Bravo

Two Zero. Along with a couple of other patrols, they were flown deep into Iraq, by an RAF Chinook helicopter, on the night of the twenty-second of January this year. They were infiltrating Iraq, to set up an intelligence gathering observation post along the main supply route between Baghdad, and north-western Iraq.'

'Anyway, the operation went horribly wrong. They couldn't receive messages on their patrol radio, so they had no way of knowing if their messages were getting through either. In addition, the weight of their kit was such that they could only carry half of it at any one time. This meant that to advance their position, they had to shuttle their equipment in back, and forth trips. By the next morning, January the twenty-third, they had only managed to advance their position by one mile.'

'Late in the afternoon of the next day, the twenty-fourth, they were discovered by what they thought at the time, was an Iraqi tank. The tank as it happened, turned out to be a bull-dozer, but nonetheless, the driver reported their presence to local Bedouins, and the Iraqi forces that were in the area.'

'Realising that they'd been compromised, they abandoned their position, and began to exfiltrate by walking in a north-west direction toward Syria. Unfortunately they came under fire, from a group of Iraqi soldiers, and an Iraqi Armoured Personnel Carrier.'

'Only one survivor of the firefight managed to escape capture. Miraculously he walked nearly two hundred miles, undiscovered through the desert to Syria in the north. All the other members of the patrol, were either captured, or killed.'

'So, as you can see, it's a ripping yarn, and your paper is going to love you for it.'

'Now with regard to the real job, I need you to do for me. I want you to request further assistance from our Station and General Support Branch Chief in Saudi Arabia. The same chap you saw last month, and just like last time, tell him I'll get the *Class Seven Authorisation* to him as soon as it comes through from the Foreign Secretary.'

'As you would also remember from last time, nothing in writing, ever, or transmitted over unsecured channels. You and I are merely human messengers in all this, relaying orders that will come from above.'

'Tell him that we have a new issue on our hands, and just like last time, we need an Increment chap to fix it. Preferably the same fellow who fixed the West African issue a few weeks ago. Anyway, the timeline for this one is going to be difficult to predict, but it'll definitely be within the next few months. It will be a quick-in, quick-out operation just like last time; probably a few days at the most.'

'I'll brief you on the finer details when you get there. Call me when you've got your meeting with the Station Chief set up.'

Tuesday (AM), 12th November, 1991.

Tuesday morning at NuForm-Craven had gone exceptionally well for Tyler Jones, and thanks be to God for that. Considering his lack of communication, it was a miracle that the

AcuWrite people had even turned up for their meeting at ten-thirty. Tyler Jones certainly hadn't reminded them; he'd completely forgotten the arrangement.

Not only did Jennifer and Jerry remember, they had brought their technical manager with them. Three heads brimming with exciting new ideas to dominate not only the UK, and European markets, but the global market as well.

During AcuWrite's meeting with the NuForm creative team, it was AcuWrite's technical manager who best identified, and articulated the needs of their end-users; their consumers, and their *raison d'être.*

Within thirty minutes the NuForm-Craven team, had roughed-out a series of graphic icons, that encapsulated these end-user needs. Each icon captured a unique feature of AcuWrite's offering, and when viewed collectively, succinctly projected AcuWrite's vision. The NuForm-Craven team, had cleverly rejigged AcuWrite's original campaign, and in the process, given it international currency. The use of stand-alone, self explanatory graphic icons, transcended the difficulties associated with language.

It was unambiguous, and it was powerful. It was a campaign that AcuWrite could roll-out globally — a campaign where the sky was the limit, and the return to AcuWrite Media, NuForm-Craven and Tyler Jones, was incalculable.

Tuesday (PM), 12th November, 1991.

Back at his desk after wining and dining the AcuWrite

people at the Michelin-starred restaurant down at Lakeside, Tyler received a call from Cyril Smart on his SIS phone.

'Good afternoon Mr Jones. Has Hersman called you yet?'

'No, not yet.'

'Well, when he does, try for Friday. If he gives you a shopping list of things he wants, tell him that I've already put together some material that should interest him; documents, and the like. I intend to give them our intelligence reports, as is, with regard to the recent illegal arms shipments to Yugoslavia. These are reports that I've only just received from our senior weapons analyst, Ivan Burzic at GCHQ. Exactly the same sort of information that they shared with us, but more up to date. Remember the envelope that Hersman handed you when you first met him. This time the information will be from our perspective. Information about the nature of the shipments, the nations and the agencies involved, and the entry, and destination points.'

'When you're in the Office for one of our meetings, I'll try to have Ivan Burzic here, so you can get to meet him. He's a very astute and interesting man.'

'By offering this sensitive, and restricted information to the Israelis we will convince them, that you are a valuable, and reliable asset. We need to gain their confidence as quickly as possible. We'll do that by overreaching to please them. This will then provide an opening to drive our own agenda, by introducing something from left-field; something dramatic. Something they wouldn't be expecting. Something they won't be able to ignore, and something that will force them to make a decision. Maybe even a decision that will benefit Mr Hersman.'

When their conversation concluded, Tyler buzzed Julie to say, 'I'm just nipping out to the supermarket for a few minutes. Anything we need?'

'Teabags, milk, a couple of boxes of tomato Cup-a-Soup, a packet of Custard Creams, and a packet of Digestives, that's about it.' She rattled off, as if she was reading from a preprepared list — and she probably was.

The real reason Tyler wanted to get out, was to access a public phone box. When talking to Smart about Hersman, he'd deliberately avoided the issue of who was calling who. Tyler felt sure that if the Office wasn't already monitoring calls to and from his personal mobile phone, they'd probably start doing it anytime soon.

With Tyler unilaterally changing the plan, by using a public phone box, it also created another dilemma. Hersman would expect Tyler's call to come from his personal mobile. That's why he had him call the number after they first met. Would he answer if the call now came from a public box, and not his mobile phone?

'Very creative. You've exceeded my estimation of you. Give me the number of the phone box, and I'll call you back,' said Hersman when he answered Tyler's call.

'Can we do Friday?' Tyler said.

'I don't know whether you noticed,' said Hersman, 'but there's another smaller cafe just a few doors back down Garrick Street on the same side. Friday eleven-thirty is OK for me. Please bring whatever you have on all recent arms shipments to Yugoslavia, and apart from that — no minders like last time.'

At that point, and just in case Tyler thought he might be

bluffing, Hersman provided a convincingly accurate thumbnail sketch of the three young MI6 officers.

'OK,' said Tyler, 'I'll be there at eleven-thirty, and do my best to bring what you want — and to leave behind what you don't want. Actually, with regard to the things you want. I understand that they are already in the process of collating, the very information that you've just asked for.'

On his way back to his office, Tyler pulled into a side street to call Smart, but a tricky situation occurred to him. Assuming his SIS, and personal phones were both being monitored, he can't very well say, *I've just had a call from Hersman.* Smart would immediately know he was lying.

When Smart answered the call from Tyler's SIS phone, and hoping that his tongue didn't dig a hole for his brain, Tyler said, 'Apropos your earlier call, I just received a message at work to call Hersman from a public phone box. When I dialled the number it diverted a number of times, but it was Hersman who finally answered. He want's eleven-thirty on Friday morning at a place a few doors down from where we met last time. Hersman also stressed, *No minders like last time.* Even though I was totally unaware of them until I was back in your office, he was able to accurately describe all three of them.'

'Give me the location of the phone box, and the number you called, but if he's diverted it a few times, and blocked the electronic ID, then there's not much we can do about it. The only number we'll have, is the number you just used to call him.'

Tyler breathed a sigh of relief, Smart had unwittingly, answered a question, that Tyler could never have asked.

After giving Smart the public phone box location and

number, Smart said, 'With regard to meeting Hersman. It seems strange that he's opted for a live drop, and not a dead drop. Anyway as I said when we spoke to you earlier, I've already prepared the stuff he now says he wants. It suggests to me, that I must have got it right.'

'Swing by the Office on Friday morning, and I'll have the envelope I want you to give to him waiting for you at the security desk. The envelope will contain the shipping manifests, and there'll also be another envelope with a hundred quid in twenties to cover your out-of-pockets. Call me straight after you've had your meeting.'

'Oh, and by the way. There's something very important I want you to drop into the conversation when you meet him, because it's not something that's mentioned in the documents you'll be giving to him. You've heard me say on a number of occasions, that we've got something big coming up with regard to Yugoslavia. Well, I need you to drop that statement into the conversation, at a point where you feel it fits, and would have the greatest impact.'

'Thanks Mr Smart, will do, I promise I won't forget.'

Only as Tyler drove back into the top of the estate, did his words to Julie come back, and whack him across the back of his head, *I'm just nipping out to the supermarket.* With an unplanned U-turn, plus a prayer that he'd be able to recall Julie's list. *Teabags, milk, a couple of boxes of tomato Cup-a-Soup, a packet of Custard Creams, and a packet of Digestives* — and his prayer was answered.

* * *

Friday, 15th November, 1991.

Before meeting Hersman, Tyler had swung by the Office to pick up the envelope, that Smart said would be waiting for him at the security desk.

He opened the outer envelope, put the envelope intended for Hersman in the breast pocket of his overcoat, and the five twenties went straight into his wallet.

Gone now, were the butterflies in his stomach, the trembling, and the paranoia. After all, he'd done his due diligence from the moment he got off the tube at Leicester Square. He had even allowed extra time for counter-surveillance as he walked to the cafe, entered the cafe, and checked out the patrons inside the cafe — including Hersman, who was already seated, and waiting.

After placing their orders with the waitress, Hersman said, 'I need to confirm with you that in a few months time, all transfers need to be made by dead drop. The usual routine, you don't need me to explain, unless of course it didn't form part of your training. You'll know when to approach the drop, by physical, or electronic flags that will be set to *on*, or *off* accordingly. In this way, if either party, or the site itself is compromised, the risk of being apprehended is reduced enormously; unlike a live drop like we're doing right now.'

'The drop point and flags, can, and will change from time to time, but the sites will always be accessible, in plain sight so to speak. The least expected place, at the least expected time, that's what all agencies strive for.'

'OK, I'm happy with that.' said Tyler. 'There'll be things though that I wouldn't like to put in writing, or say over the phone, like something that's going on at the moment. Something about which I have no detail, other than to say that it relates to Yugoslavia, and it's big.'

'Wow, that does sound interesting Mr Jones,' a suddenly animated Hersman replied, 'You must keep me informed.'

After a quick survey of the room, Tyler twisted his torso, reached around the back of his chair, removed Smart's envelope from the inside pocket of his overcoat, and slid it across the table to Hersman.

Receipt was acknowledged by a nod of his head, and making no immediate attempt to check the contents, Hersman slipped the envelope into the inside pocket of his jacket.

As they parted company, Hersman said, 'A long story, but I'll be moving to a new location, apropos my comments earlier, with regard to dead drop transfers. When that happens our one-on-one meetings, can't happen anyway.'

It seemed to Tyler that whatever this change was, it was bigger than Hersman was making out. It may even be the underpinning reason for why he'd approached MI6 in the first place. That is, if he ever did approach MI6. *Was it dissatisfaction with the Mossad as Smart had suggested, or was it something else?*

After their meeting, Tyler found a tolerably quiet and private spot on Euston Station to call Smart, from his SIS phone.

'I've just finished my meeting with Hersman,'

'Any dramas?'

'No, not really. You'll be pleased to know that I was able to tell him that there's something big coming up with regard to Yugoslavia. From the expression on his face, and the comments he made, I have no doubt that it had the desired effect. He was all ears, and definitely want's to know more.'

'That's good. Very good.'

'There was just one thing that Hersman said, maybe you need to know about; that is if you don't already know about it. Apparently Hersman's going to be moving somewhere else in a few months time. Live meetings will be replaced by dead drops. I got the impression that there's a lot more to it, but he wasn't giving much away.'

'Yes, I did suspect change was on the way for Mr Hersman,' Smart said, 'but no. I didn't know it was already afoot. Let's just say that if it's the Mossad, then they'll deal with him like you would a horse; they'll put him out to pasture until they decide what to do with him. It's another reason why we need to take advantage of these face-to-face meetings while we still have them.'

'How would next Thursday the twenty-first at the Office look for you?' Said Smart. 'In the meantime, I'll try to investigate the Hersman situation a bit more, and we need to talk about how we might handle dead drops, just in case. Say ten-thirty? Anyway, between now and then, he may well contact you with further instructions. Call me if he wants something before you and I meet on Thursday.'

Friday (PM), 15th November, 1991.

When he got off the train from London, and for the first

time in weeks, Tyler met up with Tim Hadley, and his other football mates.

Five thirty in the afternoon, and their choice of venue was totally justified on the basis; that it was almost winter, it was cold, it was raining, and it was already dark.

For Tyler it was an unexpectedly cathartic experience, because it made him realise just how much he'd changed. Here he was down at the pub, Nirvana, with mates he'd known for years, and one of whom was destined to be his brother-in-law; but things were no longer the same.

The conversation, the blokey chat, the banal and sexist talk, that now offended. It all bore witness to how much he'd changed. He just wanted it over as soon as possible, so that he could get home to his new family.

Monday, 18th November, 1991.

Monday, and back at his desk, Tyler was busy ticking-off the legacy of what was now, last Friday. He'd already attended to all the important calls, and faxes, including the revised draft proofs, that AcuWrite's Jennifer had faxed back.

Only two revisions, and they just about had it nailed. Next they'd start printing the brochures, flyers, banners, and maga-zine inserts. The magazine ad films would be prepared, and sent to the local printers in Ireland, Sweden, Germany, and Italy — and the promo film, to be used on the AcuWrite trade-show stand would be shot, edited, and voiced in their studios next week. The AcuWrite project was now self-fuelling, and was just getting bigger all the time.

With his characteristic tap on the frosted glass panel of Tyler's office door, Jim Craven suddenly appeared in his office.

Flopping into one of the guest chairs, Craven said, 'You know old son, with this newfound prosperity at NuForm-Craven, and all thanks be to you for that, it could not have come at a better time. Bill and I have been talking it over, and we've decided that I should resign as Managing Director at NuForm-Craven, so that I can devote more time to Bill's new shopping centre venture.'

'Along with Bill, I'll retain my financial interest in NuForm-Craven, but you old son, you can now be the boss. That is of course, if you accept our offer.' To underscore his statement, Craven couldn't resist an opportunity to ingratiate himself. 'From the moment you walked through that door for the very first time, I knew that all you needed was for me to mentor you, and this day would be inevitable.'

'The base salary we'd like to offer you, is thirty-five thousand pounds. As Managing Director your commission on sales will stop, and be replaced by some sort of bonus scheme, we've yet to work that out, but the car, and other perks would still continue as part of the package. Anyway, old boy, you think about it, and let me know.'

Tyler was dumbstruck. What Jim Craven was now offering amounted to almost double his current salary, even with his current commission arrangement.

Tyler's nonplussed expression didn't pass unnoticed by Jim Craven, who, seizing the moment, had already begun to leave the room, just as Julie was entering through the doorway from the opposite direction.

After Craven departed, Julie said, 'Congratulations Mr Managing Director, or should I now call you, Sir Tyler Jones. It's all right, don't get upset, I actually knew about all this before you did. You know what he's like; he's a full of himself twat at times. He whispered all this in my ear when he arrived — he's like a big kid, I guess he couldn't wait to tell someone.'

12

TIME TO REVEAL

Tuesday, 19th November, 1991.

It was after lunch when Chris Wood took the call from Cyril Smart.

'Whereabouts are you?'

'I'm sitting in the Station Chief's office. All on my ownsome. It's late afternoon here. I've got my meeting with him in the morning.'

'Well, anyway,' Smart said. 'Assuming for your sake, that this conversation is taking place in air-conditioned comfort at your end, I want to bring you up to speed in readiness for your chat with the Station Chief tomorrow.'

'This operation is in many ways a follow-on from the one a few weeks ago. Considering the briefings, and training the Increment chap received last time, it'd be best if the Chief can be persuaded to use the same fellow again.'

'The complete absence of political aftershocks, following the death of the black man. No bad press, no outrage from the Modrisian ambassador, or attaché, no adverse comments from foreign governments, no ongoing police investigations, and most importantly, the matter was never raised in parliament. In fact the matter was all forgotten within twenty-four hours, and indications are, that this operation will go exactly the same way.'

'The target this time has dual British, and South African citizenship. We are confident that once again, there won't be outrage from either government. His strongest connection has been with Israel, and the Mossad, where he's an agent tasked with arranging covert arms shipments to Yugoslavia.'

Chris Wood interrupted Smart's flow. 'Sounds like you're referring to Tyler Jones's nemesis, Aaron Hersman.'

'Indeed I am, Mr Wood.'

'We believe that Hersman's relationship with the Mossad probably soured when they, with a little help from us perhaps, became aware that Hersman had been moonlighting; an activity for which the Mossad has zero tolerance.'

'From the moment they suspected that he was negotiating an arms deal with Mr Baako Attah, Aaron Hersman would have become persona non grata. An appellation it would appear, that Hersman is currently unaware of. If they know that he's been doing deals behind their back, and because he's also negoti-ating arms shipments for the Mossad, he probably knows too much. All things considered, hopefully they won't miss him.'

'The Modrisian government would also suspect that Hers-man, although they wouldn't know him by name, would have been responsible for the murder of Mr Attah. So in getting rid of Hersman, we're not just settling a score on their behalf, we're indirectly helping the Israelis out as well. And..., we're also demonstrating to the British public, that by eliminating the man who killed Mr Attah, we're on top of our game, and most importantly, we keep them safe.'

'Tyler Jones reported to me, that at his meeting with Hersman last Friday, Hersman told him that very soon he'll be moving somewhere else. Where that is we have no idea, but it's something we need to keep an eye on. We don't want a situation where the Mossad and/or Hersman is outwardly indicating one thing, while behind the scenes, they're planning to do something else.'

'I've got Jones coming in on Thursday. Hopefully I'll have a better handle on it all after that. Jones neither knows, nor would he suspect, that we would have been involved in the death of Mr Attah. The very thought of us conducting black ops, is a thought that Mr Jones is probably incapable of conceiving.'

'Anyway, on to other matters. The British, and Israeli governments agree on one thing. We both believe that regime change would have been devastating for the people of Modrisia. By West African standards, Modrisia's current leadership delivers stable government, and a high standard of living. Regime change would have harmed the Modrisian people, and precipitated regional instability, which would have impacted our mutual strategic interests in the area.'

'Fortunately, when Attah was killed, the money he'd agreed to pay Hersman, hadn't been transferred from the Modrisian coffers. Believe me Mr Wood, no one shed a tear when The Increment removed that blot from the landscape.'

'Removing Hersman though, is more complicated than it was for the black man. We have issues that need to be resolved first. Issues, where Hersman's presence is germane to getting the outcome we want, but for which the timing is difficult to determine. It would also appear that the Israelis, for totally different reasons of course, have their own reasons for keeping Hersman around at the moment.'

'We can only guess what the Israeli agenda for Mr Hersman might look like. We each have our own, perhaps very different reasons to be interested in his future. It's a game, that's what it is, and because our agendas are so often mutually exclusive, it's going to be interesting to see who's still standing when the music stops.'

'They know we're up to something, and we know that they are too. We cooperate to a point, but neither party passes-up an opportunity to influence the other's outcomes. Not always with their best interests at heart either.'

'When Hersman asked your old friend Tyler Jones, to enter into this officially unofficial relationship, Jones made the valid point to me that, *it didn't make sense*. Jones like any ordinary person, couldn't possibly understand it. It's only people like us; people with lived experience; people who understand the rules of the game; rules that have more to do with expediency than they do with logic. That's how one should make sense of it.'

'When it comes to information gathering, it makes no difference how information arrives with the Mossad, only that it arrives. In this regard, it doesn't matter whether Hersman is acting with, or without their oversight. Information will be processed in exactly the same way, and all decisions made, will be made according to political expediency. Logic, and common-sense, as Mr Jones would understand it to be, just don't enter into it.'

'Through Hersman, they'll feed us truths, and half-truths, and via Tyler Jones, we'll do the same with them. That's how the game is played, and because of that, mis-steps from either side, can, and do occur.'

'That's where the timing of all this comes in. The Chief will want some idea of timing, and that's where we're in a bit of a quandary. The best I can do at the moment, is that you tell him, somewhere between late December, and the first few months of next year; March at the very outside. The reason for this uncertainty relates to the transfer of information that I referred to earlier. It's impossible to predict the timing of the flow, because they're the ones who are calling the shots with regard to meetings.'

'Along with our American cousins, and our other partners, we are also not happy that Israel and Russia, are directly and illegally supplying weapons to the Serbs. Diplomatic pressure at every level has failed to influence them, because within the Knesset, and the Israeli public at large for that matter, there is no appetite to support Muslims over Christian Serbs. At some stage though, they'll be forced to comply, but by then the damage may be such, that the situation in Yugoslavia will have spiralled out of control.'

'If they refuse to be influenced, by conventional diplomacy, then they leave no option, other than for us to use less conven-

tional means. So, through the agency of our unwitting partici-
pant, Tyler Jones, we will drip feed information that will test
the resolve of his opposite number's masters.'

* * *

Thursday (AM), 21st November, 1991.

'So Hersman hasn't tried to contact you since we spoke last
Friday?' Smart said, as he ushered Tyler into his office, and
toward the conversation area.

'No..., no he hasn't. I haven't heard a word.'

'In a way that's good, it gives us more time, but then time is
what we don't have a lot of at the moment. We must take full
advantage of this next face-to-face meeting with Hersman. We
want this information transferred verbally, from you to him,
and certainly not via dead drop.'

'Now, to discuss the detail behind the reason why I've
brought you in today. The sensitivity of this information, is such
that if it ever leaked outside the secret service community, the
consequences would be devastating. The ramifications would
affect every single aspect of the Yugoslav crisis, and it would
certainly affect international relations.'

'In this instance, seeing as this will be a verbal transfer of
information in the absence of credible witnesses, or other
evidence, it can always be denied.'

'I've alluded to this important, and time-critical matter on a
number of occasions. I'm talking here about the information,
you'll be verbally passing to Hersman at your next meeting.
Nothing about this must ever be committed to writing.'

'The Americans have been pressuring us to provide a quick solution to the situation in Yugoslavia. The Americans believe that to resolve the conflict, no doubt on terms favourable to them, the Serbian leader Slobodan Milošević must be eliminated. Getting rid of Milošević would also remove material support for the Bosnian Serb leader, Radovan Karadžić. Put simply, get rid of Milošević, and problem solved. That's what the Americans say.'

'I have a secret report here,' said Smart as he leaned forward, and touched a document lying face-down on his coffee table. 'In this report, our people discuss how the job might be done.'

'We'll be using Serbian paramilitary operatives who'll eliminate Milošević within Serbia. They're currently being equipped and trained, and when the timing's right, they'll be sent back in. That's why I've insisted that this is a time-critical operation; we've got a lot of work to do, and only a short amount of time to do it. The other reason that makes it time-critical, is that the situation on the ground in Yugoslavia, is getting worse by the day.'

'I need you to tell Hersman what we plan to do, and how we plan to do it as a matter of urgency. I know all this sounds stupid, considering what I said a moment ago, because why would we give Hersman and Israel, this top secret information. Information about the assassination of a State leader. A leader who has been a longstanding friend and ally of Israel.'

'The answer to this seemingly unanswerable question Mr Jones, relates to things I said to you during your first debriefing. When the Mossad, the secret service arm of the Israeli government receive information from us, we know that the first thing they do, is to put it up against information they already hold.'

'What we tell them will either reinforce, or fly in the face of what they already know, so do they believe it, or do they not believe it? No matter how they look at it, their options are limited, but the risks are enormous. Do they react, or do they sit on their hands, and do nothing. In this instance, the information is so unusual, that they may be damned if they do, or damned if they don't.'

At this point Smart lifted himself from his chair, and leaning forward, said, 'What will it be, tea, or coffee? Time for a break.'

'Coffee would be nice. Thank you. Do you need a hand?'

'No. I'm fine. Just give me a few minutes,' Smart said as he opened his office door.

After Smart left the room, Tyler stood, walked over to the window, and looked down on the slow, steady, monotonous movement of traffic on Westminster Bridge Road.

Tyler's mind could not move past Smart's shock pronouncement, about Slobodan Milošević. That Smart could discuss such a serious matter, with such casual indifference, confused Tyler.

Stepping away from the window, and walking back to his seat, Tyler's trouser leg brushed the edge of the document on the coffee table. The document spun forty-five degrees, coming to a resting position that shouted; *someone picked me up, and looked at me.*

He couldn't leave the document skew-whiff, over the edge of the coffee table, that would be tantamount to admission of guilt. With only a minute, or two before Smart would return, Tyler made the rash decision to pick the document up, and place it back down in its original position, but to have a quick peep on the way.

What Tyler saw, only served to exacerbate his existing state of confusion. The two page, double-spaced report, did not discuss, one plan to kill Milošević, as Smart had claimed; it discussed three plans.

Skimming over all three plans, Tyler noticed that the other two, would be carried out exclusively by British Special Air Service, and Special Boat Service personnel. There would be no local Serbian involvement whatsoever. It was only plan one, the plan that Smart had presented to him, that employed local forces. Thus, if the operation went wrong, Britain would simply hide behind a wall of silence, or deniability.

The second plan involved SAS, and SBS operatives drawn from The Increment. They would infiltrate Serbia to kill Milošević in an ambush. Of all three plans, this plan was cited as the one most likely to succeed, but it would be impossible to deny if things went wrong.

When it came to plan three, Smart, or someone else, had run a yellow highlighter through the text. Whereas the first two plans would take place on Yugoslavian soil, this plan would be carried out in Genève.

A high speed car crash would be staged in a Genève motorway tunnel during one of Milošević's regular visits. SBS operatives posing as paparazzi, would shine blindingly bright strobe lights into the eyes of Milošević's driver. The strobe lights were originally developed by the British SIS to blind enemy helicopter pilots as they attempted to land.

In the document's summary comments, which were also highlighted, it noted that plan three was in fact the preferred plan, not plan one. Although Special Boat Service personnel would carryout the operation, there would be fewer witnesses, and Milošević would almost certainly be killed. Once again, the downside was the lack of deniability if something went wrong.

Within seconds of Tyler placing the document back on the coffee table, there was the familiar sound of someone doing battle with a tea tray in the hallway. Smart had returned.

'Here we go Mr Jones,' Smart said as he carefully placed the tray on the coffee table. He seemed quite relaxed, and seemingly unaware that anything untoward had occurred during his absence. The fact that Tyler had positioned himself at the window, and feigned an attempt to help Smart with the tray, may have eased Tyler's immediate state of guilt-fuelled anxiety, but had it fooled Smart?

'Let's pick up where we left off then. Shall we?' Said Smart, coffee cup in hand. 'I was midway through explaining the inexplicable.'

'For Israel to be given access to this top secret information, is a two edge sword. We first need to ask ourselves some basic questions, and there are probably other questions as well.'

'Can they change the situation? Will they share the information? Can they complain to someone? And, the overarching question. Will they react, or will they just sit back, and do nothing?'

'To cut a very long story short. We believe they'll initially get very excited in an upset kind of way, then when they calm down to assess their options, they'll probably realise that they don't have any. They'll come to this conclusion reluctantly, and when they do, it'll have little, or nothing to do with protecting Milošević the man, or his designs for a Grand Serbian State. Decisions will rather be made on the basis of what's politically expedient, and best protects Israel's national interest. An example of this pragmatism might be that they'll ask them-selves: will arms sales decrease if Milošević is killed, or will they increase? You never know, he might be of more value to Israel dead than alive.'

'Yes, Mr Jones we do want you to personally relate this information to Mr Hersman, and we want it related exactly as I have related it to you. If you're unsure about anything, or have any questions, we can go over things again on the day, before you leave to meet with him.'

Thursday (PM), 21st November, 1991.

Countless, amorphous and confusing thoughts cascaded through Tyler's brain as he left Smart's office, and headed back to Lambeth North Tube Station.

He now knew what it might feel like to be losing one's mind.

It wasn't until his train pulled out of Euston Station, that some semblance of order returned to his thought processes; but not without considerable self-admonishment.

My thoughts are all over the shop. Capture one for God's sake. Latch onto it — don't let it go. Is there an end to all this, that I've got myself involved in? Where is it all taking me? Do I just follow Smart's instructions, or should I be asking more questions? Stop avoiding the issue, and start taking it seriously. Just get on with it, you lazy dude, deal with it. Get on top of it, before it gets on top of you.

The emotional rollercoaster he'd just stepped off had left him in no fit state to think logically. He was confused; there were so many questions requiring answers.

When Smart had left his room to get the coffee, Tyler thought, Surely as such a high-ranking spook, he must have known that I'd take a look at the document. After all it was he who had drawn my attention to it in the first place. Why would he verbally brief me on only one plan to kill Milošević, when there were in fact three? Why was I not briefed on plan three, the plan that someone had high-lighted as the preferred plan in the report? Why? Why would he do that?

Am I being setup? Am I being tested in some way?

What happens if I don't follow Smart's instructions, and I relate plan three to Hersman instead, because after all that's the preferred plan in the report — it's even highlighted.

Does Smart have some backdoor way of knowing what I discuss with Hersman? It seems highly probable.

Friday, 22nd November. 1991.

It was late Friday morning, when Tyler next heard from Hersman. He'd been switched through from the main NuForm-Craven line by Julie. He seemed to have, on this occasion at least, abandoned his own telephone rules. Was this an indication of trust, stupidity, laziness, desperation, or maybe even displeasure?

'Mr Jones, I'll be away for a couple of weeks, so I can't do a meeting until Tuesday the third of December. How would that be for you? Late morning, maybe where we met last time, or maybe somewhere new?'

'OK, Mr Hersman, Tuesday the third of December it is. Same place, same time.' Said Tyler, self-consciously realising that this was only the second time, that he'd actually addressed Hersman by name. All things considered, *Aaron*, didn't feel right.

'Tell me Mr Jones, has there been any further movement with regard to that big issue you referred to last time?'

'Well, actually, yes there has.'

'Will you have more to add when we meet?'

'Yes, I'm told I will. Probably a lot more.'

'Well then, I look forward to seeing you on the third, and I've got something for you too. It concerns the information you passed to me last time; the manifest of arms shipments. Our analysts did some work on it, and they think you've got a serious problem, that you may need to take care of. I'll talk to you about it when we meet.'

After Hersman's call, Tyler picked up his SIS phone, and called Cyril Smart.

'Swing by the Office on your way, like you did last time,' said Smart, 'Apropos the matter I briefed you on yesterday, we can't afford to miss this opportunity. December the third is still more than a week away, but we can use the time to review, and refine our message.'

* * *

Tuesday, 26th November, 1991.

Midmorning, as he was taking his morning tea break, Cyril Smart, put a call through to Chris Wood in Saudi Arabia.

'Have I caught you at a good time?' Smart said when Wood took the call.

'Couldn't be better. Timing is perfect. Just finished lunch. Probably the last chance to talk before I leave later tonight. A week here is about as much as I can take to get a story, even if it is a cracker.'

'Well two reasons then. I was interested to hear how you'd got on with the Station Chief, and I wanted to update you on the Jones, forward slash Hersman situation. I don't want you to put your foot in it, unintentionally of course, if Jones happens to contact you for some reason. You also need to know about these things because they're linked to what you're doing for me in Saudi Arabia as well.'

'First things first then, Cyril,' Wood interrupted. 'As you might remember, Tyler Jones, and I bumped into each other at a printing industry gig at the Courthouse Hotel. We're old school mates, and literally hadn't seen each other for years. When we met for dinner that night, we decided, well I did actually, that we should get together again, before Christmas at the latest. Strange, when I suggested that to him, I had vague plans to recruit him, and then out of the blue he phones me, all in a tizz over this Baako Attah thing, and you know the story from there. Maybe I should give him a call over the weekend, and arrange to meet up when he's back in London?'

'Yes, I would really like you to do that if you could,' said Smart. 'With all that's been happening, I was going to ask you to start shadowing him a bit more closely anyway.'

'OK, I'll get onto it then,' said Wood. 'Now with regard to the Chief, he's fine about it. He's happy to fit in with whatever. The Increment chap is going to be around for quite awhile. He's involved in training lesser SAS mortals before they go out on patrol. They don't want any repeats of Bravo Two Zero — makes for great storytelling though. Anyway, the Chief says he only needs a couple of weeks notice. Now, you wanted to say something.'

'Yes, I did. Jones has got a meeting with Hersman on Tuesday the third of December, and we think that the Mossad, or someone, will be moving him to a new location within the next few months. This means that we have to make the most of whatever time we have left.'

'I need to brief you on a few matters, that are either related to what we spoke about last week, or have happened since. When we spoke, I mentioned that via Tyler Jones and Aaron Hersman, we'll drip feed the Israelis with some information that will test their resolve.'

'Recently, the Americans have put us under considerable pressure to come up with a plan to get rid of Slobodan Miloše-vić. The Americans are convinced, that the conflict will continue to escalate unless the Serbian leader is taken out.'

'In a nutshell, and to get them off our case, we investigated the issue and came up with a report. We even developed some specialised gear for the purpose. The report proposed three ways that the job might be done; a plan one, a plan two, and a plan three. To make things easy for our cousins, we even flagged our preferred option; plan three.'

'Our Special Boat Service chaps would take out Milošević during one of his trips to Genève. We'd stage a high speed car crash in a road tunnel, using high powered strobe lights to blind his driver. Our chaps, posing as paparazzi, would be on motorbikes with the strobe lights mounted on their cameras. The strobe lights look exactly the same as an electronic flash gun. One way, or another, the plan was that Milošević would not come out of that tunnel alive.'

'What you need to know though, is that when I briefed Jones, that was not the plan I presented to him. I only presented plan one to him. In plan one, unlike plans two and three, only local disaffected Serbian operatives would be used. We would not be directly involved.'

'The takeout message we want to pass on to the Israelis, is that Milošević is on borrowed time. Plain and simple. Whether it's plan one, plan two, or plan three, is irrelevant.'

'When I briefed Mr Jones, I also told him, that the Israelis will come to the conclusion, that there's not much they can do about it, so they'll probably do nothing to warn, or protect him. They will deal with this in a pragmatic way, and any action will be predicated on political expediency. It may well emerge that Milošević is more valuable to them dead, than he is alive.'

'Now, I know what you're thinking. Why would I brief Jones on a plan, that we were never going to carry out? As I said earlier, the aim is to let the Israeli's know that history has overtaken them. Regardless of their relationship with Milošević; his fate now rests in the hands of others.'

'Briefing Mr Jones on the wrong plan is one thing, but there's something else you need to know. While he was in my office he had the opportunity to expose himself to the detail of all three plans. Not to put too finer a point on it, I offered him a bait, and he took it. The test now for Mr Jones will be, which plan he relates to Hersman? Will he relate only what he was briefed on, or will he relate another one, or maybe all three?'

'And, last. Just when you thought that that was all there was to know; here's the pièce de résistance.'

'Everything I've just told you is now totally irrelevant, and redundant. Earlier I told you that it was the Americans who'd put us up to all this. Well guess what?. The Yanks have now got cold feet, and have called the whole thing off. God knows what happened, but whatever it was, it succeeded. Bastards that they are.'

'We put a lot of work into this project, and we don't want to lose the fruits of our labour. The strobe lights, high speed car crash in the tunnel plan, is too good to discard. We may not use it for Milošević, but you never know what the future holds.'

'I know there's a risk that Jones will relate plan three to Hersman, but my guess is that he won't. If I'm proven correct, then Jones will become one of only a handful of people, who will ever know that this plan existed.'

'I wouldn't say it outside of this conversation, but I'm pretty well sure that the Americans have back-doored us. The Israelis have got to them. There's been back-channel stuff going on, that we've not been privy to.'

'Out of necessity, Mr Jones already knows more than I'd prefer him to know, which presents an issue in itself, but he wouldn't have been able to do what I've needed him to do, if that were not the case.'

'The backstory I exposed to you today, with regard to Milošević, and what we spoke about last time with regard to Mr Aaron Hersman, must never even be hinted at when you meet with Mr Jones.'

* * *

Thursday, 28th November, 1991.

'I hear from Cyril that you'll be coming down to London on the third for a meeting,' said Chris Wood. 'Now, I don't know about you, but I distinctly remember our arrangement to get together before Christmas. We had that unfortunate Baako Attah distraction of course, and while it didn't get us together in the flesh so to speak, it did result in us working for the same firm.'

'Yes, of course I remember our plan,' said Tyler. 'What about I stay over on the Tuesday night, so that we can meet up for dinner. I was going to come back home on the Tuesday, after my meeting with Smart, but I could just as easily come back the next day. I'll be staying where I was last time, at the Charing Cross Hotel, so maybe you could come over, and we could have dinner together. How would seven-thirty suit?'

'Sounds great. I'll be there with bells on.'

For Tyler, the space between his meetings with either Hersman, or Smart, had ensured that the AcuWrite project continued on its forward trajectory. While AcuWrite Media prospered, everything at NuForm-Craven prospered.

All the branding artwork had been signed-off by Jennifer, on behalf of AcuWrite. All the full page magazine ad films, had been pasted up, and sent to the various local and international printers. All the local print jobs that could be printed in-house were completed, and the promo film for AcuWrite's exhibition stands has been shot, edited, and voiced.

That night over dinner, with Annie asleep upstairs, and Cameron on and off the breast, Jemma took Tyler by surprise, 'You don't talk to me anymore about your meetings with Mr Smart, or whomever else you've got yourself involved with. You just go off to meetings, you come home, and you hardly say a word. I get the feeling that whenever we're alone you avoid the issue, it's as if I'm not part of your life anymore. Couples are supposed to share their lives. Maybe you were single for too long.'

Having said her piece, Jemma cupped Cameron's head into her breast, swung both her legs over the side of her chair, faced away from Tyler, and burst into tears.

With Jemma sobbing uncontrollably, Tyler got up, walked around the table, and knelt down in front of her, his arms around her waist, and his head to the side on her lap.

In silence, and gazing through tears, they reaffirmed their love for each other.

They held hands as they slowly walked into the living room to sit together on the sofa, where Tyler within the limits of what could, or could not be said, told Jemma about his planned meetings, and the gist of his past meetings.

13

TELLING TALES

Monday (PM), 2nd December, 1991.

In readiness for tomorrow's briefings with Cyril Smart, his meeting with Hersman, and his dinner with Chris Wood, Tyler had travelled down to London.

Perhaps out of nostalgia, perhaps out of practicality, he'd booked himself a room at the Charing Cross Hotel. For someone who embraced exercise as part of their lifestyle, both The Office, and where he'd be meeting Hersman were within walking distance of the hotel. His plan was to stay Monday and Tuesday nights, and then travel back to Birmingham on Wednesday morning.

When Tyler stepped into the hotel's warm, and cosy lobby from the cold outside, any thoughts he may have had about eating out, were instantly dispelled. The thought of looking for somewhere to eat on a cold and dark Monday night, held no appeal whatsoever.

Snug in his hotel room, Tyler changed into his fluffy white hotel bath robe, unpacked his suitcase, and sitting on the edge of the bed, he called Jemma.

Within a millisecond of the first ring burst, Jemma's phone was answered by one, very excited little girl.

'Is that you Tyler?'

'Hi Annie. . .,' But Annie was on a mission. 'Mummy's in the kitchen,' she said, as her little feet urgently transported the handset from its base station in the living room to her mother in the acoustically bright kitchen.

The squelchy muffled sounds of little fingers over the mouthpiece were suddenly replaced by Jemma, who, in a playful and echoey voice, said, 'How's my handsome man? Has he been a good boy down there in London, surrounded by all those yummy women?'

Tyler responded with silence, choosing not to deliver his preprepared script. There was no point. Jemma had done his job for him, and she had done it, ever so much better. Her words, instantly put him at ease. They were words from a woman in love. A woman who was reconnecting with her man, in the loveliest possible way. Tyler felt reassured, and safe. Everything in his world was in its place, and as it should be.

Tuesday (AM), 3rd December, 1991.

Following breakfast, and a twenty minute brisk walk from his Hotel, Cyril Smart ushered Tyler into his office, just before ten o'clock.

'Come in Mr Jones, I've got someone here I'd like you to meet. This is Mr Ivan Burzic from GCHQ. He's the fellow I told you about on the phone. Mr Buzic is our Senior Weapons Analyst, responsible for monitoring weapons systems across the whole of Europe. It's his intelligence that informs our decisions with regard to what we do, or don't do in Yugoslavia. It was Mr Burzic who prepared those illegal arms shipment manifests that I passed on to you recently.'

Tyler thought. *Why is Smart only mentioning part of the story. Why has he omitted the fact, that Burzic's manifests were handed, as is, and unread, to someone representing a foreign intelligence service, for fuck sake.*

What's Smart's game? There's got to be something going on here that I'm not getting; this doesn't make sense.

Following a few moments of embarrassing silence, it was Tyler, who broke the ice. He decided that this was not the time to vent misgivings. 'Nice to meet you Mr Burzic. Tell me, do you sit at a desk, in the same spot every day analysing data, or do you need to get out, and about, on the ground so to speak?'

'Yes, I'm afraid that I do spend a lot of my time behind a desk, in the same spot, as you say. Thankfully though, my staff do most of that day-to-day stuff. My responsibility is to analyse, and make sense of the data. There are times though, where I do need to get out in the field to collect, human intelligence. The type of intelligence that can value-add, and inform the core listening activities that take place within GCHQ.

My parents are Yugoslav, and I was born in Croatia before they migrated to Britain, so I speak Croatian, which is a tremendous advantage in this current crisis. In fact, I'll be back in

Zagreb, collecting that type of human intelligence this coming February.'

'Don't you feel unsafe going back there, with all that's going-on at the moment?' Tyler said.

'No, not really. Apart from being able to speak the language while I'm there, I'm looked after by our local diplomatic service people, so I feel quite safe. We've had a British diplomatic mission there since Croatia declared its independence a few months ago. They are currently working with the Croatian government to set up an embassy in Zagreb, sometime in the first half of next year. Actually, I have a pretty good time of it when I'm down there.'

Tyler hadn't really taken to this thickset, middle aged man. He found Burzic's self-satisfied smirk, and his cold steady squinting gaze, off-putting, so he didn't pursue the conversation any further.

Following Burzic's exit from Smart's office, Smart revisited the Milošević affair, and the story that Tyler would relate to Aaron Hersman, within the hour.

Smart reiterated every detail of plan number one, not once, but twice. To Tyler it felt like Smart was baiting him to make a comment. To perhaps reveal that, yes, he had looked at the report while Smart was out of the room, and that, yes, he was aware of the deception that was about to be perpetrated.

Smart posed a series of hypothetical questions to Tyler, presumably, to prepare him for issues that Hersman might raise — all the time stressing that his meeting with Hersman represented a once-only opportunity to benefit the people on the ground in Yugoslavia, if not the global community.

Tyler found it interesting, that at no point did Smart discuss using any form of covert surveillance during his meeting with Hersman. Maybe the Office didn't see the necessity. Maybe they didn't have the resources available. Maybe they didn't have the budget. It begged the question though — why was the matter not even discussed?

At just after eleven o'clock, Smart arranged for his driver to drop Tyler at the corner of Garrick and Bedford Streets.

As Tyler was leaving Smart's office, he handed Tyler an envelope with five twenty pound notes. 'Here's a contribution out of petty cash for your travel expenses. When you settle the account at the Charing Cross, get the receipt to me, and we'll reimburse the cost of your accommodation.'

Tuesday (PM), 3rd December, 1991.

When Tyler walked into the cafe, Hersman was already seated, and waiting.

As Tyler approached, Hersman pushed his chair back, stood up, and extended his right arm to shake hands.

'Welcome Mr Jones. I'm already into the red. You need to join me. Such a fucking cold and miserable day out there.' Hersman said as he grasped the bottle by the neck.

'I agree.' Said Tyler. 'I mean, yes, it is a fucking cold and miserable day, and yes, I will have a glass of wine.'

Hersman lifting the bottle, leaned forward, and half filled Tyler's glass.

Although there was a black, three quarter length, gabardine overcoat, and a grey woollen scarf draped over the back of his chair, Hersman was dressed in what Tyler now saw to be his uniform. Pale blue crumpled linen Jacket with patch pockets, white shirt, no tie, dark blue jeans, and saddle brown boots.

'Now Mr Jones. The longer than intended delay for our meeting was due to the fact that I was overseas for a couple of weeks. I do apologise.'

Hersman's statement told Tyler nothing. Being overseas for a couple of weeks, begged many questions; questions for which, Tyler knew in advance, answers would not be forthcoming.

As soon as the waitress had taken their orders, and with no further ado, Tyler launched into what he was sent to say.

'I don't have any material information for you today, only verbal. I've been told to tell you, in the spirit of cooperation and mutual interest, that this information is so restricted, that only a handful of people are aware of its existence.'

'As I said to you last time, the information relates to Yugoslavia. What it amounts to, is that under pressure from the Americans, the British are planning to kill Slobodan Milošević.'

'Ag. Oh man, that's big — Ag. Oh man.' Hersman responded, more than hinting at his South Africanist past.

Without pausing, Tyler related in precise detail, plan one; as rehearsed in Smart's office less than one hour before.

At no point, did Tyler even hint at the existence of alternative plans, and God forbid; that the preferred plan to kill Milošević, was inside a road tunnel in Genève.

'What's the timeline? When do they plan to do this?'

'I haven't been told. Sometime soon. I understand that their preference is for sooner rather than later,' said Tyler, 'that's all I know.'

Hersman appeared to be lost for words, as he silently, and painstakingly, divided what remained of the wine into their now empty glasses.

Returning the empty bottle to the table, and showing signs that his thought processes were now working again, Hersman said, 'Well, all I can do, is to relay what you've just told me, and I'll get back to you. Being already December, it may well be the new year.'

'I've also got something here for you too,' Hersman said, as he produced a familiar Manila envelope from the inside pocket of his jacket, 'It's our reanalysis, I emphasise reanalysis, of the arms shipment documents that you gave to me last time we met.'

'In a nutshell, you have a double agent in your organisation. Your double agent may have set out working for the British Secret Intelligence Service, but he's been turned by the newly formed, Croatian Office For The Protection Of Constitutional Order, the UZUP. They now control what he does, and how he does what he does, within your SIS.'

'We know this, because there is information within the manifests, that could have only come from the US Defence Intelligence Agency, the DIA. The British SIS assessment of the illegal arms trade in Yugoslavia, has been distorted downwards. This distortion is there in plain sight, you might say, but only if you have access to all the data.'

'Your double agent is provided access to this secret information, by his masters at the UZUP. Information that they, in turn, have received directly from the Defence Intelligence Agency, the DIA; according to a special deal that I'll explain in a moment.'

'Even agencies like the CIA, and your own MI6, don't get access to this information. The CIA, and MI6, have their own intelligence networks, plus they have access to intelligence gathered by the UN with regard to Yugoslavia. Your double agent gets all this information too, because he's one of you, but the documents you supplied to us, prove that he also has access to the intelligence gathered by the US Airborne Warning and Control System aircraft. These are aircraft that fly out of Tuzla Air Base in Bosnia and Herzegovina, and track all communications emanating from the ground, and anything that flies. There can be no delivery into, or movement through the Yugoslav states, that they don't know about.'

'The US government is deceiving the UN by manipulating and/or totally withholding this AWACS data. We believe that Croatia, unlike the UN, has access to this information, because of a deal that's been struck between the White House, and the Croatian President, Franjo Tudjman.'

'The effect of this intentional distortion of data is catastrophic. Catastrophic because it skews the day-to-day decisions Britain, and other countries make about Yugoslavia. They are making bad decisions, based on bad data. It impacts their operations on the ground, the lives of their agents, and the lives of countless innocent civilians caught up in all this mess. It is a deliberate ploy on the part of the Americans to cover up their clandestine arms deliveries into Croatia. The intended, or unintended consequence of this coverup, will be catastrophic. In a nutshell; it will increase, not decrease hostilities on the ground, which is obviously their intention. Conflict aids and abets their ambitions.'

'I need to explain the background to you Mr Jones, but before I do, let me go straight to the bottom line. Let me be totally frank with you Mr Jones. Is this issue impacting the interests of Israel, and its military support for the Serbs? Yes it is. By verbally sharing this information with you, do we seek to change MI6, and the UK's military assessment, so that it benefits Israel, and the Serbs? Yes we do. So, let me explain to you what your double agent is doing, how he's doing it, and why he's doing it.'

'As you may already know Mr Jones, there is no love lost between the Croats, and the Serbs. Ethnic tensions have existed between the two states for hundreds of years. More recently during the Second World War, Croatia actively supported Nazi Germany, and Fascist Italy. The Croatian Ustashe were responsible for murdering hundreds of thousands of Serbs, Jews, political dissidents, and Gypsies. These are historical facts.'

'In the current crisis, the Croatian President Franjo Tudjman, has negotiated a secret quid pro quo agreement with the Pentagon. The agreement allows Croatia to retain between twenty to fifty percent of the arms, and ammunition that's being flown into Croatia; what's locally referred to as *Transit Tax*. Iran Air has been operating these deliveries, but lately a whole squadron of black unmarked C-130 Hercules aircraft, fly in every night. We believe that these aircraft belong to the Americans.'

'The role that Croatia plays in the distribution of arms, and ammunition to Bosnia, and Herzegovina is pivotal. The quantity of weapons flown into Croatia directly, combined with those arriving by ship at the port of Koper in Slovenia, is massive. These supplies are then secretly transported through Croatia to the muslims in Bosnia, and Herzegovina; all this in direct violation of Article 713 of the UN Security Council.'

'So Mr Jones, Croatia retains between twenty to fifty percent of these arms shipments, which it then uses to attack Serbia itself, and the Serbs living in the Serbian enclaves within Croatia. On top of that, Croatia also receives massive amounts of illicit arms from Germany, Belgium, and the UK.'

'The arms supplied to Serbia, mostly by Israel, and Russia, on the other hand, pale into insignificance when compared with what's being shipped into Koper, and what's being flown directly into Croatia by the Americans.'

'At the Slovene port of Koper, the Slovene authorities do their own port inspections, and are not subject to international scrutiny; it's Slovenia's way of evading the UN arms embargo, and getting a cut of the action.'

'After the shipments arrive, they are then distributed to and through Croatia to Bosnia, and Herzegovina by their related military, and secret service agencies. They say that the weapons are needed to defend themselves against Serbian aggression.'

'The shipments that arrive in Koper are arranged by arms traders in Vienna, using companies that are registered in Panama, and loans that are transacted by a bank in Budapest. Perhaps unsurprising, most of the funds for these loans comes from the USA, Germany, and Great Britain.'

'To add further insult to the tragedy that is Yugoslavia; the

Italian, Albanian, and Russian mafia, like bears to a honey pot, have also written themselves into the same script.'

'And it gets even worse Mr Jones. Much worse. The American administration has also been directing a proportion of these arms to the Afghan Mujaheddin, and the pro-Iranian Hezbollah, both of whom have training bases in Bosnia and Herzegovina. In fact many of the actual Mujaheddin fighters themselves, have been flown in on these secret nighttime flights.'

'Unsurprisingly, the Croatians are none too pleased about this leakage of weapons to militant Islamists, but for practical, albeit hypocritical reasons, anything that puts pressure on Serbia directly and indirectly, helps the Croatian cause.'

'Oh, and by the way,' said Hersman, 'with regard to your double agent; this man has a name — it's Ivan Burzic.'

Ivan Burzic, the man whom Tyler Jones had just been with, no more than two hours ago, was now being accused of high treason by Hersman. The fact that Tyler had taken an instant dislike to Burzic, in no way mitigated the shock that Hersman's statement invoked in him at that moment.

Having delivered his rather complex and troubling narrative, Hersman stood up, shook hands, and left.

* * *

When Tyler stepped back out onto Garrick Street, he realised that there was no plan for how he would be getting back to the Office. Would he be hoofing it, or would he be tubing it?

But, just as on the first occasion, parked over the Kerb, and pointing back down Bedford Street, was the iridescent, dark grey, Vauxhall Cavalier.

Back in Smart's office, it was all quite predictable and as Tyler had imagined. 'Were you able to get my message across? How did Hersman react to the news? What did he say? What did you say? Did he offer anything new, or unexpected? Did Hersman say anything about another one-to-one meeting?'

'With regard to Milošević,' answered Tyler, 'Hersman seemed visibly taken aback by what I had to tell him, but beyond that he made no comment. Nor did he give any indication, as to what they might do with the information, when he took it back to his firm.'

'It was what he had to say about illicit arms shipments, that might interest you though. He gave me this envelope to give back to you; it's the manifests that you got me to give to him last time we met. It apparently contains their reassessment of the documents inside.'

'Hersman says that there's been a double agent working inside the British SIS, who's manipulating our arms shipment data.' Tyler said as he handed Smart the envelope, inexplicably stopping short of attaching Burzic's name to the accusation. A sudden, and unexpected sense of unease had prevented him from proffering a full and frank account of his meeting with Hersman.

As Tyler Spoke, Smart took the A4 sheets out of the envelope, and meticulously laid them on his desk, placing them in rows, side by side with copies of the original ones that Tyler had passed to Hersman.

'Well,' said Smart, 'this certainly does change things. It

changes things quite a lot, and unfortunately confirms my worst fears. Mossad's upward revision of our arms manifests, if correct, means that they, the Israelis, must have access to intelligence that we, and the CIA don't have. The only place this information could have come from is the DIA. The question is though, why the hell would the DIA be doing something, that's so patently stupid?'

'Intelligence communities have long suspected, that the DIA is supplying arms to radical Islamist groups in Yugoslavia. Unfortunately we've been totally unsuccessful in arguing our case with the Pentagon. We believe, that this totally illogical intransigence on the part of the US administration, is because they've been snookered by these radical groups.

The Mujaheddin and Hezbollah are obviously calling-in past debts. In this regard, one should not forget that the US comes with form. The US supplied very sophisticated weaponry to Saddam Hussein in his fight against Iran, only to have those same weapons used against them, as close as last year — it's called *Blowback*.'

'With regard to what these revised manifests might tell us about the situation in Yugoslavia, I will need time to consider. One thing that is immediately clear to me though; is that the Israelis are definitely trying to influence us in favour of not just their cause, but also that of the Serbs.'

'In a recent speech that Baroness Margaret Thatcher gave at the UN, she made the point that Croatia, and Slovenia are at a distinct disadvantage in their struggle for independence against the Serbs. She said that Croatia and Slovenia have no armies or access to weapons, other than what they've been able to capture from the Serbs. She said that we should immediately recognise Croatia and Slovenia as independent states, so that we can legally supply them with arms to defend themselves. She said that they have the legal right to defend themselves against attack from the Serbs, in their self-proclaimed Republic Of Serbian Krajina. An area that's actually within Croatia itself. Baroness Thatcher said that for Croatians, this is a *Homeland War*, against Serbia's attempts to create a *Greater Serbian* state. She said that in this instance, Serbia, and the Yugoslav army were the aggressors, and that it was a battle of democracy against communism. She said that Yugoslavia was a totalitarian communist state — a brutal state that would fall apart. She called on the international community to stop Serbian aggression — they should rather be on the side of liberty, democracy, and justice. Unlike Serbia, which has copious amounts of arms due to the stockpiling policy of the late, President Tito, Croatia only has the weapons, that they've managed to capture from the Serbs, so they're in a desperate position.'

'In a recent newspaper interview Baroness Thatcher went even further, when she stated that the current British Prime Minister, John Major, was appeasing President Milošević.'

'I guess we in the British Secret Intelligence Service, share Baroness Thatcher's views, and can therefore understand, and support, the Pentagon's secret supply of weapons to Croatia. What we, and our CIA cousins can't abide though, is the Pentagon's supply of weapons and support to Proscribed International Terrorist Groups, such as the Mujaheddin, and Hezbollah.'

'Now,' said Smart, 'with regard to this double agent issue

that Hersman has raised with you; let's examine the facts. Hersman passed to you, revised manifests, that purport to show that we have a traitor in our midst. To me, we should first question the validity of the figures provided. Are the figures a fiction, to deceive us into believing something that isn't true, and even if the revised figures are true, the only thing they prove, is that Israel has access to information that we don't have. It's a bridge too far to extend that to mean that it's proof of skulduggery, by someone on our side. Regardless, I will give serious thought to Hersman's accusations.'

Not quite what Smart had said earlier, Tyler thought, and *good reason that I didn't mention what Hersman had said about Ivan Burzic.*

'Back to the Milošević thing, and whether Hersman talked about another meeting,' said Tyler, eager to return to Smart's original conversation, 'Hersman said that he'll probably get back to me early in the new year. Do you have any backdoor way, of knowing what happens after Hersman and I meet? Otherwise, it seems to me, that it's a bit like feeling your way in the dark. Surely in a situation like this there needs to be some sort of feedback loop. I thought that's what this officially unofficial relationship was supposed to achieve. Or, is what happened today, an example of all that we can expect from it?'

Smart's eyes glazed over, and with an expressionless face he said, 'Mr Wood tells me that you two are meeting up for dinner tonight — very good.'

'Yes, he's coming over to the Charing Cross. I'm really looking forward to seeing him again. We promised ourselves, that we'd get together again before Christmas.'

'Well, you enjoy yourselves, and let me know if and when, you hear back from Hersman.'

Soon after Tyler left Smart's office, Chris Wood called his SIS phone to reconfirm their arrangement for dinner.

'How about we meet in the main dining room at seven-thirty,' said Tyler. 'I'll make a booking for us when I get back to the hotel.'

'A great idea,' said Wood. 'A heads-up though. You may not have worked it out yet, but Six mealtimes are an entrée to the good life. Fuck knows where the money comes from, but they've never balked at one single bill I've submitted. We could eat at the Ritz — Cyril Smart's not averse to lunching there with his Cabinet Minister mates. If we went there instead of the Charing Cross, they wouldn't bat an eyelid.'

'Thank's Chris,' said Tyler. 'Probably sounds crazy, but the way I feel at the moment, I just couldn't be fagged walking up to the Ritz.'

'As you please. Seven-thirty in the dining room at the Charing Cross it is.'

'Hard to believe it's only been a couple of months, since we bumped into each other,' Tyler said, as they took their seats in the dining room. 'So much has happened, in such a short space of time,'

'Yeah, I suppose you're right. For me things have gone on pretty well much the same, but then my life's probably more all over the place than yours. Lately though, I guess the changes for you, have been out of the ordinary too.'

'That's an understatement,' Tyler quipped. 'Every morning when I first wake up, there are a few milliseconds where my brain still thinks it lives inside the old me. Then there's literally, a clunk inside my head as it synchromeshes with the new-me cog. I'm still waiting for this phenomenon to stop, but in a way, I'm not sure I want it to. On the other hand, I have this weird feeling, that I'm losing contact with the real me in the process.'

'Oh, don't give it another thought, you'll get used to it. Just think of all the benefits. Think of all the lurks and perks; things that the plebs can only dream of. Then there's the thrill of knowing stuff, that ordinary folk never get to know about, or wouldn't believe even if they did.'

Tyler found Wood's comments crass, but agreed with him anyway. He was in no mood, to face the semantics that would otherwise follow. Better to just agree, move on, and enjoy the evening.

'So, what have you been up to Chris?'

'Well yes, I just got back from the latest perk two weeks ago today, to be precise. I was in Saudi Arabia for a week, chasing down a story on behalf of the London Leader. I'd been given a heads-up, on this intriguing story about a covert British SAS patrol with the call sign Bravo Two Zero.'

'Bravo Two Zero, was an eight man patrol, that secretly went into Iraq to gather intelligence, with regard to destroying Iraqi Scud missile launchers.'

'They were discovered, less than two days into their operation, and there was a firefight. As a result, one man was killed, two men died of hyperthermia, four men were captured, and one man escaped. The man who escaped walked nearly two hundred miles through the desert to Syria, and nearly died in the process.'

'I was in air-conditioned digs, but for a lot of the time I was out in the heat interviewing people. A week was about as much as I could take. I was certainly glad to get back home, and to cooler weather. Anyway, as early as next week, you'll be able to read all about it in the Leader.'

'The story is a real scoop, because it lifts the lid on a covert British operation, that happened as recently as January this year. There's no plausible deniability with this one. There are too many first hand witnesses from both sides; all eager to tell their tale. Apropos that, this story could easily get me *Journalist of the Year,* at next year's, *British Press Awards.*'

With their main courses delivered to the table, and as the remains of their first glass of wine disappeared, Chris Wood said, 'Cyril tells me that you've been doing some work with the Israeli's. Something about what's going on in Yugoslavia. What's that all about?'

'Well it started, that night when I called you I guess, and you arranged for me to meet Cyril Smart. One thing led to another, and in a way I felt obliged to continue with it. I was originally influenced, perhaps misguidedly, by the perception that because of what I'd witnessed, I was in some sort of danger. In that regard, I'm still not really sure whether I made the right decision. Something tells me that I might have jumped out of the frying pan, and into the fire.'

'Being new to this game, I'm not even sure whether we're

allowed to be talking about all this. Don't take that the wrong way, because it's certainly not directed toward you personally, but who do you trust in this business? Are we allowed to talk shop amongst ourselves, simply because we work for the same firm? Or, do we walk on eggshells, skirting around things with euphemistic newspeak.'

'Relax,' said Chris Wood. 'You think too much. You worry unnecessarily. We're both sworn to secrecy, so you're not going to go over there, and blab all this, to the people sitting on that table, are you? You're talking to me, not them, and yes, it is OK, because we do work for the same firm.'

'Well it's just that I've learned first hand, and the hard way I suppose, that things are not always how they first appear, in this business. Or maybe better put, things can be manipulated so that they appear the way another party wants them to appear.'

'I'm sure Chris, that in your relationship with Cyril Smart, he's told you about this Aaron Hersman. Hersman's the person who's responsible for getting me into this mess in the first place. He's the person I overheard, along with the West African man Baako Attah in the lounge, up the top of those stairs over there.'

'I have to tell you that in my brief conversations with Hersman, I didn't find anything he said to be more, or less believable than that told to me by Cyril Smart. In fact I shouldn't say this, but at times, what Hersman has said is more plausible, than what Cyril Smart may have said with regard to the same issue.'

'Hang-on,' said Chris Wood. 'I thought that this bloke Hersman, was the reason why you called me, shit scared at ten o'clock at night? Why would you believe one word that this prick says to you. And, how come you don't seem so shit scared of him anymore? We all know he's a killer, that's why you called me. He's a heap of shit. Don't tell me that you've switched sides. Have you?'

'No Chris, of course I haven't. It's just that as I said, I've now been exposed to differing, but equally plausible points of view with regard to the same issue. I didn't ask to be put in this position. At the end of my first meeting for instance, Hersman told me, that he had had nothing whatsoever to do with the killing of Mr Attah.'

'Of course the prick would say that. Wouldn't he?' Wood said. He threw you a bait, and you took it. This man is a professional, and you're a novice. His job is to sow seeds of doubt in your mind, that's how he'll get more out of you. It's the information outside the script that he's after.'

'He's grooming you, so he can get your personal thoughts about whatever it is that the Office has sent you with. Thoughts, where you might just give something extra away, because of everything you've been exposed to. It's this additional, often intangible information, that he'll then use to value-add the original script that you were sent with.'

Tyler listened, and carefully considered Chris Wood's comments, but he chose not to bite. Now was not the time to pursue the matter, at least not until he'd had more time to think about it. Maybe he'd come out the other side agreeing with Chris Wood. At the moment though, that seemed extremely unlikely.

The only thing, Tyler Jones could be sure about now, was that Chris Wood had successfully managed to extract his personal thoughts, and feelings.

Paradoxical, Tyler thought. *The very thing that Wood had only just a few moments ago, warned him about with regard to Hersman.*

It was just after ten o'clock when Tyler returned to his room after accompanying Chris Wood, out to the hotel forecourt to catch a taxi.

Back in his room, Tyler's mind was confused and disturbed. A confusion that he knew would take time to resolve. First things first, and because of the hour he needed to call Jemma. Resolving confusing and disturbing thoughts, would have to wait until later.

'Hello you,' he said when she answered. 'I'm sitting here on the bed in my lovely warm hotel room, I've just got back from accompanying Chris Wood out into the cold to catch a taxi.'

'Can I come to your hotel and sit with you, and maybe watch a bit of TV, or even a movie? Or, maybe we can just skip the movie, and snuggle up with a cup of tea in bed? I really miss you Mr Jones. Anyway how did your dinner go with your old friend Chris Wood?'

'Oh..., OK I guess.'

'You don't sound overly enthusiastic.'

'Oh well, there are just a couple of things, I need to think through, that's all. I don't think we clicked, in the way that we used to click. I guess our relationship was already changed, because of the huge amount of time that had passed since we last saw each other, and then there's this MI6 thing on top of that. Maybe, considering the circumstances, the way I feel at the moment is normal, and I've just got to get used to it.'

'Oh my darling does worry so much, but you know, I worry about the same things too. Even after you opened-up to me the other night, I have to say, I still have misgivings about it all.'

'Never mind sweetheart,' said Tyler. 'It's obviously something I've got to work through; to make sense of it all. I'm sure it'll all work itself out. Anyway, talking about more mundane matters, how's your day been?'

Tyler's question had the desired diversionary effect, because Jemma responded, 'Oh, mum came over for lunch while Cameron was still asleep, and when he woke up we all got in the car and went into town. The Christmas decorations are all up in the city, which was just lovely for the kiddies; even little Cameron was wide-eyed. We walked down New Street and Broad Street, and went to see Santa and the Christmas lights at the Bull Ring Centre; which was all pretty tacky. Just a shame that Lewis's Department Store's gone. Corporation Street is not the same without Lewis's Santa, and the Uncle Holly Grotto. At least Annie managed to experience it all at an age where she might just be able to remember.'

With their conversation over, and having said their goodbyes, Tyler boiled the kettle, made himself a cup of tea, switched on the TV, and sat up in bed to give greater thought to his evening with Chris Wood.

In his conversation with Jemma, he'd deflected her away from any forensic analysis of the issue. He knew that he needed to give it his full, and undivided attention, but it was something he needed to do alone in the quietness of his own mind.

What was it about the evening that had left him feeling so uneasy? Was it something Wood had said? Was it something more subtle, and nuanced, like body language?

And, then it came to him. He had been preached to and patronised, for daring to discuss his innermost thoughts and feelings. More importantly, he had been interrogated. This had been an interrogation, that's what it was. Why?

This was not a meeting of two old friends and equals, each respecting one another's opinions, regardless of whether they agreed, or not.

He had been seduced by what he now saw to be, the misguided trust, he'd placed in another person. A person whom he'd considered to be a friend. A friend with whom he could reveal his innermost thoughts in confidence, and not be judged.

Tyler thought, *What's next? Was this an aberration on Wood's part, with the whole matter starting and stopping with him, or was it contrived; the purpose for which, might offer possibilities that are even more disturbing.*

If it was simply insensitivity on Wood's part, which is highly likely, then that's probably the beginning, and the end of the matter. On the other hand if it was contrived, was it contrived by him, and him alone, or were there others involved? If others were involved, who might they be?

Sitting up in bed with an empty tea cup in his hand, and staring at a television, that was on, but may as well be off, Tyler's mind had been working ad nauseam, analysing every aspect, of his time with Chris Wood.

It was only as he swung his legs over the side of the bed, to make another cup of tea, that it came back to him.

As he'd been leaving Smart's office this afternoon, Smart, flustered by his question, about whether he had a back channel, feedback loop, a question Smart obviously did not want to answer, Smart had said, *Mr Wood tells me that you two are having dinner this evening.*

Tyler thought. *How did Smart know that Wood and I were having dinner together tonight? Did Smart know because Wood had mentioned it to him in passing, or did he know because the idea had been his all along?*

Was Wood acting on Smart's orders, and if he was, what were those orders, and what was Smart hoping to get out of it?

The phone was ringing, when Chris Wood stepped back in to his flat.

Picking up the kitchen cordless phone, and walking to the Thames facing floor to ceiling window in the living room, he took the call.

'Good evening Cyril.'

'Apologies for the late hour, but I just needed to know how you fared with Jones.'

Wood glanced at his watch, it was just after ten-thirty.

Leaning into the corner of the window, and gazing down at the moving ribbon of red, white, and flashing orange lights on Tower Bridge Road, Wood said, 'To answer your question Cyril, it went very well. I gleaned a lot. Maybe things I wouldn't have expected. Mr Tyler Jones is a good man. He's ideally suited in so many ways, for the tasks you've assigned him, but it would appear he has difficulty, separating his thoughts from his feelings.'

'In his conversations with this Hersman character,' Wood continued, 'Even if they are brief and relatively superficial, they've nonetheless caused him to compare the rightness, or wrongness of what we say, and do, as opposed to what they say, and do.'

'He hasn't switched sides, nothing as dramatic as that, but what it amounts to, is that we may have his mind, but we only have half his heart. I'd have to say, that he's ambivalent when it comes to the moral and ethical values of us, compared with them. In Jones's own words, *Who do you trust in this business?*'

'Oh dear. Oh dear. Oh dearie me,' said Smart. 'That's a worry. I'm obviously going to have to manage Mr Jones with much greater care than I've done thus far. I might need more help from you. I'll need to take away what you've just said, give it some more thought, and get back to you.

I was planning to get Mr Jones involved beyond simply passing, and receiving documents and messages, but now, thanks to what you've just told me, I'll possibly have to figure out another way to do the job.'

'While we're on a secure line; another matter,' Smart continued. 'Apropos what I had you discuss with our Station Chief in Saudi Arabia. Once we get Christmas out of the way, I need you to come in for a briefing. I'll need you to do a few things to support our SAS friend during the time that he's back here with us. The detail about which, I'll go into when we see each other at the time.'

'Thanks Cyril, just let me know when you want to do it.

Perhaps to end our conversation, on a positive note. Following my dinner with Jones tonight, I can one hundred and one percent assure you, that Tyler Jones has no inkling whatsoever, of what you told me, about the Americans getting us to scrap the plan to kill Milošević; who really killed Mr Baako Attah; or, your forthcoming plans with regard to Mr Aaron Hersman.'

* * *

Wednesday, 4th December, 1991.

It was just after midday when Tyler arrived back at New Street Station to meet Jemma, and the children at the platform gate. Back in Jemma's car, they headed to the new IKEA store in Wednesbury for lunch, and some Christmas shopping.

With Cameron asleep in his pram, and Annie totally absorbed, running between the children's play area in the restaurant, and their table, Tyler told Jemma about his time away in London.

Within the framework of what he could, and couldn't say, he adroitly avoided anything that may lead to questions he wanted to avoid at all cost. Questions that might expose his deep-seated insecurities, and answers for which he didn't currently possess.

He had told the truth to Chris Wood at dinner last night when he'd said, 'I'm still not really sure whether I made the right decision, or not. Something tells me that I might have jumped out of the frying pan into the fire.'

Throughout the course of their lunchtime conversation, Jemma had contributed only constructive, and optimistic comments. Tyler sat in awe, as she demonstrated her uncanny ability to see things differently; to think outside the box, and to discretely and tactfully, pick-up on things he'd missed.

He was so proud of this woman, and so grateful that this package of God-given abilities, had chosen him above all others. As time had passed, and as this occasion had demonstrated; she was the Yin, to his Yang. By the same token, it terrified him. Jemma had contributed so much to his personal development, and in such a short space of time, how could he ever cope without her? This was his secret, and his alone. He owed all his recent achievements to her. Without her, he would be nothing.

As they finished their lunch, and before trekking through the store to buy Christmas decorations, Jemma leaned across to Tyler, kissed him, and said, 'I think you should be extra circumspect, when dealing with Mr Wood.' With a silent and wry facial expression, Tyler acknowledged receipt of her apt advice.

In the tradition that is IKEA, they stacked-up their dirty plates and utensils, separated the scraps, and dutifully took it all to the *Return Your Trays Here* area.

Before entering the IKEA labyrinth, they had deposited Annie in Småland, where she so desperately wanted to be, and pushing the still sleeping Cameron in his pram, they set off in search of Christmas decorations.

Thursday, 5th December, 1991.

Back at work for the first time since Monday afternoon, Tyler's Thursday morning was totally devoted to catching-up.

Julie had arranged three neat piles of date, and time ordered phone call dockets, faxes, and letters on Tyler's desk.

Bypassing the lot, Tyler chose to start his day with a touch-base call to Jennifer at AcuWrite Media. Commonsense, once again dictated that NuForm-Craven's number one customer demanded priority.

Tyler's instincts were well placed when Jennifer, totally oblivious to Tyler's recent absence, said, 'What a coincidence, I was just about to pick up the phone and call you. I wanted to arrange a meeting, your place, or ours, whatever suits. Some-time over the next couple of weeks I'd like to go through your involvement in our marketing campaigns for the coming year.'

After setting a time to go down to AcuWrite's offices before Christmas, Tyler went back to restoring his desk to a pile-free zone.

When Tyler was down in London, the thought that he was now the managing director, of a small, but not insignificant firm; finally registered. Accompanying that recognition, came thoughts with regard to the responsibilities that went with the position of Managing Director. He could now, within reason, make decisions that would not only impact the firm's future, but also the welfare of every single employee as well.

Maybe now as managing director, it behoved him to demon-strate, in some material way, his appreciation.

They had never been mistreated by Jim Craven, but then they'd never been rewarded with praise, or generosity either.

Tyler called Julie into his office, and together, they began to plan a staff Christmas party; something that should have been given thought to, well before Thursday the fifth of December.

After much calling around to local, and not so local restaurants and pubs, they finally found one where a group booking of twenty-five people, for the evening of Friday the twentieth, had been cancelled only five minutes earlier. The perfect date, and just the right number for NuForm-Craven staff and partners. Sixty-five quid a head, comprising, a three course à la carte dinner, an open bar of house red, and white wine, all festivities, a dance floor, and a live rock band.

Everything they were seeking, and to top it off, Tyler authorised up to six bottles of Veuve Clicquot non-vintage Champagne at thirty-five quid a pop.

In addition, limos would be ordered to ferry people to and fro the venue, each staff member would receive a five percent Christmas bonus, and they'll all receive a five percent increase in their salary, as from the first of January, 1992.

Mission completed, and as Julie rose to leave his office, Tyler indicated for her to sit back down.

'There is something else, something quite important, that I need to talk to you about, in total confidence. Something I need your help with,' said Tyler as he got up from his desk, and removed a plain B5 Manila envelope from the safe that stood in the back corner of his room.

'Inside this plain envelope is another envelope. The envelope inside is addressed, but it's not stamped. Now here's the somewhat embarrassing bit. In the unlikely event that I am killed in a car crash, or go missing, or something. I want you to remove the letter, run it through the firm's franking machine, and post it on the same day. You won't recognise the recipient's name, or address, and there is no return address on the back either.'

'Please promise me that you'll do what I've asked, and please don't discuss this matter with anyone else, or pass the responsibility to anyone else, if the occasion should ever arise.'

'And just in case you wonder,' added Tyler, 'there will be no repercussions for you, if you ever need to do this little job for me; no one should ever know about it. It's totally between you and me, and hopefully it's something that you'll never need to do anyway.'

'I think you know me well enough to know that I'll do exactly what you ask, and in the way that you ask,' said Julie, as she once again rose from her chair to leave his office. 'Obviously it's something that's important to you, and that's all that matters to me — I don't need to know any more.'

Friday, 13th December, 1991.

If it hadn't been, for an unexpectedly lengthy phone call, at the end of the day, Tyler would have already left, and Jim Craven would have missed him.

It had been over a week since the staff had learned about the Christmas party, their Christmas bonus and their pay rise, and every day Tyler, had half expected that Craven would come in, and admonish him. Craven would see Tyler's decisions as unnecessary generosity.

Regardless that it had been Craven after all, who'd personally anointed him, Tyler felt uneasy, and found the remnants of his past relationship with Craven, hard to shake off.

Because Craven, had suddenly appeared in the hallway without notice, Tyler's anxiety about what Craven may, or may not approve of, never got the chance to kick in. In a relaxed voice, Tyler said, 'Hello Jim. What do we owe the honour; and the pleasure, of course?'

'Just passing, and thought it was a good chance for a quick catch-up beer.' Craven responded, as he reached into the bar fridge for a couple of Heinekens, before taking them over to the conversation area of his old office.

'Won't hold you up old boy, and no doubt we'll get together again before Christmas anyway, but Julie told me about the great things you've been doing, and what you've got in the pipeline too. NuForm-Craven today — NuForm-Jones tomorrow. Good for you old son, that's what I say.'

Listening to Craven, Tyler realised he had had nothing to worry about; Craven was in the building to boast, not to criticise.

YUGOSLAVIA MAP 1991*

PLACES MENTIONED IN STORY INDICATED BY A STAR (★)

*Outline Map of Yugoslavia Created by Mr. Misa. Wikimedia Commons

14

NEW BEGINNINGS

Early January, 1992.

For Tyler Jones, 1992, propelled by the closing successes of 1991 had got off to a great start. 1992, possessed all the signs of being a great year in the making.

In the lead-up to Christmas, everything had seemed to fall into place. The office Christmas party was a night to remember, and the staff reaction to their Christmas bonuses, and their new year pay increases, had been positive and predictable.

AcuWrite Media's request for a meeting had been addressed, when Tyler drove down to their offices just before Christmas. Jerry and Jennifer took the wraps off their marketing plan for 1992, revealing their corporate strategy, market objectives, and their month by month promotional campaign for the year ahead. They also produced a supply partner contract for Tyler to peruse and sign, and discussed how NuForm-Craven might best serve their needs for 1992.

Tyler quickly realised that the £250K spend, that Jerry had spoken about, when they were all together at lunch was no boast, and probably a gross underestimation of what they would spend with NuForm-Craven this year.

This meeting alone, provided Tyler with all the assurances he needed to create NuForm-Craven's budgets, forecasts, and cash flow projections, for 1992.

Christmas Day at Jemma's mum's place was delightful, and had totally allayed any insecurities that Tyler may have had, with regard to whether Jemma's family would accept him, or not.

Jemma and Tyler had said goodbye to 1991, with a slap-up New Year's Eve party, for family and friends at Jemma's house.

During his Christmas/New Year break from work, Tyler had given little thought to MI6, and his cover story life.

Friday, 10th January, 1992.

When Tyler next heard from Hersman, he bypassed the switchboard, by calling Tyler's desk phone number directly.

'How would next Thursday the sixteenth suit you?' Hersman said. 'Late morning for coffee, perhaps somewhere different, say eleven-thirty. I'll call you on your mobile, an hour, or so beforehand. Somewhere different, but easy to get to.'

'We need to talk about that issue you raised with me last time. My masters have some strong opinions they want me to convey to you. Not something I care to discuss over the phone. They also want to know if any action was taken with regard to the illegal arms trade data. The documents that I passed back to you last time we met.'

For Tyler, Hersman's first comment was predictable, but his second comment, sent a shiver up his back. When he'd debriefed with Smart, back on the third of December last year, he had obfuscated by deliberately withholding Ivan Burzic's name. The man who Hersman had identified as a double agent, and the same man Tyler had met in Smart's office earlier that day. He now needed to fix this misstep, before it developed into an issue.

After terminating Hersman's call, Tyler crossed out next Thursday and Friday in his diary, and made a booking for Thursday night at his favourite London bolthole. He then called Cyril Smart to tell him about Hersman's call.

'I'm relieved,' said Smart 'that's very good news indeed. We've been in limbo waiting for feedback. Did he have anything else to say?'

'Well, yes he did. With regard to the Milošević matter, his masters apparently want him to communicate something that he wasn't prepared to discuss on the phone. With regard to the data manipulation issue, he named Ivan Burzic, that man you introduced me to earlier in the day as the person responsible. He says that Burzic, is also working for the Croatian Office For The Protection Of Constitutional Order.' Surprising himself that he even remembered, such a complicated piece of information. 'He wants another face-to-face meeting, late morning next Thursday.'

'Oh, my...,' said Smart, '...this is certainly a surprise. How does he know all this? Surely he must have said more — he must have elaborated.'

'No, no, he didn't. That's all he said. He was unequivocal with regard to Ivan Burzic, being a double agent.'

'Well then, if that's the case,' said Smart, 'I need to get to the bottom of all this — that's a very serious accusation, and against one of our most senior people.'

We'll need to meet before you see Hersman next Thursday, so we can discuss how you can best handle the situation with him. How would nine-thirty in the morning, and then again for a debrief at two in the afternoon suit you?'

When Smart hung-up from Tyler, he immediately put a call through to Chris Wood.

'Just a heads-up Mr Wood. Tyler Jones has called in, to say that he's got a meeting with Hersman next Thursday morning. As it transpires, Hersman has raised a new, and very serious accusation, so I need to have Jones in, for a briefing before his meeting with Hersman, and then again afterwards.'

'The accusation relates to our senior weapons analyst, Ivan Burzic, whom I think you've met. Serious questions about Burzic's loyalty have arisen since Jones met with Hersman last time. In a nutshell, the Israelis are now alleging that Ivan Burzic is a double agent, and the person responsible for deliberately distorting those arms shipment figures. Let's face it though, even if he is, it may not be such a bad thing from our point of view.'

'Anyway, what this tells me, and the reason why I'm calling you now, is that not only is this Hersman still around and active, but this new issue suggests that he still has work to do. It's in our best interests, that we just keep following the bouncing ball, until we better understand what's going on. Depending upon what comes back from Jones after he meets with Hersman, I'm hopeful that I'll have a better sense of timing with regard to that other matter we're dealing with. Then, as I mentioned last time, I'll need to brief you on the logistics of how we best manage the operation.'

'Thanks Cyril. Apropos something else you said to me last time. If Jones stays in London on the Wednesday, or Thursday night, do you need me to meet with him, or maybe even have dinner with him again?'

'No, not at the moment. Let's just see how his meeting with Hersman goes. Keep it free though. If I need you, I'll give you a call.'

Thursday (AM), 16th January, 1992.

'Come in Mr Jones,' Smart said as he opened the door to his office, and beckoned toward the conversation area, 'Good timing, I'm still trying to get a grip on this Ivan Burzic, double agent thing.'

'There are aspects of the situation that perplex me,' Smart said. 'I still ask myself the same questions about those arms shipment figures, that I raised with you when we were together back in December. What's their agenda, and why now out of the blue, do we now get this accusation about Burzic? What's Israel's interest in all this?'

'Even if Ivan Burzic is a double agent, and he has access to the AWACS data that he's excluding, or distorting; how does that help Croatia and harm Israel's cause? At the moment, I can't accept one word of it.'

'Well, if that's the case, what am I going to tell Hersman, when he asks me about it?,' said Tyler.

'You'll just have to say that we're still working on it. Anyway, it's probably not in our strategic interest, to give too much away with regard to what we're thinking, and doing at the moment.'

What a waste of time this has all been, thought Tyler. *Smart's up to something. I can see excellent reasons, as to why what Burzic's doing is helping Croatia. I can also see why the Israelis, on behalf of the Serbs, would be upset. By lowering, or totally excluding illegal arms deliveries, it makes it appear that the Croats are receiving little, or nothing; when in fact, they receive literally tons, via their transit tax arrangement. What Smart is suggesting, is also designed to add credence to Baroness Thatcher's pleadings at the UN; that Croatia, and Slovenia, be recognised as independent states, so that they can receive the arms they need to defend themselves against the Serbs.*

Burzic's actions also achieve another objective. The UK arms shipment assessments make it appear that the Moslems in Bosnia, and Herzegovina are also being deprived of weapons to defend themselves. If Hersman is to be believed, they are actually receiving shiploads, and planeloads, mostly through Croatia; courtesy of the President of the United States. The DIA is also supplying both arms and men, to the Mujahedin and Hezbollah, in Bosnia and Herzegovina. Both of whom are proscribed international terrorist groups.

* * *

Soon after leaving Smart's office, Tyler received Hersman's, call with regard to their meeting point.

'How about the coffee bar on the lower ground floor at Selfridges Department Store in Oxford Street?'

Pondering for a few moments, Tyler said, 'Yeah, that should be OK, I've got time to get the tube up to Oxford Circus, and then walk. It'll probably be just as quick, as trying to change lines.'

When Tyler approached the coffee bar, Hersman was already there. He was seated on one of the bar stools at the very end of the service counter area, and far away from where other people preferred to sit.

Tyler had done as he'd suggested to Hersman on the phone. He'd taken the Bakerloo Line to Oxford Circus, come up onto the north-western side of Oxford Street via Exit Four, and leisurely walked along Oxford Street, to Selfridges.

Every aspect of Tyler's journey had been positive, and gone like clockwork — until now. For some inexplicable reason, a heavy dark cloud had suddenly descended upon him.

As Tyler pulled himself up onto the counter stool next to Hersman, his sense of unease was amplified significantly.

'Good morning Mr Jones,'

'Good morning Mr Hersman.'

'Let me order,' said Hersman. 'Mine's an espresso. What's for you?'

'If I could have a Cappuccino, that'd be lovely. Thank you.'

After placing the order directly with the barista, Hersman

said, 'Any word on what's happening with regard to the arms shipment assessments?'

'No, unfortunately not,' said Tyler, 'they're still investigating the issue. Apart from personally meeting Ivan Burzic for the very first time a couple of months ago, and even then for only a few minutes, I've had nothing further to do with the man. I know very little about him.'

Leaning his head in toward Tyler, Hersman said, in a voice reminiscent of the time when Tyler heard him admonish Baako Attah, 'My masters have told me to tell you, to tell your masters, not to fuck with us and waste our time.'

'One of the things I said to you when we first met, was that there are things you think you know, but you don't know all there is to know.'

'This was the case with the Milošević fairytale that you recited to me so carefully the last time we met. It was a load of crap and you know it. This isn't a matter of information sharing, for the purpose of helping each other. No, this is a crass example of your lot sending you, with information that's been strategically manipulated to deceive us.'

Tyler's mind was instantly thrust into lockdown. How could he possibly respond to the unknown? What could he say in reply, that wouldn't make an already bad situation worse?

Tyler knew that Hersman was telling the truth, but he couldn't acknowledge it. He had seen evidence of Smart's deception on a number of occasions. What else was there that Smart hadn't told him about?

In the absence of knowing what that might be, he also risked lapsing into a bout of verbal diarrhoea if he responded.

The very situation that Chris Wood had warned him about when they'd had dinner together, at the Charing Cross Hotel.

Demonstrating remarkable perception, Hersman said, 'I'll ease your embarrassment, Mr Jones, by reminding you of a couple of things.'

'You told me that Mr Milošević would be killed by local Serbian paramilitaries in Serbia, when in fact the plan was always for your black-ops people, to kill him in a Genève road tunnel.'

'Another thing you said Mr Jones, was that this operation would be carried out sometime over the next few months, sooner rather than later. Well, we know for a fact that neither plan will ever be carried out. All plans to kill Milošević have been scrapped. And, worse still, your people knew all that when they sent you last time.'

'How do we know these things?' Hersman continued, to Tyler's unexpressed relief. 'We know these things because the Americans told us. They shared your firm's full report with us. The report that considered three ways to kill Milošević, not just the fairytale you related to me. The real plan was always to kill Milošević in a road tunnel.'

'Fortunately, the Americans lost their appetite for the project, when we politely explained what the consequences of their actions might be.'

'For all these reasons, I'm told to tell you that for the time being at least, it's best that we cease our back-channel meetings.'

'For your sake Mr Jones,' Hersman said, as he gently placed his right hand, on the top of Tyler's left wrist. 'I won't embarrass you by discussing these matters any further. I can sense your discomfort, and your need to be alone with your thoughts. Where this leaves you with your firm, is something, that you will need to work out for yourself.'

Tyler did not respond. He simply stared into the rapidly drying, froth at the bottom of his coffee cup — words had deserted him.

Hersman removed his hand from Tyler's wrist, pressed both hands on the counter, straightened his back, and slid off his stool. 'Hopefully we can meet again Mr Jones, perhaps under different circumstances. I wish you well with whatever it is, that you now need to do.'

'Thanks Aaron.' Tyler said, without deflecting his gaze from the bottom of his coffee cup.

Thursday (PM), 16th January, 1992.

When Tyler walked back into Smart's office after lunch, he had no doubt about how he was going to handle the situation.

'Well Mr Jones, I'm eager to know how you got on with Mr Hersman this morning.'

'I rather think you're going to be less than pleased when I actually tell you,' said Tyler. 'It went very badly. Badly for me that is. What it means for you and MI6, I have no idea.'

'First. Hersman was visibly annoyed that I came along with nothing about Ivan Burzic. He was even more annoyed, that the information I'd given him last time about Slobodan Milošević, *had been strategically manipulated to deceive* — his words.'

'He claims that the plan to kill Milošević, was never the intended plan. Apparently the real plan was to kill him in a road tunnel crash. And anyway, the Americans had decided to scrap the whole operation.

'Oh dear,' said Smart, visibly shaken by what Tyler had said. 'This is not the outcome I had expected. Hersman must have offered some rationale for why he said what he did.'

'Oh yes,' said Tyler. 'He certainly did. He said that the Americans had provided them with an MI6 report that canvassed a number of ways of killing Milošević. I presume he was talking about the same report that you had in your hands, when you briefed me. Hersman also said that they, that is the Israelis, had persuaded the Americans to call the whole operation off. They apparently knew all this stuff, before I even met with Hersman last time.'

Following a momentary, and expressionless pause, Smart said, 'Coffee, or tea?'

When Smart returned with the tea tray five minutes later, Tyler had seen his absence as a ploy to buy thinking time, and to remain in control.

'What did Hersman say about the future?' Smart said as he handed Tyler his cup of tea.

'Oh,' said Tyler, 'he was very clear about that too. As things stand, there is no future, they don't trust us. I did get the feeling though, that they'd be prepared to review their decision, if circumstances changed.'

'So, no further meetings eh,' said Smart. 'Leave it all with me. I'm going to have to give it some thought, and get back to you.'

'Where does all this leave me?' Said Tyler.

'In the short term,' said Smart, 'it changes nothing, but in the longer term, and if this deadlock can't be broken, we may need to review our relationship.'

Thanks for nothing, you useless pompous-arsed prick, Tyler thought, but the words never survived the journey to his lips.

As Smart returned his empty tea cup to the tray, he said, 'Why don't you give Mr Wood a call, and arrange to meet him for dinner tonight. Go somewhere nice on the Office, and have a chat. It'll help you feel better.'

* * *

Before Tyler would have reached the ground floor foyer, Smart had dialled Chris Wood's SIS mobile phone.

'Good, I've got you,' said Smart. 'Jones has just left my office. We can discuss the detail some other time, but his meeting with Hersman this morning didn't go well at all. As a consequence, I need to reconsider Jones's future with us. I've suggested that he contact you, and maybe meet up for a chat over dinner tonight. How are you placed? Did you end up keeping the evening free?'

'I did indeed keep the evening free Cyril. Do you want me to give him a call, or do I wait for him to call me?'

'I'd give it an hour, or so, and if you haven't heard from him, give him a call. Maybe say something along the lines of *Mr Smart was concerned about you, and asked me to give you a call to make sure you're OK. Maybe we could meet for dinner?*.'

It was four-thirty in the afternoon, in an emotionally flat state, that Tyler succumbed and called Chris Wood. The extreme circumstances of his day, plus his immediate need for company, had overridden any earlier decision to have no further tête-à-têtes with Chris Wood.

'Strange you should call,' said Chris Wood, 'I was just about to call you. Cyril called, to say that things hadn't gone well for you today. He wanted me to make sure that you were OK, and suggested that a dinner out on the firm might cheer you up.'

'I'm reluctant to admit it, but Smart's probably right,' said Tyler. 'Whereabouts, and what time?'

'How about I make a booking at the Savoy, River Restaurant, for seven-thirty,' said Wood. 'If you haven't already noticed, the Savoy's just down the Strand a bit on the same side as the Charing Cross, if you're heading toward Aldwych.'

'That'd be great,' said Tyler. Still raw from his last dinner with Wood, and in an attempt to circumvent a similar situation happening again, he added, 'If I could please, just ask that we don't talk shop tonight. I've had a shit day, and my brain's addled. I've had it up to my eyeballs at the moment.'

'That's fine,' said Wood. 'I'll be more than pleased to just sit there, and watch the boats out the window.'

'Thanks Chris.'

When Tyler arrived at the Savoy, Wood was waiting at the entrance to the restaurant, and together they were shown to their table, by a waiter wearing white cotton gloves.

Settling into his river facing chair, leaning back, and inter-clasping his fingers behind his head, Tyler said, 'This is far, and away the most relaxing thing I've done all day. How great is this. Floodlit gardens, and through the trees, boats moving up and down the Thames.'

'Well Tyler,' said Wood, 'that's what we're here for. To relax, and enjoy ourselves, courtesy of the firm.'

Beginning with a leisurely consumed aperitif, then followed by the two course dinner option, nobly accompanied by a bottle of Bordeaux, their evening was all mapped-out.

'Apropos what you said on the phone, and in no way wanting to discuss the specifics of work and your day,' said Chris Wood, 'but Cyril told me, that what happened today, may prove to be a game-changer for you. So, if the nature of your extra-curricular activity with MI6 changes, or maybe even comes to an end, how are you going to feel about it? Would you be relieved, or would you miss it? Speaking for myself, and I'm sure you would have guessed it anyway. I couldn't live without it. To me *Six*, is tantamount to a drug of addiction.'

'I don't think it'd be like that for me.' said Tyler. 'Even before accepting the job, I'd asked myself that very same question. How would I feel if I turned the opportunity down, and it never presented itself again, or as you say, if I took it up and then it all of a sudden came to an end.'

'So as you can see, for me, it's a bit of a dichotomy,' Tyler continued, 'and I think I opened-up too much about it when we had dinner last time. It's not at all in my own best interests to go there again; other than to say, that my thinking, particularly after the events of today, probably hasn't changed much.'

True to his word, Chris Wood, did not pursue the matter any further. Tyler had voluntarily reaffirmed his already stated position. There was nothing more to discuss.

* * *

'Well, how did it go?' Said Smart, when he answered Chris Wood's call.

'Oh, much as you would have expected Cyril. I've just got back, and it was enjoyable, thank you very much. As for learning anything new from Jones, that was never going to happen. When he finally called me, he made it abundantly clear that he didn't want to talk shop. My assessment would be, that Tyler Jones's attitude hasn't changed one iota from when we had dinner last time. What I told you after that occasion, applies equally now.'

'Oh dearie me, what a shame,' said Smart. 'I had hoped that Mr Jones may have had, a change of heart — so to speak — pun intended. Considering that this obviously hasn't happened, it's further complicated, because the Israelis want to call-off our back-channel relationship via, Hersman and Jones. Where that leaves Mr Jones, I've yet to decide. Anyway, putting all that aside, we do now need to focus our attention back onto dealing with that outstanding matter. Nothing changes there. How are you placed for a chat? Maybe sometime tomorrow if you can manage it?'

Friday (AM), 17th January, 1992.

'Good morning Mr Wood,' Smart said as he ushered Chris Wood into his office.

'Good morning Cyril.'

'Tea, or Coffee?' Smart said with a quizzical gaze, as he picked up his handset, and waited for the catering extension to respond. All proof that according to circumstances, he was quite capable of enlisting the services of others if it suited him.

Seated in the conversation area while waiting for their morning tea to arrive, Smart briefed Wood on Tyler's meeting with Hersman. 'This changes nothing with regard to our plans for Mr Hersman, and the reason why we're having this meeting today.'

Cleverly using the language of the *collective,* rather than *individual* responsibility, Smart said, 'We may have underestimated the American and Israeli's propensity to backdoor us, but the fact remains, that for the sake of our relationship with the Modrisians, and to maintain the confidence of the British taxpayer — we need to show them a scalp.'

'Before you arrived, and just to double-check,' continued Smart, 'I phoned the Station Chief, to action our request. He's received the *Class Seven Authorisation*, so the SAS operative is cleared to leave, and will arrive in about two weeks time.'

'Our job in the meantime, is to put the required logistics into place. For security reasons, fewer than a handful of people will ever be involved, or have knowledge of this operation. Therefore, teamwork per se, and as we normally view it, will not be a feature of this operation. It will just be a few select individuals; each assigned a specific task to perform.'

'Tomorrow, a surveillance officer will begin assembling a profile of Mr Hersman. By the time the SAS operative arrives, we'll know where Hersman comes from, where he goes, why he goes where he goes, and who he sees. We'll know what time he gets up in the morning, what time he goes to bed, and what he eats for breakfast.'

'Our SAS man, will perform his duties based on that information, plus of course, his own assessment of the situation. At the end of the day though, he will be the final arbiter, as to how and when, the job will be done.'

'Your role in all this Mr Wood, will be to provide logistical support, to help him do what he needs to do. You will not be required to play an active role, per se. You'll know the operative, only as Sergeant James, and it will just be you and I, who will actually get to meet the man.'

'The name James, may be his first name, or it may be his last, or it may be neither, I don't know. In many ways your role Mr Wood, apropos what I've just said, will be the next most important to Sergeant James himself, because you'll be the person who supports him. We'll work out the specifics of what that'll be, when Sergeant James gets here.'

'None of these things are things that concern, or involve Mr Jones. They should therefore, never be discussed with him. He is not to be in the loop. In fact, because of the almost counterintuitive relationship, that seems to have developed between Jones and Hersman, he mustn't have the slightest inkling of what's going on. Imagine for a moment that Jones gets wind of our plans, and out of some sort of misguided loyalty, he communicates that information to Hersman. What a mess that would be.'

'As if we haven't got enough of a mess to cleanup, with the Milošević fiasco.'

* * *

Friday (PM), 17th January, 1992.

After dinner on the Friday evening, and with the little ones asleep, Tyler told Jemma about his meetings with Smart, his meeting with Hersman, and his subsequent dinner with Chris wood.

'For obvious reasons, I can't go in to the nitty-gritty, but my meeting with Hersman did not go very well. In a nutshell, at our previous meeting a few weeks ago, I was sent along with information that turned out to be fabricated, and designed to mislead the Israelis. Anyway, they called it out for what it was, got very angry, and have suspended our back-channel meetings.'

'Oh my darling, that's terrible. Do the Israelis blame you personally, for doing this?'

'No, I'm pretty sure they wouldn't,' said Tyler. 'They would know that the decision to feed them crap, would have come from someone well above my station. Apparently, their lot would do the same to us in a heartbeat. The Mossad has a reputation for playing hardball.'

'What about your relationship with MI6?' Jemma said. 'If the Israelis have cancelled these meetings, where does that leave you? I actually find all this very hard to fathom. This man Hersman kills the man from Modrisia, and because of what you witnessed, you get all worried that he'll be coming after you. Then you get involved with Chris Wood, Cyril Smart and MI6, because they tell you that they can help protect you. Then later, when you actually get to meet this Hersman, you start to think that he's not such a bad fellow after all, and that maybe they have deceived you.'

'After what Hersman told you yesterday, and the fact that you aren't so afraid of him anymore, why don't you just give it all up? There's nothing to worry about anymore. Just walk away. It seems to me, that you'd actually be doing MI6 a favour. Now that these meetings have been called off, they're probably trying to get rid of you anyway.'

15

GIVE AND TAKE

Monday (AM), 3rd February, 1992.

'Thanks for coming in Mr Wood,' Cyril Smart said, as he indicated for Wood to take a seat.

'I've decided to let Tyler Jones go, regardless of any future relations with the Israelis. If Hersman's not going to be around, Jones has no further role to play. I have the feeling that Jones and Hersman, may have become a little bit like, Tweedledum and Tweedledee.'

'I'm on the horns of a dilemma,' Smart continued. 'Even when we were still moving forward with the plan to kill Miloše-vić, at the urging of the Americans, there was always the question of how would the Israelis, and the Russians react. When the plan was abandoned, ironically at the behest of the Americans, the opportunity was there to leak the abandoned plan to the Israelis, simply to test their reaction.'

'We now know, that initially at least, the Israelis took it seriously. What we couldn't have foreseen, was that they'd run straight to the Americans, and using whatever lever it is that they hold over them, they'd be able to prise everything out of them — including the fact that the whole operation had already been abandoned.'

'It just so happened, that right from the outset, Tyler Jones was in the ideal position to communicate the plan via Aaron Hersman, and I had carefully groomed him for that purpose. For Jones to pull this off, it was necessary to expose him to far more information than I would have liked. Anyway, what's done is done. All that remains now, is how we deal with the consequences; hence my dilemma. If I let Jones go, because quite frankly I have no further use for him, then all this top secret information goes out the door with him.'

'Naturally, I'll get him to re-sign his agreement to be bound by the Official Secrets Act, but then what good did that do us with the *Spycatcher* fiasco a few years ago. Our ex MI5 officer, Peter Wright, wrote his memoirs in breach of the Act, and was charged with treason by the British Government. Wright, who was living in Tasmania by that time, was defended by a very clever Australian barrister, Malcolm Turnbull. Turnbull won the case, Wright's book was published, and Wright walked away scot-free. The British Government was humiliated, and Wright made a small future, from book sales generated by the publicity.'

'On the other hand, would keeping Jones in the Six family, protect us any more. We don't have the budget, to justify paying hush money, in the form of wages. Rightly, or wrongly, I've made the decision to let him go, and I'll call him in to tell him, in a few days time.'

'Talking about changes, has there been any movement with that Ivan Burzic, double agent thing, that you told me about?' Said Chris Wood.

'Timely you should ask that question, Mr Wood. It's only now, that I've finally got to the bottom of what's been going on. I'm expecting to have the matter resolved, within the next few days.'

'Anyway, onto other matters,' Smart pivoted. 'We've discovered most of the pieces to the puzzle that is, Mr Aaron Hersman, and the pieces fit together very nicely. The other big news is that Sergeant James, is flying in to Middle Wallop Airfield later tonight, on an Army Air Corps flight. After he arrives, we've got him booked in at Fred and Meg's place in Pimlico. Anyway you'll get to meet him, here in my office, tomorrow morning.'

'What were the things, that you learned about Hersman?' Said Chris Wood.

'Oh, we learned quite a lot about Mr Hersman, thank God — quite a lot. Looking at it now, some of it was predictable, while some of it was less than predictable. The predictable bit is that being of the Jewish persuasion, he has a bolt hole, in the Brent Cross area, just inside the North Circular. Most weekdays, he walks to the Brent Cross Underground Station, just after the morning rush hour, and travels down to London. His usual destination is the Embassy of Israel, in South Kensington.'

'The least predictable, but most useful observation, turned out to be that he's a creature of habit. He enters onto platform two at Brent Cross Station, no more, or no less, than two minutes either side of nine-thirty.'

'Very interesting,' said Chris Wood. 'This Sergeant James fellow, should be pleased to hear that.'

'Yes, I would imagine so. Anyway, let's have a meeting with Sergeant James, here in my office, sometime tomorrow morning. That is if you can manage it, and if Sergeant James's flight gets in on time tonight.'

'Cyril, you know that the London Leader, is a very benevolent, and philanthropic institution, especially when it comes to their top journalist. Tell me the time, and I'll be here?'

'Say I call you first thing in the morning after I find out what's happening with Sergeant James, and we'll take it from there.'

* * *

Monday (PM), 3rd February, 1992.

Jennifer from AcuWrite Media, called Tyler with an invitation to attend a meeting, on Thursday the twenty-seventh of February. The purpose of the meeting, was to get all of AcuWrite's European supply chain partners, together in one room for a day. The venue would be the Courthouse Hotel; the same hotel where the Industry Forum was held, last October. Tyler accepted Jennifer's invitation, and immediately called his favourite bolthole in London to make a booking.

Cyril Smart also called, and arranged a meeting, for this coming Thursday at ten. Smart proffered no reason for the meeting, and Tyler didn't ask for one — he already knew the reason. Apart from Smart checking if Tyler had heard from Hersman, there was no further conversation.

Tyler and Jemma, had discussed Tyler's relationship with MI6, on a number of occasions since he'd returned from his last meeting with Smart, a couple of weeks ago. Perhaps the only surprising thing, was that it had taken Smart more than two weeks to get back to him. Tyler and Jemma had already decided, everything considered, that Smart would let Tyler go. At least Tyler was now prepared for it. He was not only prepared for it — he had begun to warm to the idea.

* * *

Tuesday (AM), 4th February, 1992.

Sergeant James, a handsome, fit, and healthy looking individual in his early thirties, was sitting in Smart's office when Chris Wood arrived at ten o'clock. Dressed in casual clothes, Sergeant James exhibited no sign, that he may be tired, or stressed, and he sported a tan that was conspicuous, because of its absence on everyone else.

'Good timing Mr Wood.' Said Smart, as he introduced them. 'Sergeant James, this is Officer Wood. Officer Wood will act as your facilitator. Although not directly involved in your operation, he'll nevertheless provide you with whatever support you need.'

'That packet on my desk, contains over one hundred photographs, of the target. Photographs taken in every possible location and from every possible angle. There's also a map of the area, with the route that the target takes to the Brent Cross

Station each morning. Our surveillance officer, has highlighted the route for you, and also some possible hide sights, with their ingress and egress points for you to consider.'

'Actually, I'd like to get the train out there this afternoon.' said Sergeant James, 'So I can get a feel for the area, and then tomorrow, I'd like to be there first thing, to observe the target for myself, if that's OK?'

'Of course.' said Smart, as he unfolded the map that he'd just referred to. 'The target will emerge from somewhere along here in Golders Manor Drive. We're not quite sure where he starts from at this stage. Regardless, it doesn't really matter, because once you pick him up, he'll walk to the end of Golders Manor Drive, where it meets Heathfield Gardens as a T-junction, he'll then turn left into Heathfield Gardens, and cross the road, before turning right, into the laneway that leads into the back entrance, of Brent Cross Station.'

'Anyway,' said Smart, 'all of this is your call, not ours. Would you like Mr Wood to accompany you today?'

'No. At this early stage I'd rather be on my own. Once I've got a plan worked out, that'll be when I'll need Mr Wood to help me. See it like perfecting a magician's trick. Pulling it off rests with the sleight of hand at the beginning and end of the trick, the middle bit, is the easy bit. I'll explain it in detail of course, when I've had a chance to choreograph the performance.'

* * *

After his meeting with Cyril Smart, and Chris Wood, Sergeant

James was driven back to Meg and Fred's safe house in Pimlico, to change his clothes, and fetch his subminiature camera and mini binoculars. Leaving the building dressed in his grey military fatigues, and black waterproof thermal jacket, he headed for Victoria Underground, to begin his journey to Brent Cross.

It was just after midday, when Sergeant James stepped off the train at Brent Cross Station. The sky was leaden, it was freezing cold, but there was no rain, and there was no wind. The bitumen pavements were the dark grey of dampness that never dries out, and putting aside the odd bird tweet, and the noise of distant traffic, it was deadly quiet. Most importantly, there were very few humans. All the conditions, that Sergeant James had wished for.

Leaving the station by the back entrance, and following the map that Smart had provided, he walked, in the reverse direction, the route that the target takes on his way to the Brent Cross station each morning.

To get a global appreciation of the area, he walked to the very end of Golders Manor Drive, turned right into Golders Green Road, and then right again into Highfield Avenue, before reentering the station, through its main entrance on Highfield Road.

During the course of his walk, took a series of photos with his Minox camera. Photos that captured the environs surrounding every leg of his journey.

When Sergeant James reentered the Station, through its short-term carpark, he took full advantage of the paucity of human activity. With his Minox camera discretely cupped in his left hand, he photographed all the publicly accessible areas. He then walked through the subway passage, under the railway tracks, and up the stairs onto the southbound platform, where he then took photos of the environs surrounding the platforms.

From the London end of the platform, he photographed the terrain on both sides of the line, between the end of the platform, and the North Circular Overpass, one hundred yards away. He noted that on both sides of the line, there was a wide verge of trees, and thick, seemingly impassable undergrowth.

Using his binoculars, he meticulously examined the terrain to find a suitable hide site. A hide site that had safe ingress, and egress points, was inconspicuous, and had a clear line of sight to the platform. A line of site, that would not put innocent bystanders at risk.

With all these preliminary tasks completed, his job now, was to catch the next train back to London, go to his room, and develop the two 36 exposure cassettes, that he'd run through his camera.

Tuesday (PM), 4th February, 1992.

Sergeant James was well accustomed to pressure, so to get back to Pimlico, lock himself in his room, process his films, and possibly miss out on dinner, was all in the line of duty. The fact that it was eighteen hundred and thirty hours, he was tired, he'd had a busy day, and another one was coming up tomorrow, was beside the point — this was all part of his mission.

Using his portable Minox daylight developing tank, he

developed the two 36 exposure film cassettes, that he'd run through his camera.

After converting his bathroom into an improvised dark-room, he cut the negatives into strips, laid them directly onto a ten-by-eight sheet of photographic paper, and exposed it using his bedside table lamp. The exposed sheet, was then developed, fixed and rinsed in his hand basin, before being gently dried, using his hair dryer.

At just on twenty-thirty hours, he slung his jacket over his shoulder, and left his room. In his jacket pocket, folded along the spaces he'd left between the groups of negatives, was the contact print.

He'd also brought with him his Minox loupe, a small magnifier, specifically designed for viewing subminiature prints. All he needed to do now, was to find somewhere to eat that was quiet, and where he could study his prints.

At an Indian restaurant close to Victoria Station, he was able to eat, and leisurely examine his photos. After close on an hour of frustration, coupled with concern that he might be displaying strange behaviours, Sergeant James decided to decamp, and continue the process back in the privacy of his own room.

His frustration arose, from his inability to choose a suitable hide site. He was in a quandary. Usually there was a location that screamed; choose me, choose me, but not on this occasion. Every position seemed to have a major downside attached to it. Nothing was black and white, at best it was shades of grey. It was a mess, and it worried him.

He thought, *Maybe in the morning, when I'm actually there, and I get to see the target, in situ, the answer will come to me. Somehow, I need to have a plan ready, for my meeting with Smart and Wood tomorrow afternoon.*

* * *

Wednesday (AM), 5th February, 1992.

When he'd flown in on Monday evening, Sergeant James, based on the brief he'd been given, had brought a selection of hand picked weapons. For security reasons, his tactical weapons bag, that contained these items, had been stored at the Middle Wallop, AAC base.

The bag contained, a Glock semiautomatic pistol, a Scorpion battle knife, and a Knights SR-25 carbine rifle, with its riflescope, bipod, and detachable sound suppressor.

Sergeant James had chosen the carbine variant of the SR-25 rifle from the armoury, because it was shorter and lighter. It was also better suited for when the target would be reasonably close, but the shooter's manoeuvrability and concealment, would be less than ideal.

Eight in the morning, and on the train to Brent Cross, Sergeant James's mind was not so much focused on his tools per se, but rather, the conditions that surrounded their use.

This morning he would observe the target, and based on his scoping of the area yesterday, select a hide site. The site needed to be inconspicuous, have an unimpeded line of sight to the target for about five seconds, and could be entered and exited quickly.

If he didn't use the riflescope, or the bipod, he'd have the

SR-25 out of the bag and assembled, along with the gas suppressor, in less than a minute, and afterwards he'd do a break-down, in even less time. Again, these were all issues he must decide before his meeting with Smart and Wood later in the afternoon.

Tomorrow, Thursday, and with Chris Wood as his assistant, he would rehearse the plan and tweak it, if required. On Friday, at zero nine thirty hours, the final plan would be actioned.

Arriving at Brent Cross Station just before nine, Sergeant James headed toward the intersection of Golders Manor Drive and Western Avenue. From this position, the target could not escape detection, because Sergeant James would have a clear view in all directions.

Sergeant James's patience was rewarded when the target, confirmed from the photos supplied by Cyril Smart, crossed the intersection, along with some other pedestrians. Sergeant James, initially shadowed them from the opposite side of the road, before crossing, to fall in about twenty yards behind.

Predictably, they all turned left when they reached Heathfield Gardens, before crossing to the laneway, that leads into the back of the Brent Cross Station.

Keeping his target in sight, Sergeant James followed him through the ticket barriers, into the subway passage, and up the stairs onto the southbound platform.

At nine thirty-five, Sergeant James watched as the target boarded the train, and the doors closed behind him.

Back in the now almost empty ticket hall, Sergeant James, focused his attention, on the position of all the Closed Circuit Television Cameras, and the public and staff facilities. Apart from two ticket booths, only one of which was open, the station seemed to be unmanned. The CCTV cameras were all predictably directed, toward the ticket barriers, entrances, and other public areas. There was a staff access door to the side of the ticket booths, hinting that there was almost certainly, an office on the other side.

As Sergeant James walked toward the front Highfield Avenue entrance, he noticed that there was a locked wooden door on the left hand side wall. He decided that it probably opened to stairs, that would be used to access the Neo-Georgian/Art Deco roof perimeter of the building.

After walking through the short-stay car park, to Highfield Avenue, he then looped back into Heathfield Gardens, to reconnoiter the same walk he'd taken the day before.

It was only toward the end of his walk, that he began to form a plan. Nothing tangible, nothing concrete, just a nascent plan that he'd need to put more structure to. At least it was a start, and that helped to put his mind at ease. His meeting with Smart and Wood, was now only two hours away.

Wednesday (PM), 5th February, 1992.

'Good afternoon Sergeant James,' said Cyril Smart. 'I was just reassuring Mr Wood that when he's with you tomorrow, and again on Friday, it will only be as your facilitator.'

'That's right,' said Sergeant James, 'When we discussed the operation last time, I said that the sleight of hand in the beginning and ending, would determine the outcome. It's in these thimble and pea moments, that I will need Mr Wood to be my eyes and ears. Just a few critical moments, that's all; at no stage will Mr Wood be directly involved. To anyone observing, we will be as strangers, always twenty, or more yards apart.'

'I've spent quite a bit of time today, surveying the area around the Brent Cross Station, and it's this beginning and ending bit, that's caused me the greatest grief. It's been difficult to find a hide site that's inconspicuous, got line of sight to the target, can be got in and out of quickly, and when entering and particularly leaving, won't invite attention. I realise now, that I underestimated just how difficult this task was going to be; anyway I think I've now got it all sorted.'

'In a nutshell, the best hide site is on the flat skirt at the rear of the station roof. The corner of the roof that looks down on the laneway, that leads to the back entrance of the station from Heathfield Gardens. I'll be able to setup a hide there, establish a secure mobile phone link with Officer Wood, so I can track the target's progress, and then drop him, just as he turns to enter the station from the laneway.'

'There's an unmarked, plain wooden door, just inside the main entrance, that almost certainly provides access to the roof. There's probably a stairwell on the other side.'

'The door, has a commercial grade, key entry, night-latch lock, you know the type, where you turn the key, and push on the door at the same time to open it. The door will have an automatic door closer fitted on the other side, to guarantee that it closes and locks again, when you let it go.'

'Anyway, I'll crack the lock tomorrow, while Mr Wood keeps a look out. Thankfully, I've got a bump key in my kit for that type of lock.'

'With all this in mind,' said Sergeant James. 'I need you to get a couple of things for me, if you would be so kind Mr Smart. I'll need some overalls in my size, for any of the public utilities, like gas, water, electricity, or telephone, take your pick. I'll also need you to get me one of those small portable tents, the type that telephone technicians use to protect them from the weather, while they're working down a pit on connections.'

'The way I'll be dressed will allow me to pick the lock in plain sight, and the tent will provide cover while I'm up on the roof. My intention is to set up the tent tomorrow, and leave it there, ready for Friday.'

'When we finish our meeting, I'll head back up to Middle Wallop to pick up my kit, and to do some target practice.'

'It'd be great if those items, could be at my digs by the end of the day. I'll need to have them, before we leave in the morning at the latest. I'd also like Mr Wood, to be outside my place at seven-thirty in the morning, so we can get on up to Brent Cross, by eight-thirty to start setting-up.'

Before Sergeant James left the AAC base in Middle Wallop, he'd already decided, not to use the SR-25 riflescope, or the bipod. With the target so close, less than twenty yards, his mechanical iron sights were good enough. He'd drop the target with a couple of head shots. If he wasn't going to use the riflescope and bipod, it got rid of some unnecessary gear in his bag, and would also save some valuable set-up and break-down time on the day.

When Sergeant James, arrived back, at the safe house in Pimlico, two packages were leaning against his bedroom door.

The smaller of the two, contained a pair of *North-West Water* overalls and a North-West Water hard-hat, while the larger package, contained a tandem pit guard tent, with a collapsible steel frame, and a folding pedestrian barricade.

Cyril Smart, had made good.

* * *

Thursday (AM), 6th February, 1992.

At seven-thirty, and as expected, Chris Wood was waiting downstairs, ready for their morning of setup, and rehearsal. With Sergeant James dressed in his North-West Water, maintenance technician outfit, they walked, talked, and planned on their way to Victoria Station.

Arriving at Brent Cross after travelling in different carriages, they walked separately through the ticket barriers, across the hall, and toward the main entrance. When Sergeant James reached the locked wooden door, and while Chris Wood, inconspicuously kept watch from a distance, Sergeant James placed his bags down, got his ring of bump keys out of his pocket, and proceeded to work on the lock. To a passer-by, the scene would be interpreted as a maintenance guy, fumbling through a set of site keys, until he found the right key.

Within sixty seconds, he'd cracked the lock, and with his foot wedged in the door jamb to prevent the door from closing, he pulled the keys out of the lock, put them back into his pocket, scooped up his bags from the floor, pushed the door open, and disappeared inside.

The plan now was for Chris Wood to move out into the car park and keep watch, while Sergeant James, assembled the tent on the roof. The section of roof that looks down on the laneway, leading to the back entrance of the station. If it were not for a line of trees and shrubs, anyone standing on the station platform might just be able to see Sergeant James, up on the roof. So too, might a person looking out an upstairs window of a residence bordering the station, or laneway.

Although it was extremely unlikely that he'd be spotted, Sergeant James had decided, that the risk wasn't worth taking. The success of the operation, rested upon the element of surprise. His decision to pose as a maintenance technician, for a major utility, and to work from inside a tent, seemed a logical and necessary precaution. Otherwise it would only take one busybody to phone the police, and the operation would need to be called off.

Chris Wood had been standing in the freezing cold car park, for over twenty minutes, before he received the preplanned single ring burst, on his SIS mobile phone. The signal from Sergeant James, to say that the tent was setup, and that he was now ready for the rehearsal.

Chris Wood would now move to Golders Manor Drive, where he'd identify, and shadow the target. Once identified, he'd call Sergeant James from his SIS phone to report the target's dress attire, and his real-time position, as he walked to the station.

'He's in Golders Manor Drive ... He's just crossed Western Avenue ... He's wearing a charcoal grey woollen beanie with a wide turned-up cuff ... He's about to cross Heathfield Gardens ... He's crossing Heathfield Gardens, and he's about twenty yards from the entrance of the laneway.'

'Right, I see him ... He's in the laneway ... The grey woollen beanie with the wide cuff ... Come on, give me more head ... A few more steps ... *Click-Click* ... I've got him ... *Target Down.*'

* * *

'Come in Mr Jones,' said Cyril Smart, 'Take a seat over here.'

'Thanks Mr Smart,' Tyler said as he moved toward the conversation area in Smart's office.

'Based on what happened, when you met Hersman last time, and my phone call to you on Tuesday, you've probably guessed why I might need to see you.'

'A couple of things, seem pretty clear to me. First, the Israelis attitude with regard to our officially unofficial, back-channel relationship, vis a vis yourself and Mr Aaron Hersman, now seems to be a thing of the past, and second; that the original threat Hersman posed to you, no longer seems to exist.'

'Under those circumstances, and because we, that's MI6,' Smart continued, 'are not in a position to pay for services unnecessarily, we'd like to terminate our arrangement with you at the end of February. That's on Saturday the twenty-ninth. Yes, we do have twenty-nine days in February this year.'

'As an Agent, your relationship with MI6 was always going to be, on an ad hoc basis. There was a job to be done, and you were there to do it.'

'If it transpires, that circumstances change, and the Israelis want to reengage, then we can reconsider the matter if, and when that happens.'

'To be honest,' said Tyler, 'I was expecting it. How do you want to handle it? Is there anything else that I need to do?'

'Well, now that you raise it. Yes there is. Over there on my desk, is a document for you to sign. The document reaffirms your previous agreement with us, with regard to you being bound by the Official Secrets Act.'

'What about the MicroTAC phone?' Said Tyler.

'Oh yes, I did think about that too. Because we might have some trailing issues, perhaps some unfinished business, maybe best you hang on to it until the end of the month. We can get it off you then.'

'With regard to trailing issues,' Smart continued, 'If Aaron Hersman, or anyone representing him, tries to make contact with you, please call me immediately. Since you had your last meeting with Hersman, we've received absolutely nothing back from the Israelis.'

'Oh....,' said Smart, 'there is though, just one other small matter, that might be of interest to you — rather sad, actually.'

'Mr Ivan Burzic, the man that you met here in my office a couple of months ago from GCHQ, and the man Hersman claimed was a double agent — well he died in Zagreb only yesterday. He was visiting our diplomatic mission, when he unfortunately slipped and fell under the wheels of an oncoming tram; right outside the Palace Hotel where he was staying. Two of our people were with him at the time, and they say, that he probably slipped on a patch of black ice. There was absolutely nothing they could do to save him — it was all over in a few moments.'

A chill passed through Tyler's upper body, as he gave

thought to Smart's callous reporting of Burzic's demise. *This is proof that Smart has known all along that Burzic was a double agent. In fact Smart has known from the moment I gave him that newspaper after my very first meeting with Hersman. The newspaper that had the envelope inside, with the illegal arms shipment manifests. The sheets that Smart had laid out in rows, so carefully on his desk, and studied so intently.*

Smart has simply left it to the Mossad to expose Ivan Burzic as the double agent. How clever of him. All he had to do, was to sit on his hands, and wait. Burzic's guilt was confirmed from the moment, I passed Burzic's own manifests, unopened and unread to Hersman. Then, from the moment the Mossad amended those documents, by factoring-in the missing AWACS data, and handed them back — Ivan Burzic's fate was sealed.

When it finally came time for Tyler and Smart to shake hands, and say goodbye, Tyler detected, an uncharacteristic awkwardness, on Cyril Smart's part.

* * *

Thursday (PM), 6th February, 1992.

When Tyler returned home from London, there, looking out of her bedroom window was the beaming face of his preschool, super spook detector.

Predictably, she was the one who opened the front door, before he had time to insert his key in the lock.

'Where's mummy?' said Tyler.

'She's in the kitchen. Where else would she be?' Annie said, with an incredulous look on her face.

'Well it's not even five o'clock, what say we surprise mummy by taking her out to dinner. I'm thinking, that it might be nice if we all went back to that Cafe. You remember, the place where you had that yummy Latin American food, and played with that little boy. What was the place called? What was the boy's name?'

'Oh Tyler, you're hopeless. It's called Cafe Sofrito, and the boy's name was, Julian,' she quickly said as she excitedly pivoted, to run down the hallway, and tell her mother the good news.

'My lovely young family, have returned to Cafe Sofrito. Bienvenido a nuestro restaurante.' The waiter said as he escorted them to the same table as last time; the one with space for Cameron's pram.

As they seated themselves, and aware that on this occasion, there was no playmate for Annie, the waiter reached into the large front pocket of his apron, and pulled out a spiral bound notepad, and some coloured pencils.

'Can I serve you the same drinks as you had last time? The Jugo for the young lady, and the Casablanca Valley, Sauvignon Blanc-Semillon, for her lovely parents?'

'Of course,' said Jemma, as Tyler nodded approval, and said. 'That would be lovely. Thank you.'

When the waiter departed, and with Annie eagerly exercising her artistic talents with the materials provided, Jemma said, 'This is such a lovely idea of yours. We seem to be so busy these days. The only time we ever get to sit down, and talk, is after you've had a meeting with Smart.'

'Yes, you're right,' said Tyler, 'it has been a bit like that, but hopefully all that'll change from now on. Smart gave me the sack today, and apart from this AcuWrite thing in a couple of weeks time, that's it for trips down to London for the time-being. It's all over for me at MI6, on the twenty-ninth of the month it seems.'

'So he actually did it.' said Jemma, 'What did he say?'

Tyler responded, by offering Jemma a version of events, that whilst accurate, honoured his commitment to The Official Secrets Act, by excluding any identifying details, relating to operational matters. He was also careful to couch events, in terms that hopefully wouldn't hook back into previous conversations with Jemma — the testy conversations about MI6. The bottom line metaphor being, that the cure may have been more harmful, than the complaint.

His stratagem with Jemma, ably assisted by the simultaneous return of the waiter with their drinks, had seemed to work.

Carefully placing their drinks on the table, and as Tyler handed the menus back, the waiter said, 'And will your food orders be as they were last time, or do you prefer something different?'

'No, we'd like to have all the same things again please. We really enjoyed what we had last time. It was lovely. What a feat for you to remember what people ordered after so long, and when we've only been here once before?'

'Gracias. You are more than generous. I only remember what lovely people, such as yourselves order. Please enjoy your drinks.'

The waiter had moved no more than a few steps from the

table, when Jemma, having bided her time, said to Tyler, 'So, you tell me, if it's all over at the end of the month, what happens after that? Do you really feel any safer? Maybe you just traded enemies, by getting involved with these people.'

'Yes, maybe,' said Tyler. 'It has been a five month roller-coaster ride, the like of which I could never have imagined, and I would never want to take again. With the benefit of hindsight, if I had known then what I know now, yes, I might have chosen differently. But, having said that, what I learned about Hersman, which was important to me at the time, I would never have learned if I hadn't accepted Smart's offer.'

'Do I believe,' continued Tyler, 'that Smart used my over-heard conversation, plus the violent death of Mr Attah, to reinforce my fear, yes I'm sure he did. Did Smart lie to me when I first met him about MI6's involvement, then no he didn't. He just manipulated the information, so that I'd jump at the quid pro quo he was offering.'

'Looking back now, I realise that you were right. It would have been better to have just walked away, but then, I'd have been forced to live with uncertainty. The least expected thing to come out of all this for me, was that Hersman did not turn out to be the ruthless killer Smart had made him out to be. Although I never reported it back to Smart, Hersman told me, that he had had nothing whatsoever to do with the death of Mr Attah, and I tend to believe him. On the other hand, maybe you can't believe anything a spook tells you?'

'So why didn't you report what Hersman told you back to Smart?'

'It would have made no difference whatsoever to the situation, and anyway, another thing that Hersman told me early on, is that what I choose to report, or choose not to report to MI6, is the only power I have. I gave great thought to what he said, and decided that he was right.'

'What's evident to me now is that all along, Smart's real reason, for putting all that upfront effort into me, was never intended to protect me from Hersman. It was always about grooming me for his hair-brained scheme to leak some highly secret, and controversial information to the Israelis. Precise details about which, because of the National Secrets Act, and for your own safety sweetheart, I can't talk about.'

'All the work Smart put into me, from the moment we met, and I accepted his offer, was to lay the ground for that moment. All the briefings, and all my training at Fort Monckton; it was all for when I'd reveal this disturbing piece of secret information to Hersman, and the Israelis.'

'What MI6, never considered though,' Tyler continued, 'was the possibility, that the Israelis already knew all this. They already knew everything that MI6 knew, and more. Plus, they'd already used the information, to cut a deal with the Americans. A deal that would work against MI6, and British interests, with regard to their involvement in the breakup of Yugoslavia.'

'Oh my darling,' said Jemma, 'actually, I'm not surprised, I guessed as much. I knew there were things you weren't telling me, because you either didn't want to, or you weren't allowed to. I'm just so glad, that you're able to express your feelings to me now that it's all over. You know I've been worried sick about you.'

Reluctantly, they were forced to pause their conversation, when the waiter returned to deliver their food to the table.

For Jemma, Tyler's visible eagerness, to get back to their conversation, came as a pleasant surprise.

It was the waiter's *Buen apetito*, as he departed their table, that provided the cue to resume.

'When Smart had me communicate this top secret information, to Hersman, he'd deliberately introduced an error, into the most critical part of it all. He did that to not only incite the Israelis into doing something, that might be strategically bad for them, but also, to test my loyalty to MI6. By devious means, he had simultaneously made sure that I too, had been privy to this critical flaw in the information. He did that deliberately, because he knew it would conflict me ethically if I was forced to lie to Hersman. Conflict me such, that I might even be tempted to tell Hersman the truth, because the situation that MI6 was forcing upon me, was morally, and ethically bankrupt.'

'As it happened,' said Tyler, 'I did in fact transfer the flawed information, just as Smart had instructed me to do. I did it, because I'm sure a feedback loop exists between someone on the Israeli side, and Smart. What I've only recently realised though, and I can't endanger you by telling you too much about it, but the bottom line is that this information I've been exposed to, is so sensitive, that only a few people are in possession of it. Others may know, the *What it's all about* aspect, while others, may know the *how* aspect, but fewer than a handful know both the *what* and *how* of it all.'

'The *what* aspect is bad enough,' Tyler continued, 'but the *how* is absolutely explosive. Explosive because, if the *what* was ever to be carried out, and the *how* became public knowledge, then the international fallout for MI6, and the British Government would be catastrophic. That's how bad it is.'

'There's also another, perhaps more upsetting immediate matter, that once again I can't talk about, other than to say that I learned today, that a man died as a result of information Smart had me pass on to Hersman. Smart used a trick that Hersman had warned me about when I first met him. Smart had me transfer information that I thought I understood, but as Hersman had warned me, I didn't know all there was to know. Smart only told me, what he needed me to know to achieve his desired outcome. He manipulated me to do something, that I would never have done, if I'd known all there was to know. It's terrifying to contemplate what else, might still be out there — chickens yet to come home to roost. The immediate troubling question for me is: how much responsibility must I assume for the death of this man? How much did my role contribute to his demise? Or, is it my role to simply follow orders, ask no questions, and don't think about it, even if I do become aware that it's a matter of life, or death.'

'I'm sure I'm over catastrophising it,' said Tyler, 'as I did in the beginning with Hersman, but as I recently commented perhaps unwisely to Chris Wood, I may have jumped out of the frying pan, and into the fire.'

Friday (AM), 7th February, 1992.

At seven-thirty, and just as he'd done yesterday, Sergeant

James, dressed in his North-West Water outfit, had met Chris Wood on the pavement outside the MI6 safe house in Pimlico.

As they walked to Victoria Station, Sergeant James said, 'It's the same thing as yesterday, only this time, it's for real. I need you to identify the target, and call me with what he's wearing, and again like yesterday, we keep the line open, but unlike yesterday, I don't want you to shadow him down the laneway. I want you to keep walking on around to the station's main entrance, on Highfield Avenue. This means that not only will you avoid seeing something, that you'd rather not see, but it will also provide you with plausible deniability. You can't be expected to describe something you didn't see. From a time perspective, and walking at a normal pace, you should get to the ticket hall around the same time as I do. When you get back there, just shadow me and observe, don't acknowledge me in any way whatsoever. Get the same train back as me, and just like yesterday, we travel in different carriages, and we only meet up again when we're both back in Cyril Smart's office.'

'Oh, a couple of other, quick things,' continued Sergeant James, 'Just to be on the safe side, and in case you need it for some reason, here's an extra key I've had cut for the lock on the wooden door.'

'Let me also explain to you, what you'll hear through our open line connection when the target goes down. It's also what a person close-by would hear, above the ambient noise of the railway station. The gas suppressor, that I will fit to the rifle, is not the fictional *silencer*, of crime novels and movies — there *will* be noise. There *will* be an audible *Crack*; a crack, with all the harmonics of the full sound removed. There'll only be two of these sharp cracks — *Crack-Crack*, and that's it.'

'If we get separated for whatever reason,' said Sergeant James, 'we meet-up back in Smart's office for the debrief. If things go horribly wrong for me, and you happen to be around, be a bystander, *do not* get involved no matter how much you might feel tempted.'

Arriving at Brent Cross Station, and stepping from their carriages, they went their own separate ways, each with a series of tasks — tasks that when combined, were designed to do a job.

Chris Wood called Sergeant James at just after nine-twenty. 'Target has just crossed Western Avenue ... Target is wearing exactly the same clothes as yesterday, including the beanie ... Target turning left into Heathfield Gardens ... Target crossing Heathfield Gardens ... Target about to enter the laneway.'

'Right, I see him ... Target confirmed ... A few more steps ... *Crack-Crack*.'

* * *

Chris Wood was only one house, past the opening of the laneway, when he heard the anticipated *Crack-Crack,* through the earpiece of his SIS phone. It was exactly how Sergeant James had described it would be.

After pressing the *End* button to disconnect the line, and following Sergeant James's earlier instructions, Wood walked on, turned right into Highfield Avenue, right again into the car park, and then into the station through its main entrance.

He deliberately slowed his pace as he entered the building, and was passing the hallway door, but Sergeant James wasn't there, and he wasn't in the ticket hall either. He was probably up on the platform waiting for the train that was due in less than one minute, at twenty-five to ten. Chris Wood rushed through the ticket barriers, the subway corridor, and along with a number of other passengers, ran up the stairs, before stepping out onto platform two.

People were moving toward the doors of the train, that had not yet come to a stop, and yes — there he was. There was Sergeant James. Chris Wood's brain told him that it was Sergeant James, because at that moment, that's the image it wanted to see. In reality, he was looking at the back of a man wearing a grey woollen beanie with a wide cuff.

A wave of fear and confusion overcame Chris Wood as he thought. *If the target is still alive, and about to board the train, then where is Sergeant James? How could the target have escaped two shots from a professional marksman?*

Going against his gut feelings, and the express instructions of Sergeant James, Chris Wood left the platform, and returned to the ticket hall; in the belief, that there had to be a logical explanation for what was happening.

Sergeant James will probably be there, waiting for me in the ticket hall, but then, that doesn't make sense either. For Sergeant James to be waiting, the target should be dead, not alive and getting on a train. Maybe he shot the wrong man? But then where's all the commotion? Maybe Sergeant James had fired, but missed his target, aborted the operation, and was already on his way back to Smart's office. But then, wouldn't he have called to tell me, if that were the case?

Waiting for the moment when no one was looking, Chris Wood drew the key that Sergeant James had given him from his pocket. Inserting the key into the lock, he realised that the key was unnecessary, merely pressing against the door had opened it. Someone had snibbed the latch open from the inside. It only had the appearance of being locked.

Ascending the stairs, he opened the roof door to the sounds of traffic and birds. To his immediate left, on the section of the roof skirt that covers the back entrance to the station, he could see Sergeant James's tent. The zippers were closed, and the tubular steel frame was secured against the wind, by piles of strategically placed bricks. Everything looked normal, nothing seemed out of place; it was just how Chris Wood imagined it should look.

Pulling up the rear zipper, exposed Chris Wood to an image that his mind could not make sense of. It was as if Sergeant James's head, was the disassembled pieces of a jigsaw puzzle. Chris Wood knew it was him, but somehow his brain was refusing to accept the images his eyes were transmitting.

Associated with the catatonic state that had now claimed him, was the morbid inability to look away. The longer he looked, the harder it became. If he could just identify the pieces, and reassemble them, then everything would be OK.

Chris Wood desperately did not want to live with this image for the rest of his life.

The moment that Wood, forced as he was, to accept the inevitable; that no amount of wishful thinking was ever going to put Sergeant James's head back together again, his catatonic state instantly changed to one of blind panic.

Trembling uncontrollably, he frantically pulled the tent zipper back down, and left the roof via the same route that had brought him to the place, he was now so desperate to leave. Pausing against the tiled wall of the ticket hall to catch his breath, he reached into his coat pocket, pulled out his SIS phone, and pressed the one-touch button for Cyril Smart's number.

'Oh Dear,' said Smart, 'Oh dear, this is bad — this is very bad indeed. Are you sure?'

'Of course I'm sure. Do you want me to hang about here, go home, or come back in to see you?'

'I think you should go home Mr Wood, make yourself a cup of tea, and lie down. Second thoughts. Before you do that, go back and take the snib off the door, and make sure that the door's firmly closed and locked. You don't need to do anything else. Just go home.'

'I'll notify our dry cleaning team; they're the ones who deal with situations like this. Before cleaning up, they'll look at the scene forensically, and adjust it. They'll do whatever they need to do, to ensure that the take-out message of what happened on the roof this morning — is our message, and not someone else's. I imagine that this process will take a few hours, and then of course, we'll need to notify the local police.'

'Do try to put all this out of your mind, and I'll see you in my office, first thing on Monday morning — all the forensics should be in by then.'

* * *

Monday, 10th February, 1992.

'Do take a seat Mr Wood.' Said Cyril Smart, extending an arm toward the conversation area of his office. 'I've got two important pieces of information for you.'

'First things first,' said Smart. 'Sergeant James was killed by two close-range shots to the back of his head, but then, you probably don't need me to tell you that.'

'No, I certainly do not.'

'Well what I can tell you though, Mr Wood. Oh..., before we start. Tea, or coffee?' Smart said as he lifted the handset on the coffee table to call catering.

'Coffee please.'

'Yes, what I can tell you, is that, the bullets that killed Sergeant James, came from a Glock 20 pistol, and they were fired at very close range; probably less than a couple of feet. Glock only released this model a few months ago, but for a number of law enforcement agencies around the world, it's already standard issue. It would have been nice, if the gun had been a bespoke weapon, with a unique signature, one that's linked to a particular person, or an agency that we know. There is though, one somewhat quirky, and unexpected aspect, to the killing of Sergeant James. The shots were fired through a feather pillow. Forensics found microscopic fibres in his brain matter, and around the scene.'

'That's bizarre,' said Chris Wood. 'That's Hollywood gangster stuff. Executing rival gang members, or traitors, with a pillow pressed against their head.'

'Yes I know, it does all seem a bit strange, but that's what they found. There is a logical explanation for it though. The Glock 20 pistol makes a lot of noise, and the aftermarket gas suppressors are still in their infancy. They're also huge and weighty attachments, and they don't work very well. Tests our people did down at Monckton, proved that a feather pillow, outperformed the lot. It would actually be much easier to stuff a feather pillow into a backpack, than to carry in a hand gun fitted with a suppressor. A feather pillow can be compressed to only a fraction of its normal size.

The appeal of the Glock 20 therefore, is that it fires powerful 10mm cartridges, but the design of the gun results in very little recoil action. It's also very light, small, and easily concealed. Fitting a gas suppressor would completely destroy all that.'

'Who would have done such a thing,' said Chris Wood, 'Who would have done it, and why?'

'Yes, well that's the question, isn't it Mr Wood? Who would have done it, and why?' Smart said as he stood up, and opened the door for the tea-lady. After handing Chris Wood his coffee, he took his cup and saucer from the tray, and walked over to the window. 'Well we know it wasn't Hersman. He would have been the logical contender, but to be Sergeant James's killer, he would have needed to be in two places at the same time, so it obviously wasn't him. Was it the Israeli's, was it the Americans, or was it even the Russians? Who knows? We simply don't know.'

'And now Mr Wood,' continued Smart, 'talking about the Russians, I've got that second bit of news that might also surprise you. When you saw Mr Aaron Hersman, getting on that train at Brent Cross Station last Friday morning, you were the last person in our community to see him.'

'Early Friday afternoon he took a BA flight, from Heathrow to Helsinki, and without leaving the airport, he booked and paid cash for a direct flight to Moscow, with Aeroflot. We understand that officers from the newly formed Foreign Intelligence Service, the SVR, were there, waiting to greet him at Moscow airport.'

'We now have a better understanding, of those reports we were getting through Tyler Jones. Hersman had mentioned to Jones, on a number of occasions, that he'd soon be moving somewhere else. Jones along with myself, had got the impression that the move was permanent, and Hersman wasn't all that pleased about it. Jones was right about the permanence, but we may well have been wrong about whether Hersman was looking forward to it, or not. Recently Hersman also had a number of unexplained short trips to unknown overseas destinations, so it looks like he'd been planning his defection for some time.'

'While that might explain Hersman's behaviour,' said Chris Wood, 'it doesn't explain how he survived our attempt to kill him? It seems unthinkable, that Hersman could have known in advance that Sergeant James would be taken out instead — and right at the very moment that Sergeant James, was squeezing the trigger on him.'

'I was there. I was the only person privy to the audio of what was happening inside the tent, and besides, even if he did know, he would have had to be a lunatic to take that sort of risk. I don't believe anyone would do that. To knowingly be a decoy for someone trying to kill them. Maybe Hersman was oblivious to everything, and he was just an unwitting beneficiary of a miracle. A coincidence of place and time.'

'Wow, now that gets really spooky,' continued Wood, 'Hersman was never the target. Hersman was just the unwitting decoy so that someone else could kill Sergeant James. All along the target was Sergeant James — it was never Hersman. Surely it wasn't our lot? Please tell me that we were not mixed up in all this.'

'Oh, and on another matter dear man,' Smart pivoted, 'I had that meeting with Tyler Jones yesterday morning. I've terminated our arrangement with him, effective the end of the month. As you, and I agreed last time; it would have been disastrous, if Jones had ever got wind of our plans with regard to Hersman; even more so, when you consider what transpired on Friday. I'm sure you agree.'

'Yes, I understand Cyril.' Said Chris Wood.

Walking from the window, and placing his cup and saucer back on the coffee table, Smart took his coat and Fedora off the stand at the doorway, and ushered an incredulous Chris Wood out of his office, into the lift, and back down to the lobby.

BRENT CROSS MAP

BRENT CROSS TUBE STATION (FRONT & REAR ENTRANCES), NEO-GEORGIAN / ART DECO ROOFTOP

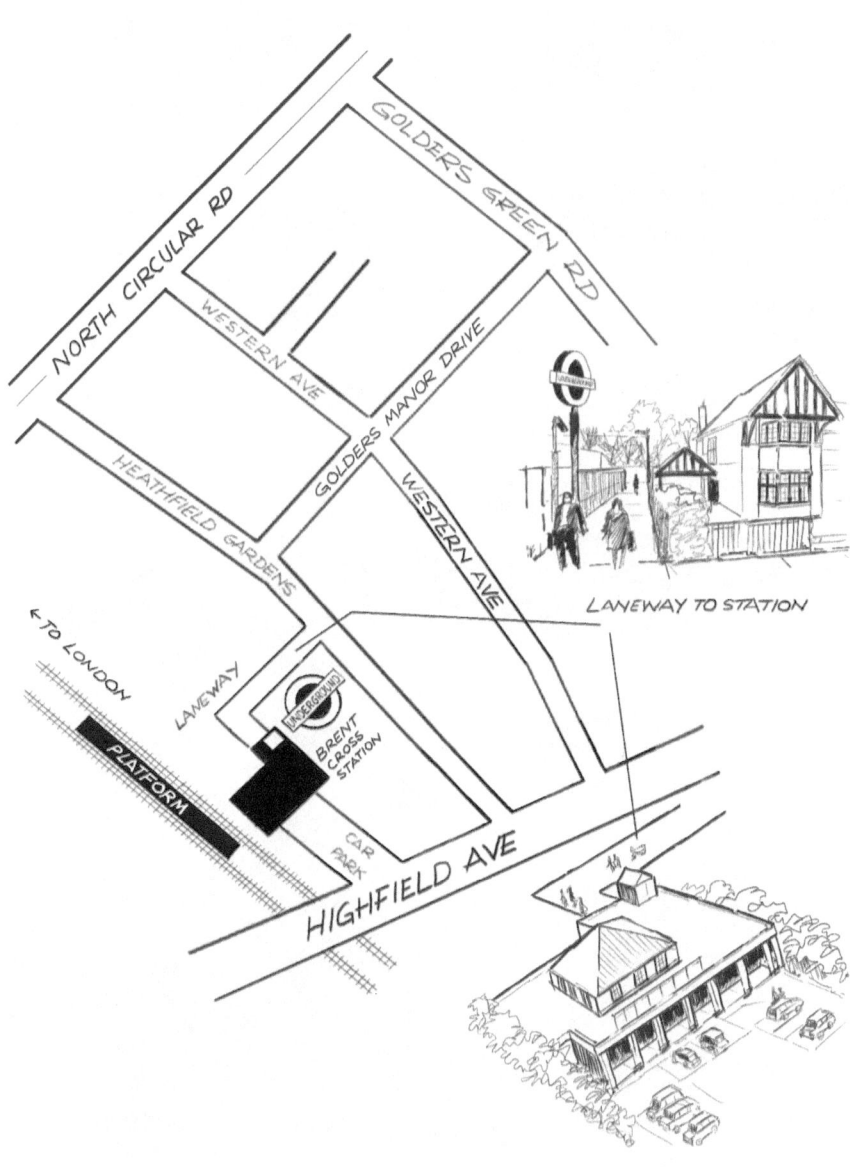

16

SAFE AT LAST

Tuesday, 25th February, 1992.

When Tyler had confided in Jemma, about the more troubling aspects of his time with MI6, at dinner two weeks ago, he had totally underestimated the consequences.

Exposing his innermost thoughts and feelings, had set off an unexpected, and somewhat counterintuitive reaction.

Rather than a sense of relief, that usually comes from getting something worrying off one's chest, and out of one's mind, Tyler had descended into a state of malaise. A flatness that was with him when he woke in the morning, and it was still with him when he went to bed. A flatness, that was both physical, and mental.

He only started feeling better, when he realised that there was a direct connection between how he was feeling, and the stress that he'd endured over the past few months. He was run down, his batteries were flat. More energy had been going out, than had been coming in.

Now that his stint with MI6 was over, it was as if a weight had been lifted from his shoulders. It was time to balance the books, and recharge his physical, mental, and emotional energies. He was run down, his batteries were flat. More energy had been going out, than had been coming in.

Another positive factor that aided his recovery, was the change he'd seen in Jemma. She was once again radiating the loveliness that had attracted him to her in the first place. Her natural beauty, her quick wit, her ability to think outside the box, and her good-natured generosity. Since leaving MI6, the love of his life, had been returned to him undamaged.

He would now start hiring new people, and get back to his plans for growing the business. When he'd gained the die-for account of AcuWrite Media, it had come at the best, and the worst possible time. On one hand, it had almost certainly been the catalyst, for why Jim Craven had relinquished his position, and passed it on to Tyler. On the other hand, Tyler's commitment to MI6, had distracted him from what should have been his main game — getting new customers, and growing the business.

It can be expected that a firm shall derive eighty percent of its revenue, from twenty percent of its customers, but to have one single customer, contributing the lion's share of the revenue, then that's untenable in the longer term.

Notwithstanding the skewed customer base at NuForm-Craven, Tyler nonetheless felt that he needed to reaffirm his relationship with AcuWrite Media. A commitment he'd recently neglected — even though AcuWrite Media seemed unaware. At this delicate time he could not afford to lose his number one customer. He needed to take full advantage of the upcoming AcuWrite partners' meeting, in two weeks time.

Tyler also saw the meeting, as an opportunity to kill two birds with one stone. While he was down in London, he'd stay on for the Friday night at his own expense. This would give him all day Friday to visit prospective clients. People who'd shown interest, by leaving their details with Julie during some of his recent absences. Staying over, and coming back on the Saturday, also offered a bonus opportunity. Julie had suggested that while he was down in London for the Friday night, he should take-in a West End show.

Feeling better about himself, he was now looking forward to the future again; everything seemed to be falling into place. Even the situation with regard to Jim Craven had been resolved, when Craven relinquished his position as managing director at NuForm-Craven; the company that bears his name.

* * *

Wednesday, 26th & Thursday, 27th February, 1992.

When Tyler checked-in at the Charing Cross Hotel, late on the Wednesday afternoon, it was as if he was coming home. A feeling amplified when the girl on reception had said, *Welcome back Mr Jones*, and in his room, a basket of fruit with a hand written note, that affirmed his status as a valued guest.

Settled in his room, Tyler perhaps out of habit, reached for his SIS mobile phone to call Chris Wood. He hesitated when it occurred to him, that if he followed Julie's advice and went to a show tomorrow night, tonight was the only night that he would have to himself.

Chris Wood had demonstrated that he was less than a good friend. Considering his break with MI6, it was probably better, that he relegate the past to the past, and move on.

With a busy day ahead, and the need for an early night, Tyler switched on the TV, got undressed, put on his bathrobe, and ordered a meal from room service. After dinner, he sat up in bed chatting to Jemma, until it was time to turn off the light. He would need all his wits about him, in readiness for tomorrow's meeting.

After breakfasting in the hotel restaurant, Tyler chose to walk to the Courthouse Hotel, confident that his memory from the last occasion wouldn't let him down; and it didn't.

Arriving at the Courthouse Hotel at twenty past nine, Tyler intuitively headed downstairs without bothering to seek directions. Once again his instincts were proven correct, because ahead of him he could see Jerry Blair welcoming people, this time into Chamber V. Chamber V, was the room directly across the hallway from where they were last time in Chamber I. This was apparently not an occasion, where Jennifer's presence was required.

Chamber V was setup as a boardroom, with twelve places at the table. Five places were reserved for AcuWrite people, and seven places for suppliers. The AcuWrite people were from manufacturing, purchasing, distribution, sales, and marketing, and the invitees were people who supplied raw materials, equipment, logistics, financial services, legal services, packaging, and in Tyler's case; graphic design and printing.

The day was programmed to be full-on, plus there was a dinner planned for the evening. There would be a one hour break for lunch, and then a two hour break between the last session, and the dinner. During the late afternoon break, Tyler's planned to leave the hotel, and walk down to the half price ticket booth, in Leicester Square.

The meetings ended with Tyler feeling that he had gained a unique insight into the operations of a large multinational corporation. Tyler had not had any prior experience of the Corporate world, its language, and its culture; so the opportunity to attend this meeting was huge. He was so grateful, that ActWrite Media's Jennifer had included him.

It was also clear to him, that the AcuWrite Media account with NuForm-Craven was safe, both in the short, and the longer term. His despair for the future, seemed to have all been related to his recent bout of depression. In that regard, the meeting had reinvigorated him, by giving him ideas for growing NuForm-Craven's business. He had seen how the existing one-stop-shop offering of NuForm-Craven could be extended to provide bespoke laser-cut paper, card, or even plastic packaging.

AcuWrite Media's current supplier of packaging, whose representative was also at the meeting, was not offering that kind of service. Tyler figured that NuForm-Craven could do the job, better, faster, and almost certainly, for less cost.

Over dinner, Tyler had arranged to discuss the possibility with the manager of Europe's largest manufacturer of CO_2 Laser cutting machines. In just one day, Tyler had learned that in the corporate world, loyalty counted for little.

At just after five in the afternoon, Tyler was out on the street, and headed toward Leicester Square. It was freezing cold, it was dark, and ice had already formed on the windscreens of parked cars — but, he was on a mission. The mission being; to follow Julie's instructions, and take-in a West End show while he was down in London.

While waiting in the queue at the Clocktower Ticket Booth, he'd already settled on *Me and My Girl* at the Adelphi Theatre. His decision, assisted by the fact that the Adelphi Theatre was only a short distance down the Strand, on the opposite side from the Charing Cross Hotel.

Tomorrow, Tyler would visit the two firms, where Julie had secured appointments, and pitch his firm's points of difference. Fortunately, both appointments were in the central London area, and within easy reach of the Charing Cross Hotel.

He would be able to get back to his room with enough time for a hot bath, and an early dinner, before walking down to the Adelphi Theatre for Me and My Girl, at seven-thirty.

Friday (PM), 28th February, 1992.

For Tyler, *Me and My Girl*, had turned out to be, perhaps unexpectedly, an enjoyable evening. The story of Bill Snibson, and his sweetheart Sally, echoed for Tyler, aspects of his own relationship with Jemma. He saw himself, somewhat, in Bill, and in Sally, he saw the intrinsic qualities of his beautiful

Jemma; the girl who hid her light under a bushel. And the songs; *The Lambeth Walk*, and *Leaning On A Lamp-post*, had induced a state of sentimentality, that had brought tears to his eyes.

When Tyler exited the Adelphi, he just wanted to get back to his warm hotel room as fast as he could. To switch on the TV, make a cup of tea, get into bed, and make his promised bedtime call to Jemma.

People were walking away from the theatre in every direction, in minus two degrees of cold. They had looks on their faces, like they knew where they were going, and they couldn't get there fast enough. Others, seemingly oblivious to the cold, were rabbiting-on in small groups on the pavement, directly in front of the theatre entrance.

Responding to the impenetrable barrier, that these people presented, Tyler made the decision not to cross the Strand at that point, but to rather walk on down, and cross later. Anyway, this side of the Strand, with its pubs and restaurants, seemed much more inviting than the other side. Paramount though, was to get back to his room, and get out of the cold as fast as he could.

As he approached the forecourt of Coutts Bank, he glanced back over his left shoulder to check the traffic, before crossing to the Charing Cross Hotel on the other side of the Strand. As he did, a person overtook him, and brushed against his right shoulder, knocking him slightly off balance.

Now alongside, and slightly ahead of Tyler, the man made a sudden, and vigorous quarter turn, swinging his right arm around such that Tyler thought, *This guy's taking a swing at me.*

The man, as with many others that night, was wearing a dark grey woollen overcoat, with its collar turned-up against the cold, and a grey Fedora on his head.

With only a fleeting glimpse of the upper left side of the man's face, and a whiff of floral scent, Tyler's world suddenly became surreal — he had just seen the face of betrayal. How could he have allowed himself to be so stupid.

The projectile, even if inaccurately administered to the upper chest, was designed to kill. No great outward damage, front, or back, but devastating internal injury. Death was inevitable. Death was instant, or so close to instant, that any delay may well serve as a plus for the assailant.

The bespoke, segmented and hollow-pointed, 5.6 mm short bullet, had been designed to be used at point-blank range. Upon impact, it would breakup into numerous divergent pieces, and because of its lower velocity, it was eighty per cent quieter. Its design fell well outside, The Hague Convention On War and War Crimes.

Tyler felt an intense searing pain in his chest, and the sensation as if a hand-grenade had gone off inside him. He instantly crumpled, and fell backwards, his head hitting the pavement with a sickening thud. He lay there, flat out and motionless, eyes wide-open, staring up into the dark night sky.

There were no outward clues, as to what might have happened to him. The blood that was seeping from his chest and his back, was at this point contained, and therefore hidden inside his thick waterproof Parka jacket. Outwardly, there was only a soft gurgling sound, and intermittent twitching of his lower extremities. To a casual observer, he may well have been lying on the pavement for any number of reasons.

A small crowd of mostly young Friday night revellers, quickly formed a circle around the body that lay on the pavement. They had faces of bewilderment and suspended emotion, as their brains tried to make sense of what confronted them. A sight that almost certainly, none had witnessed before, and none would likely witness again.

As they struggled with their emotions, reactions ranged from stunned silence, to chatting, and even tittering. It was tantamount to the free entertainment of watching a man die.

Tyler's brain was running on rocket-fuel, as it attempted to process vast amounts of disparate information simultaneously. His mind at that moment was like crystal, but his limbs were fast becoming numb, and his eyesight and hearing were fading. it was as if someone was simultaneously turning down his volume and brightness controls.

He was aware of the giants who were standing, staring down at him. Their faces seemed so far away. The rhubarb, rhubarb, rhubarb of their voices, and the words that no longer registered, or had meaning.

Although his mind was racing, there was no pitstop for family, or friends — not even for Jemma, Annie, or Cameron, and certainly not for the Manila envelope, sitting in his safe at work.

His focus was now totally directed toward himself, and his immediate predicament. He instinctively knew that this was the end, and perhaps the thing that surprised him most, was just how relaxed and accepting of it he was.

Holy Fucking Shit — the wrong place at the wrong time. Or, is it the right place at the wrong time? Or, is it the wrong pla...

In almost no time at all, a windowless dark grey Transit Van, approached from the direction of the Adelphi Theatre, and crossing to the wrong side of the road, parked contraflow, against the kerb in the bus lane.

A man in a dark grey woollen overcoat, got out of the front passenger seat, and opened the rear doors to two men, dressed in khaki overalls.

Simultaneously, a London ambulance with no flashing lights, or siren arrived, and slowly reversed up over the curb, silent, save for its ear-piercing, back-up beeper.

The three to four deep, circular crowd of now completely silent onlookers, courteously parted to allow the ambulance first-responders, and the two men in khaki overalls to access the motionless body that lay on the pavement.

The ambulance officers spent a few minutes going through the motions of checking Tyler for vital signs, making notes, and briefly answering two-way radio calls. When all this seemingly futile activity was over, the men in khaki overalls moved in, and systematically removed all personal items from Tyler's pockets. They placed the items into a large clear plastic zip-lock bag, and without comment, handed the bag to the man in the grey woollen overcoat at the rear of the Transit.

The ambulance officers, gently lifted Tyler's body onto a trolley, and after covering him with a red woollen blanket, slid the trolley into the back of the ambulance. The ambulance then slowly departed in the direction of Trafalgar Square, and ironically, straight past the front door of Tyler's Hotel.

The two men in khaki overalls, got into the back of the Transit, while the man in the grey overcoat, having removed what appeared to be Tyler's personal mobile phone from the plastic bag, got into the front passenger seat.

As the Transit edged away from the curb, the man could be seen gesticulating vigorously, as he spoke to an unknown recipient, on the other end of the mobile phone line.

To a passer-by, the only evidence that something may have happened, on the pavement outside Coutts Bank, were two police cars parked in the bus lane, and a small group of people milling about. People transfixed, or in quiet conversation, as they contemplated the meaning of life.

The fact that the police only attended, after it was all over, begs many questions.

17

HOPE (EPILOGUE)

Monday (08:25), 2nd March, 1992.

When Julie Clarkson arrived at work to find Bill Barrett standing in reception, and Jim Craven in Tyler's office with a man whom she didn't recognise — the nausea she'd woken-up with, worsened, and the toilet bowl could not come fast enough.

Seedily reentering the hallway from the ladies toilet, Julie observed that the door to Tyler's office was now closed, but through the frosted glass partitioning she could see Craven and Barrett, standing in muted conversation with a man in a mid-grey suit.

Sitting at her reception desk — her little patch of normalcy, and security — did little to allay the waves of nausea that were once again washing over her; or to settle the anxiety that was interfering with her ability to press the correct button, and take the phone system off night-switch.

When the door to Tyler's office finally opened, the dapper, bespectacled man in the grey suit emerged. After donning his overcoat, he walked briskly past Julie's reception desk, and descended the stairs, back down to the front entrance.

As Craven and Barrett left Tyler's office, Julie could see from the looks on their faces, that whatever it was that had happened, it wasn't good. *Maybe*, thought Julie, *they've just given Tyler the sack; taken back the day-to-day running of the firm, and the man I just saw going down the stairs, is his replacement.*

'Unfortunately, we've just been given, some terribly bad news.' A visibly shaken Bill Barrett said in a soft, and considered voice. 'Our managing director, Tyler Jones, has been found shot dead in London. The man you just saw leaving, is from Military Intelligence, who for reasons we don't understand, because he wouldn't tell us, is investigating the matter. At the moment, all we know is that the poor chap is dead, and that his partner and family have been notified.'

Jim Craven, who had now found his voice said, 'Bill, and I are nipping out for a cup of coffee to discuss the matter, but in the meantime, we've decided to close the business for the day, while we sort out what to do. We'll inform the design, marketing, and accounting people up here, and then go downstairs to tell the others on the floor. The message will be that Tyler has been killed in London, and that at this stage, we have no further details.'

'What we'd like you to do Julie, before you head off home, is to put a short message on the line, to say that due to unforeseen circumstances we'll be closed all day today, but open again tomorrow morning, and then lock the place up. In the morning,

I'd like to get a temp in, whilst you and I sit down, and you fill me in on all the stuff that only you would know about.'

When all the other employees had left, and Julie, after numerous failed attempts, had finally managed to record a new outgoing telephone message — she slipped into Tyler's office, opened the safe, and removed the B5 Manila envelope.

Following the instructions that Tyler had given her in his office last December, the instructions about what to do if anything untoward should happen to him, Julie carefully opened the envelope to reveal the smaller envelope inside. The person it was addressed to, Mrs Mavis Hadley, Tyler had suggested at the time, would mean nothing to her, and it didn't.

Now surrounded by an aura of euphoria, a phenomenon well known to people suddenly confronted with tragic loss, as their consciousness refuses to acknowledge the reality of what has happened; Julie ran the letter through the firm's franking machine, popped it into her handbag, and left the building.

MIND MAP

HOW PEOPLE AND PLACES RELATE TO EACH OTHER

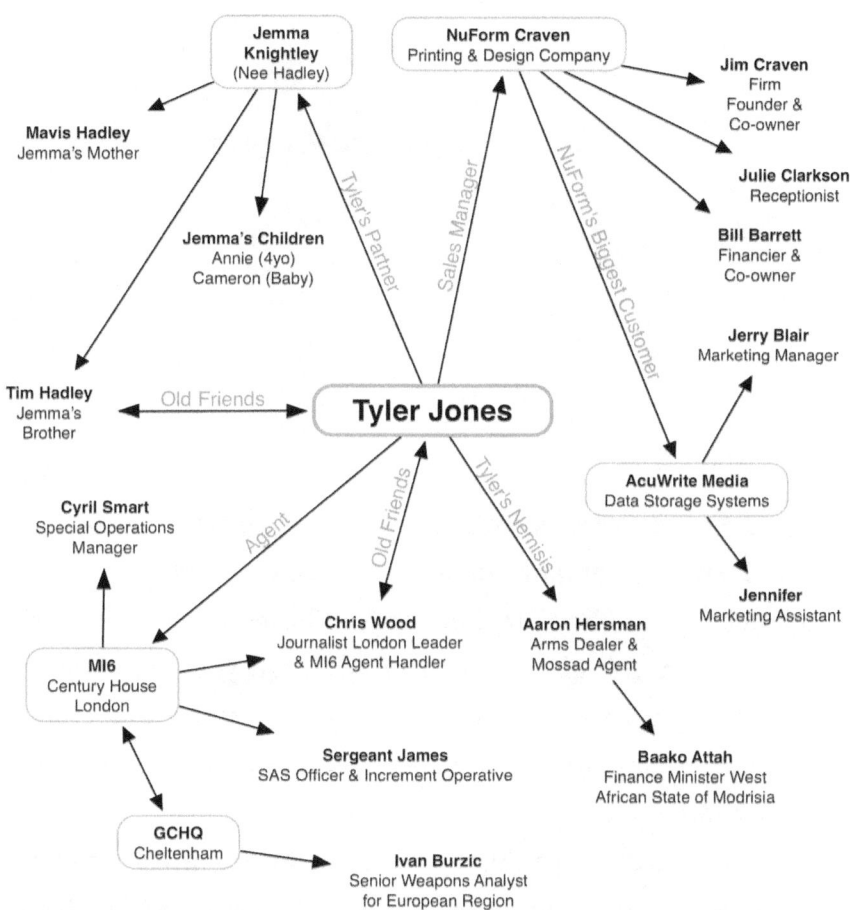

AUTHOR'S AFTERWORD

Dear Reader,

Diagrams and maps are strategically placed throughout this book. Their placement generally relates to what has just happened, or is about to happen in the story. For logistical reasons this hasn't always been possible, so you may need to view diagrams, before or after their place in the text. These visual aids are an attempt to bring context and added meaning to the written word.

A map of the Birmingham/Kings Norton area was also considered for inclusion, but abandoned because its complexity might confuse. Worth mentioning though, is that, with the exception of *Lifford Circle* (where Jemma Knightley lives), all geographic locations in the Birmingham area, exist, or did exist in 1991.

The reason why Iraq and Yugoslavia even feature in this

story, is because of what was going on within the secret service agencies of the world's major powers, during 1991 and 1992.

The release of pent-up ethnic hatreds during the breakup of Yugoslavia was bad enough, but outside interference from the major powers was unforgivable. Self interest and political expediency, fuelled the Yugoslav crisis for the best part of a decade. While posing as innocent bystanders and/or reluctant participants, the major powers, mostly through their secret service agencies, forced their way into the conflict. They also created the myth of good guys and bad guys, both for the ethnic groups within Yugoslavia and for themselves as participants. The truth is, that there were no good guys. All actors left this conflict with blood on their hands, and bad Karma.

Although Wrong Place Wrong Time is a work of fiction, there is more than a grain of truth to many of the scenes, but I can't be more specific than that. I will though, try to answer a couple of questions that may have crossed your mind.

What was the seed from which Wrong Place Wrong Time was germinated?

You will no doubt, recall the scene where Tyler Jones overhears a conversation in the upstairs lounge at the Charing Cross Hotel. It was me who overheard that conversation; well not quite. It did take place in the upstairs lounge at the Charing Cross Hotel, and it did take place in the exact spot where I seated Tyler Jones in the story. It was circa 1981, not 1991, and my overheard conversation was not between a Mossad agent, and a West African politician; it was between a British spook and an official from one of the Gulf States. Their conversation concerned the inducements necessary to facilitate the illegal supply of sophisticated British weaponry.

Tyler Jones's overheard conversation, was not just an attempt to turn my truth, into Tyler's fiction. It was my attempt to demonstrate that a blurred line exists within all of us, when it comes to separating truth from fiction. Sometimes, as in my case and Tyler's case, that truth is so surreal, that to anyone outside of the experience, it may well register as fiction, or *Fake News*.

Did I ever work for MI6? No, I did not.

Did I ever have a relationship with a similar agency? I probably did.

When writing Wrong Place Wrong Time, I called upon my own lived experiences, plus information gathered from international newspapers, long read articles, published papers, journals, and government and UN reports. Some of this material, print and microfilm, was physically accessed by me, at the State Library of Victoria, but most was accessed from reputable sources digitally, via the internet.

Public email services, and internet search engines, did not exist in 1991. This means that all the online reference material available today, has been digitised after the event.

Unfortunately, many of the original web links no longer work, or are hidden behind paywalls. Regardless, I've still been able to provide you with an extensive list on my Reader's Club page. This information clearly demonstrates the nefarious activities our governments and their secret service agencies were up to at the time. Some of it, as is the case with the war in Iraq, even more damning with the benefit of hindsight.

And last, but certainly not least. Thank you for investing a little slab of your life to read *Wrong Place Wrong Time*. Maybe you and I can meet again when *Fruit Of The Dead* is born.

Join the Leslie Henry Reader's Club

- Access to research material.
- Deleted scenes.
- Book club notes.
- Previews of *Fruit Of The Dead* (when available).

Visit: leslie-henry.com and enter your email address.

I promise that you'll only ever receive an occasional news-letter, and of course, your email address will never be used for any other purpose.

Website: leslie-henry.com
Email: info@leslie-henry.com

Leslie Henry.
Melbourne, September, 2019.

ABOUT THE AUTHOR

Leslie Henry is an emerging writer of espionage and intrigue. He is also a published and successful author (under another name), in the area of natural medicine.

During the first half of the 1990s, Leslie Henry took up residence in the UK, living just one street away from Windsor Castle and the Queen of England. Many of the scenes in Wrong Place Wrong Time, were inspired by what was happening in London at that time.

Leslie Henry now lives with his wife and eleven year old daughter, on the picturesque Mornington Peninsula, just south-east of Melbourne, Australia.

Join the Leslie Henry Reader's Club

If you would like access to some of the research material used when writing this book, two deleted scenes (because they contributed little to the plot), book club notes, and previews of my next book, *Fruit Of The Dead (when available)*.

Visit: leslie-henry.com and enter your email address.

I promise that you'll only ever receive an occasional newsletter, and of course, your email address will never be used for any other purpose.